**I stared where my godson was staring,
up at the Red Moon, which seemed smaller.**

*The Red Moon shrank in the sky, from basketball-size to
melon-size.*

*The murmur spread to the Casuni and Tassini ranks,
then to the more worldly Marini soldiers, and finally to my
troops.*

*Overhead, the Red Moon, our key to victory, had become
as tiny as a crimson pea.*

Then it winked out altogether.

Praise for the Jason Wander Series:

*"Th[e] authentic voice is captivating, as is Buettner's facil-
ity with crisp, clear action, whiz-bang plotting and clever
twists."*

— *Science Fiction Weekly*

*"[E]ntertaining homage . . . Buettner shows the Heinlien
touch."*

— *Denver Post*

ORPHAN'S TRIUMPH

★

ROBERT BUETTNER

www.orbitbooks.net

New York   London

Copyright © 2009 by Robert Buettner
Excerpt from *The Company* copyright © 2008 by K.J. Parker
All rights reserved. Except as permitted under the U.S. Copyright Act of 1976, no part of this publication may be reproduced, distributed, or transmitted in any form or by any means, or stored in a database or retrieval system, without the prior written permission of the publisher.

Orbit
Hachette Book Group
237 Park Avenue
New York, NY 10017
Visit our Web site at www.orbitbooks.net

Orbit is an imprint of Hachette Book Group. The Orbit name and logo are trademarks of Little, Brown Book Group Limited.

Printed in the United States of America

First Orbit edition: June 2009

10 9 8 7 6 5 4 3 2

For our new boys, alphabetically,
Evan, Grant, and Jereme

Though Father of the great victory, I was laid upon the battlefield of Mantinea, bleeding from my wounds. I commanded my soldiers to lift me up, that I might see my orphans triumph, and I bade them make a lasting peace. But I died too soon to see these things, as all soldiers do.

     — Epaminondas' Lament,
       attributed to Xenophon, ca. 364 BC

ORPHAN'S
TRIUMPH

ONE

Blam-blam-blam.

The assault rifle's burst snaps me awake inside my armor, and the armor's heater motor, ineffectual but operating, prickles me between the shoulder blades when I stir. The shots' reverberation shivers the cave's ceiling, and snow plops through my open faceplate, onto my upturned lips.

"Paugh!" The crystals on my lips taste of cold and old bones, and I scrub my face with my glove. "Goddamit, Howard!"

I'm Lieutenant General Jason Wander, Colonel Howard Hibble is an intelligence Spook, and both of us are too old to be hiding in caves light-years from Earth.

Fifty dark feet from me, silhouetted against the pale dawn now lighting the cave's mouth, condensed breath balloons out of Howard's open helmet. "There are dire wolves out here, Jason!"

"Don't make noise. They're just big hyenas."

"They're coming closer!"

"Throw rocks. That's what I did. It works." I roll over, aching, on the stone floor and glance at the time winking from my faceplate display. I have just been denied my first hour's sleep after eight hours on watch. Before that, we towed the third occupant of this cave across the steel-hard tundra of this Ice Age planet through a sixteen-hour blizzard. This shelter is more a rocky wrinkle in a shallow hillside than a cave.

I squint over my shoulder, behind Howard and me, at our companion. It is the first Pseudocephalopod Planetary Ganglion any Earthling has seen, much less taken alive, in the three decades of the Slug War, since the Blitz hit Earth in 2036. Like a hippo-sized, mucous-green octopus on a platter, the Ganglion quivers atop its Slug-metal blue motility disc, which hums a yard above the cave floor. Six disconnected sensory conduits droop bare over the disc's edges, isolating the Ganglion from this world and, we hope, from the rest of Slug-kind.

Two synlon ropes dangle, knotted to the motility disc. We used the ropes to drag our POW, not to hog-tie it. A Slug Warrior moves fast for a man-sized, armored maggot, but the Ganglion possesses neither organic motile structures nor even an interface so it can steer its own motility disc. Howard was very excited to discover that. He was a professor of extraterrestrial intelligence studies before the war.

I sigh. Everybody was somebody else before the war.

Howard would like to take our prisoner to Earth alive, so Howard's exobiology Spooks can, uh, chat with it.

That means I have to get us three off this Ice Age rock unfrozen, unstarved, and undigested.

I groan. My original parts awaken more slowly than the replaced ones, and they throb when they do. Did I mention that I'm growing too old for this?

"Jason!" Howard's voice quavers. He was born too old for this.

I stand, yawn, wish I could scratch myself through my armor, then shuffle to the cave mouth, juggling a baseball-sized rock from palm to palm. Last night, I perfected a fastball that terrorized many a dire wolf.

As I step alongside Howard at the cave mouth, he lobs an egg-sized stone with a motion like a girl in gym class. It lands twenty feet short of the biggest, nearest wolf. The monster saunters up, sniffs the stone, then bares its teeth at us in a red-eyed growl. The wolf pack numbers eleven total, milling around behind the big one, all gaunt enough that we must look like walking pot roast to them.

But I'm unconcerned that the wolves will eat us. A dire wolf could gnaw an Eternad forearm gauntlet for a week with no result but dull teeth.

I look up at the clear dawn sky. My concern is that the wolves are bad advertising. The storm we slogged through wiped out all traces of our passing and, I hope, kept any surviving Slugs from searching for us. But the storm has broken, for now. I plan for us to hide out in this hole until the good guys home in on our transponders.

If any good guys survived. We may starve in this hole waiting for dead people.

We don't really know how Slugs track humans, or even if they do. We do know that the maggots incinerated Weichsel's primitive human nomads one little band and extended family group at a time—not just by waxing the whole planet, which the Slugs are capable of. And the maggots had rude surprises for us less primitive humans when we showed up here, too.

I wind up, peg my baseball-sized stone at the big wolf,

and plink him on the nose. I whoop. I couldn't duplicate that throw if I pitched nine innings' worth. The wolf yelps and trots back fifty yards, whining but unhurt.

Howard shrugs. "The wolf pack doesn't necessarily give us away. We could just be a bear carcass or something in here."

I jerk my thumb back in the direction of the green blob in the cave. "Even if the Slugs don't know how to track us, do you think they can track the Ganglion?"

Disconnected or not, our prisoner could be screaming for help in Slugese right now, for all we know.

Howard shrugs again. "I don't think—"

The wolf pack, collectively, freezes, noses upturned.

Howard says, "Uh-oh."

I tug Howard deeper into the cave's shadows and whisper, "Whatever they smell, we can't see. The wind's coming from upslope, behind us."

As I speak, Howard clicks his rifle's magazine into his palm and replaces it with a completely full one. I've known him since the first weeks of the Blitz, nearly three decades now, and Colonel Hibble is a geek, all right. But when the chips are down, he's as infantry as I am.

Outside, the wolves retreat another fifty yards from the mouth of our cave as a shadow crosses it.

My heart pounds, and I squeeze off my rifle's grip safety.

Eeeeerr.

The shadow shuffles past the cave mouth. Another replaces it, then more. As they stride into the light, the shadows resolve into trumpeting, truck-sized furballs the color of rust.

Howard whispers, "Mammoth."

The herd bull strides toward the wolf pack, bellowing, head back to display great curved tusks. The wolves retreat again.

Howard says, "If we shot a mammoth out there, the carcass would explain the wolf pack. It could make an excellent distraction."

He's right. I raise my M40 and sight on the nearest cow, but at this range I could drop her with a hip shot.

Then I pause. "The carcass might attract those big cats." Weichsel's fauna parallels Pleistocene Earth's in many ways, but our Neolithic forefathers never saw saber-toothed snow leopards bigger than Bengal tigers.

Really, my concern with Howard's idea isn't baiting leopards. Saber teeth can't scuff Eternads any more than wolf teeth can. I just don't want to shoot a mammoth.

It sounds absurd. I can't count the Slugs that have died at my hand or on my orders in this war. And over my career I've taken human lives, too, when the United States in its collective wisdom has lawfully ordered me to.

It's not as though any species on Weichsel is endangered, except us humans, of course. The tundra teems with life, a glacial menagerie. Weichsel wouldn't miss one mammoth.

So why do I rationalize against squeezing my trigger one more time?

I can't deny that war callouses a soldier to brutality. But as I grow older, I cherish the moments when I can choose not to kill.

I lower my rifle. "Let's see what happens."

By midmorning, events moot my dilemma. The wolves isolate a lame cow from the mammoth herd, bring her down two hundred yards from us, and begin tearing meat from her woolly flanks like bleeding rugs. The mammoth herd stands off, alternately trumpeting in protest at the gore-smeared wolves, then bulldozing snow with their sinuous tusks to get at matted grass beneath. For both species, violence is another day at the office.

Howard and I withdraw inside the cave, to obscure our visual and infrared signatures, and sit opposite our prisoner.

The Ganglion just floats there, animated only by the vibrations of its motility plate. After thirty years of war, all I know about the blob is that it is my enemy. I have no reason to think it knows me any differently. For humans and Slugs, like the mammoths and wolves, violence has become another day at the office.

Howard, this blob, and I are on the cusp of changing that. If I can get us off Weichsel alive. At the moment, getting out alive requires me to freeze my butt off in a hole, contemplating upcoming misery and terror. After a lifetime in the infantry, I'm used to that.

I pluck an egg-sized stone off the cave floor and turn it in my hand like Yorick's skull. The stone is a gem-quality diamond. Weichsel's frozen landscape is as full of diamonds as the Pentagon is full of underemployed lieutenant generals. Which is what I was when this expedition-become-fiasco started, three months ago, light-years away in a very different place.

TWO

"HAS SHE SHOT ANYBODY YET?" I picked my way through the scrub and scree of Bren's Stone Hills, wheezing. The planetologists said the Stone Hills were analogous to Late Cretaceous cordillera on Earth, which didn't make them easier to climb.

The infantry captain alongside me, burdened by his M40 and his Eternad armor, wasn't even puffing. "No, General. But I'd keep my head down. She's not very big, but she's the best shot in my company."

We ran, crouched, as we crested the ridge, to a sniper team prone on a rock ledge. Below us the Stone Hills dropped away to the east to the High Plains. In the early morning, moons hung in the sky like ghosts. One glistened white, the other blood red, with a drifting pterosaur silhouetted against it.

Six hundred yards downslope, pocketed in rocks but a clear and easy shot from our high ground position, a figure in camo utilities crouched among boulders. A hundred yards downslope from the soldier, a dozen Casuni tribesmen, sun glinting off their helmets and breastplates, half surrounded her, screened from her by scrub. Each

Casuni carried four single-shot black-powder pistols huge enough to bring down a small dinosaur, and none would hesitate to use them. Really, the standoff just looked like a dot sprinkle to me, because I was wearing utilities myself, without the optics of Eternad armor's helmet.

The sniper's spotter had his helmet faceplate up and peered through a native brass spyglass. He passed the glass to me and pointed. "The Blutos chased her up there at sunset yesterday, General. You can see the snapper curled up alongside her."

Through the spyglass, the dozen burly, black-bearded Casuni looked small. But the distant soldier looked about twelve years old, gaunt, with hair like straw and big eyes. Her file said she was twenty-one, a private fresh out of Earthside Advanced Infantry Training, with just two weeks on Bren. The snapper, its hatchling down as gray as the surrounding rock, was already the size of an adult wolf.

I rolled onto my side, toward the captain. "What set her off?"

"Last week bandits ambushed the convoy that was shipping replacements out here from Marinus. Her loader bought the farm. He'd been together with her since AIT. She took it hard."

"He?"

"Nothing like *that*, sir. Infantry can be close without—"

I raised my palm. "I didn't mean *that,* Captain. When I was a spec four, I was a loader for a female gunner. Just sounded familiar."

The captain wrinkled his brow one millimeter. He was a West Pointer, and the notion that the commander in chief of offworld ground forces was a high-school dropout grunt typically ruffled Pointers' feathers. But maybe his discomfort grew from the way I said it. Because I felt a catch in my throat. That long-ago female gunner and I had grown infantry-close, and in the years later, before her death, as close as family.

The captain continued, "An adult female snapper dug under a perimeter fence and maimed three Casuni at the sluice before the security Casunis brought her down. The private down there found the female's cub wandering outside the wire. The private's trying to make a pet of it. But the Casuni say it's sacrilege to let the cub live."

Grown snappers are ostrich-sized, beaked carnosaurs. They're quicker than two-legged cobras, with toxic saliva and the sunny disposition of cornered wolverines. A snapper's beak slices the duckbill-hide wall of a Casuni yurt like Kleenex, and Casuni mothers have lost babies to snappers for centuries. Nothing personal. Snappers are predators, and human babies are easy protein in a hard land. But in Casuni culture, even Satan is better regarded than snappers.

I sighed. "No animal-rights activists here." Over the thirty thousand years since the Slugs snatched primitive Earthlings to slave on planets like Bren, humans had adapted to some strange environments, none harsher than the High Plains of Bren. The Casuni had evolved into flint-hard nomads, following migrating herds that resembled parallel-evolved duckbilled dinosaurs, across wind-scoured plains that resembled Siberia. I turned to the captain. "Why haven't you puffed her?" On Earth, any suburban police department could neutralize a hostage situation by sneaking a roach-sized micro 'bot up close to the hostage taker, then snoozing the hostage taker with a puff of Nokout gas.

"A creep-and-peep team's inbound from the MP battalion in Marinus, sir. But it'll be six hours before they ground here and calibrate the Bug."

As the captain spoke, two Casuni began low-crawling through a draw, screened from the girl's sight, working their way around toward high ground off her left flank. One of the Casuni must've been careless enough to show an inch of skin, because the girl squeezed off a round that cracked off a rock a foot from the crawling man, exploding dust and singing off into the distance.

The girl called downslope in Casuni, her voice thickened by her translator speaker, "Stay away!"

I said, "We don't have six hours."

The captain shook his head. "No, sir, we don't. That's the only reason I set up a sniper to take her out. It makes me sick to do it. But I know a major incident with the Blutos could freeze the stone trade."

He was right. If the Casuni killed an Earthling, it would be a major incident that could jeopardize the fuel supply of the fleet that stood between mankind and the Pseudocephalopod Hegemony. If the girl killed a Casuni, it would also be a major incident. And given her advantage in skills and equipment, she was probably going to kill a bunch of them as soon as the Casuni got in position, then rushed her.

But if *we* shot her, it would still be a major incident. The terms of the Human Union Joint Economic Cooperation Protocol, known in the history chips as the Cavorite Mining Treaty of 2062, reserved the use of deadly force to indigenous civilian law enforcement. Casuni civilian law enforcement resembled a saloon brawl, but I don't write treaties, I just live by them.

I stood and brushed dust off my utilities.

The captain wrinkled his brow behind his faceplate. "Sir?"

"I'll take a walk down there and talk to her."

The captain stared at my cloth utilities, shaking his head. "General, I don't—"

The sniper's spotter swiveled his helmeted head toward me, too, jaw dropped. "That's suicide. Sir."

THREE

AFTER FIFTEEN SECONDS, the captain swallowed, then said, "Yes, sir."

The spotter scrunched his face, then nodded. "I think there will be time if we take the shot as soon as she turns and aims at you, General."

"No shot, Sergeant."

"Of course not, General. Until she turns and—"

"No shot. I'll handle this."

The spotter, the captain, and even the sniper stared at me.

Then the captain pointed downslope. "If the Casuni rush her, do we shoot? And who do we shoot?"

"The Casuni won't rush her. That's why I'm going now." I shook my head, pointed at the sky. "It's six minutes before noon. At noon the Casuni will pause an hour for daily devotions. That's our window to talk her down."

The captain stood. "Then I'll go, sir. I'm her commanding officer." He rapped gauntleted knuckles on his armored chest. "And I'm tinned up."

I pulled him aside, then whispered to him, "Son, you're

right. If I were in your boots I'd be pissed at me for pulling rank." I tapped my collar stars. "But I need you up here to be sure your sniper doesn't get the itch."

I had given him a ginned-up reason, and he was smart enough to know it. But the captain was also smart enough and resigned enough that he just nodded his head. There was no percentage in arguing with the only three-star within one hundred light-years. Besides, he probably figured his sniper could take the shot before I could get myself killed, anyway.

Twenty minutes later, I had crept and low-crawled to within fifty yards of the girl and she hadn't spotted me. Downslope, I heard the twitter of Casuni devotion pipes. The warriors would all be head-down and praying for an hour, during which we could clean up this mess, before they rushed her. I kept behind a rock ledge as I cupped my hand to my mouth. "Sandy?"

"Who the hell's out there?"

"Jason Wander."

"Bite me. The old man's pushing paper back in Marinus. Whoever you are, I can't see you, but I can hear you well enough to lob a grenade into those rocks. So back off."

"Sandy, I really am General Wander. I came out from Marinus to award a unit citation. When I heard what happened, I came here. I'd like to talk to you." I paused and breathed. "I'm going to stand up, so you can see me, see that I'm unarmed."

"I'll drop a frag on your ass first!"

Ting.

The M40 is an excellent infantry weapon, except that it makes a too-audible "ting" sound when it's switched between assault-rifle mode and grenade-launcher mode, as a grenade is chambered in the lower barrel.

So far, so good. My heart thumped, and I drew a breath, then let it out.

I stayed behind cover, levered myself up on my real arm, and glanced back to confirm where I was in relation to the sniper farther up the hillside. Then I got to my knees, spread my arms, palms out, and stood.

The girl had swung around from facing the Casunis downslope and now faced me, her unhelmeted cheek laid along her rifle's stock as she trained her M40 on my chest. She lifted her head an inch, and her jaw fell open. "General?"

I nodded, then called, "Mind if I come closer? Then neither of us will have to yell. We won't wake the baby."

The voice of the captain upslope hissed in my earpiece. "General! Sir, you need to move left or right a yard or two. You're blocking the shot."

Which was the idea, though the captain hadn't anticipated it until too late. They don't teach enough sneakiness at West Point.

The girl jerked her head, motioning me closer, but she kept her finger on the trigger. "Two steps! No more."

I took the two steps, which brought me within fifteen yards of her, then shuffled until the distance between us was down to ten yards.

She poked her M40 forward, then growled, a pit bull with freckles. "I said two steps, dipshit! Sir."

In my ear, the captain said, "Sir, move left or right! Not closer! Now you're obscuring her even more!"

The rifle quivered in the girl's hand.

I swallowed. There's a class in MP school that teaches

how to talk jumpers down. I never took it. There was probably a series of soothing questions to ask, but I didn't know what they were.

So I said, "Tell me what happened, Sandy."

"The Blutos tried to kill the baby."

"And you're tired of seeing things killed." Even though her "baby" was a killing machine growing deadlier by the day. I kept my arms out, palms open toward her as I inched closer.

"The other Blutos—the caravan raiders—killed my loader. I couldn't do anything to stop it."

"I started out as a loader. I was there when my gunner died, too. It's an empty feeling."

I wasn't lying, either, about the feeling or the death. But my gunner's death had come less than three years ago, though it had come in combat and while I watched, unable to prevent it.

Her gun's muzzle dropped an inch as she nodded. "It feels like there's a hole in my gut."

"The hole heals. It takes time, but it heals." I didn't tell her how much time, or how disfiguring the scar could be.

I stepped forward. The voice in my earpiece whispered, "Sir, the psyops people predict that she'll shoot. Just kneel down and we'll take her out."

She came up onto one knee, her M40 still trained on my chest. "What about the baby?"

I could see the snapper infant now, curled up asleep, tail over snout, on a bed of leaves the girl had prepared for it among the rocks. Empty ration paks littered the ground, where the girl must have been hand-feeding the little beast. Regardless of the girl's maternal instincts, within a week the snapper's predatory instincts would take over, and the monster would snap the girl's hand off at the wrist if she held out a snack. The exobiologists said snappers were the most implacable predators yet discovered on the fourteen planets of the Human Union.

I said, "We'll care for it for a while. When it's old enough to fend for itself, we'll release it into the wild."

In fact, the Casuni would insist the devil's spawn be gutted on the spot and its entrails burned. And with three of their own maimed by the beast's mother, we would have no choice but to turn the little snapper over to the Casuni like a POW.

Harmonious interface with indigenous populations wasn't all handing out Hershey bars. Sometimes it required tolerating customs we found barbarous. I used the moment to inch closer, within three yards of her. One step closer and I could lunge forward, grasp her rifle's muzzle, and twist it away.

Her rifle's muzzle came up again and she snarled. "Liar!"

Crap. I've always been a lousy liar.

She fired, point-blank.

FOUR

"SIR?" The whisper was old, gravelly, and familiar. It came from close to my ear, so I heard it over jet-engine shriek.

I opened my eyes, focused, and saw Ord, gray eyes unsmiling, and above him the interior fuselage ribs of a hop jet. I asked, "Sergeant Major? What happened to the girl?"

Ord jerked his buzz-cut gray head, and I followed his eyes. A corpsman knelt beside the private, who lay strapped to the litter next to the one I lay on. Her eyes were closed; her chest slowly rose and fell. Joy juice from a suspended IV bag trickled down a transparent tube into her forearm. A purple streak began at the point of her jaw and traced halfway back to her ear.

Ord said, "Her jaw's not broken, but you dropped her with a right as you went down, then landed on top of her. That kept her outfit from shooting her and gave them time to get downslope and put cuffs on her." Ord frowned. "Sir, if you don't mind hearing my opinion . . ."

I had minded hearing Ord's opinion ever since he was my drill sergeant in infantry basic, but he never hesitated to share it with me anyway.

"You took an unnecessary risk."

I shook my head. "No risk. I heard her shift her rifle to grenade mode. I never heard her shift back, and I talked my way to inside five yards from her."

Ord nodded. "An M40 grenade doesn't arm for five yards. So all she did when she pulled the trigger was wallop you in the chest with a low-velocity lump of unexploded shrapnel."

I smiled a little at the cleverness of me.

Ord, as usual when I did that, frowned. "She could have flicked the selector switch back to rifle in an instant and killed you. She could have shot you in the head, instead of the chest, and killed you. That would have decapitated the offworld chain of command. If your sucker punch hadn't knocked her flat, the sniper would have killed her anyway. That would have precipitated a crisis with the indigenous population."

"But none of that happened. Now she gets a ride home. At worst, a Section Eight discharge. At best, administrative punishment and another chance in the army. The army gets a Band-Aid bill for me. I could see she was too distracted to realize she was still in grenade mode."

Ord stared at me. I suppose he stared the way the caveman who discovered fire stared at the first idiot who stuck his finger into the flame. "Even so, sir, you could have allowed someone in armor, her commanding officer, perhaps, to make the approach. Or waited until the creep-and-peep team could have neutralized the situation."

I glanced at the 'Puter on Ord's wrist. A normal transport hauling a creep-and-peep team from Marinus would still be hours away. But only about an hour had passed since I stuck my chest in front of an almost-live grenade.

"That captain said the creep-and-peep team was coming out on a tilt-wing. Six hours. Why did the Spooks divert a hop jet to get out here faster? And why did you come out here on it?"

Ord peered at the IV bag alongside me, and the tube that ran from it into my forearm. "Sir, no need to get into that now. Your—ah—heroics left you with a hairline fracture of the sternum and related soft-tissue damage. The corpsman here just upped your dosage." Ord smiled. Everybody in my platoon in basic knew an Ord smile meant that whatever the smile-ee thought was about to happen, he was sorely mistaken. Ord patted my shoulder. "Just relax for now, General."

"I feel fine. Sergeant Major, answer my—"

The engine whine faded into nothing, and then another voice replaced it.

"—pleasure to have a casualty that outranks me, for a change." I woke to the voice of the light colonel who commanded the infirmary at Human Union Camp, Marinus. Cocoa-skinned, gray-haired, and clad in short-sleeved blue scrubs, he stood in a white-painted single-bed room, staring at the chart reader in his hand. Hippocrates Wallace bared his forearms even though they were slick and puckered with burn scar tissue. I was there when he got burned. He had been a flight surgeon during the First Battle of Mousetrap. He was the only person I knew who had earned a Harvard Med School degree and a Silver Star.

I started to cough. Through the dope, pain penetrated my chest like a dull ice pick twisting. I froze my shoulders and tried to refrain from breathing while I hissed, "Pleasure? You this compassionate with all your patients, Wally?"

He toggled through my overactive medical history with his thumb. "Oh, suck it up, Jason. A cracked sternum's little potatoes for you."

I asked, "What about the girl?"

"Your victim? The private won't be playing the harmonica for a while. Jaw contusions and some dental work. She's on the stockade ward. I might move you there, too."

"Now you're a criminologist?"

"No. But I've got an honorary degree in watching screwballs. If you threw yourself into that situation to save the girl, to balance the scales for your perceived inadequacy because Congresswoman Metzger died on Mousetrap, you're a little nuts. But if you were trying to commit suicide by lunatic, you're a lot nuts. In which case I'm required by regulation to decertify you for command."

"I'm fine. Half the Pentagon and two-thirds of Congress are crazier than I am, and nobody decertifies them."

Wally snorted.

I said, "Remember, *Colonel,* I'm the biggest stud duck within two billion cubic light-years. I could fire you before you could decertify me."

Wally sighed. "If only. Then *I'd* be the one who got shipped back to Mousetrap, where the sports holos are only two weeks behind and a man can get plotzed on scotch instead of fermented groundfruit juice."

I narrowed my eyes at him, about the only body parts I could move without wincing. "Who's getting shipped back to Mousetrap?"

He raised bushy eyebrows. "Didn't Ord tell you? You are. Ord got one of those hard-copy encrypted chips that Hibble insists on sending. Why do you think the Spooks pulled an orbit-capable ship away from shuttling back and forth to the Red Moon? And used it to double time Ord out to the Stone Hills to deliver your Spook-o-gram?"

I sighed. "Wally, not even I am supposed to know where those shuttles are going. So don't spread that around."

Wally leaned down to me and whispered, "I don't need to. Everybody on this post knows that whole Moon's a Cavorite nugget. Though it beats the fecal matter out of me why the Spooks care. The Stone Hills mines produce Cavorite faster than Mousetrap can build ships to use it."

I changed the subject. Partly because I didn't want to know how much other classified material was common knowledge in my command. Partly because I was curious about Howard Hibble's summons to Mousetrap. "How soon can I travel?"

"Given the diminished recuperative powers of a man your age—"

"You're as old as I am."

"Exactly. It takes me three days to recuperate from shining my shoes." Wally shook his head. "I can't sign off that you'll be ready to tolerate escape-velocity G forces for at least a week."

Howard was a devious geek, but if he sent a Spook-o-gram, something was up that I couldn't wait a week to hear about. "Release me to travel tomorrow and I'll smuggle you back a case of scotch."

Wally raised his eyebrows higher. "Single malt?"

I managed a shallow nod. "And if you don't share your amateur shrinkology with Sergeant Major Ord, I'll make it sixteen-year-old."

"Done. I'll shoot you up with healing accelerants, but I

can't immobilize that fracture, so don't blame me when it hurts like hell. And the shrinkology was Ord's in the first place, so don't blame me if he brings it up."

The next morning, Ord and I caught a lift aboard what everybody was supposed to think, but nobody actually believed, was a hop jet shuttling us to rendezvous with the *Abraham Lincoln*, in parking orbit above Bren. Wally was right about the fracture, which hurt like hell. I clamped my jaw while I blamed him anyway, every minute that the hopper boosted.

We shared the hopper with one passenger, who spun his seat to face Ord and me once the engines went silent. His nameplate read "Applebite."

Like the rest of Howard Hibble's freak show, also known as Military Intelligence Battalion Bren, Reinforced, our companion wore army utilities, topped with a twentysomething's straw-colored chin and skull fuzz, which had no recent experience with a barber or a razor.

Ord eyed the kid's crooked-pinned captain's brass with the enthusiasm of a jockey aboard a pig.

I asked, "How goes Silver Bullet, Applebite?"

Howard Hibble's supergeeks had the military bearing of Cub Scouts, Mensa-level intellects, and the xenophobia of Cold War spies. Applebite's eyes widened, because even the code name for the Cavorite weaponization project was classified. He slid his eyes to Ord and said nothing.

I sighed. "The sergeant major's clearance is higher than yours, Applebite. Besides, in about forty minutes, he and I are gonna watch you board a ship that's not even supposed to exist."

Finally, Applebite shrugged. "We're close, sir. But . . ."

I smiled. From three decades of war, we knew that

the man-sized armored-maggot Slug Warriors were as replaceable to the Pseudocephalopod Hegemony as fingernails were to us.

The only way to win the war was going to be to destroy the single cognitive center that ran the organism. A center that was probably the size of a planet. But we had learned early in the war that the Slugs had a way to neutralize nukes. So for the last thirty years, the Spooks' job had been to think up a silver bullet that could kill a brain bigger than Mars.

"But even if you make a silver bullet, you don't know where to shoot it?"

Applebite scratched his chin fuzz and smiled. "We don't. But finding the homeworld's not my job."

Even after almost four decades, now that we finally had ships numerous enough and good enough that we could chase down Slug ships like wolves on cattle, we couldn't find the Slugs' homeworld. If we could find it, we were, apparently, almost ready to pour Cavorite on it like salt on a garden snail. A simile that delighted me.

Our hopper shook, the broken edges of my breastbone rubbed against each other, and I stiffened like somebody had cabled an Electrovan battery to my chest. We decelerated and matched circumlunar orbit with an unmarked vessel that had once been a Metzger-class cruiser and was now Silver Bullet's headquarters. Cavorite was less toxic to humans than to Slugs, but the Spooks still chose to orbit the Red Moon rather than set up camp on it. Applebite's drop-off at the research ship wasn't recorded by its Spook crew on the hopper's flight log, and a half hour later Ord and I were piped aboard the *Abraham Lincoln* before her foremast watch finished breakfast.

Thereafter, we spent a steady week at .6 light speed, and my breastbone started to knit, thanks to Wally's accelerants.

Less happily, Ord hadn't heart-to-hearted me about my mental state. Nominally, commissioned officers outrank senior noncommissioned officers. But if a good sergeant hadn't privately advised the Old Man, who was typically younger than the sergeant, after the Old Man screwed up, it meant the time bomb was still ticking.

I watched the stars around us stretch from light points into glowing spaghetti, then disappear altogether as their light, and the *Abe*'s mile-long mass, got sucked into the Temporal Fabric Insertion Point that would spit us out inside the Mousetrap interstellar crossroad. As we jumped, I muttered to myself, "Howard, you mendacious son of a bitch, this better be worth the trip."

FIVE

ORD AND I WERE SPECTATORS on the *Abe*'s bridge when she popped out into the Mousetrap, light-years as the crow flies from the Bren II Insertion Point, where the *Abe* went in. Vacuum is vacuum to my untrained eye, so the new space we saw on the screens looked as black and starry as what we left behind. Except the *Abe* got lit by sixteen pings within its first three seconds in new space.

All sixteen pings got instantaneous, correct electronic responses back from the *Abe*'s electronic countermeasures array. If they hadn't, the *Abe* would have been trading real bullets with a Scorpion interceptor squadron. Scorpions were single-seat Cavorite-drive fighters, so small and stealthy compared to a conventional starship like the *Abraham Lincoln*, or like a Slug Firewitch, that they're scarcely noticeable. Scorpions may be too delicate to survive a jump, but they sting, as the Slugs had learned the hard way.

The Mousetrap was a point of nothing in a universe mostly filled with nothing. But clustered in the Mousetrap, "close together" by astrophysical standards, were a double handful of the useful kind of black holes the

Spooks called Temporal Fabric Insertion Points. A T-FIP's enormous gravity tacked together folds in the fabric of conventional space, so an object that could slingshot through a T-FIP jumped out light-years away from where it went in.

The Mousetrap was the most strategically valuable crossroad in human history because every one of the fourteen warm, wet rocks that constituted the planets of the Human Union could be reached in just days or weeks by jumping a ship through one or another of the Mousetrap's T-FIPs. Humans could easily colonize the Milky Way and defend ourselves via the Mousetrap's shortcuts. Unfortunately, the Pseudocephalopod Hegemony, which viewed humans as a virus, could just as easily exterminate us via those same Mousetrap shortcuts.

Mankind guarded the Mousetrap like its collective life depended on it, because it did.

So, ping challenges and visual confirmations notwithstanding, four Scorpions assumed station around the *Abe,* shadowing her like a potential Trojan horse. Well, the *Abe*'s crew knew that the Scorpions were there, even though the *Abe* couldn't find them with its sensors. Ten escorted hours later, the great orange disk of the gas giant Leonidas filled the *Abe*'s visual displays, like Jupiter with blue stripes. One hour after that, Leonidas's only satellite became visible, a spinning, twenty-mile-long nickel-iron mote against the planet's glowing bulk.

The one thing in this universe more valuable to mankind than the empty space of the Mousetrap was the only habitable rock within the Mousetrap, from which the empty space could be defended.

Ord peered at the moonlet known as Mousetrap as the

Abe drifted closer. Half of Mousetrap's lumpy surface sparkled with silver solar arrays, even more than on our last trip through. He grunted, "Must make more electricity than Hoover Dam, these days."

The *Abe*'s engineering officer, who stood watching the displays alongside us, inclined her head toward Ord. "Actually, Sergeant Major, Mousetrap generates enough power to lift the Hoover Dam into low Earth orbit. The smelting plants are power hogs."

Too many miners, most of whom had been Bren slaves risking death for emancipation, had died boring a core out of Mousetrap's centerline. From Mousetrap's north pole to its south pole, sealed at each end with massive airlocks, ran a great tunnel that had been carved out. Into the tunnel's walls had been carved vast living, mining, and manufacturing spaces, in concentric rings around the core canal.

A vessel like the *Abe,* or like the Slug vessels from which we copied Cavorite drive, could thunder up to Mousetrap at thousands of miles per hour, or even per second, then stop on a dime, without spilling coffee within the vessel's gravity cocoon. Also without denting the ship or the moonlet. I had seen it done.

But a *Bastogne*-class cruiser's fender bender would dent even the national debt. Therefore, the *Abe* drifted, slow and nose-first, "down" toward Mousetrap's north pole like a cherry toward the top of a sundae. The outer doors irised open on an airlock chamber bigger than a volcano crater. The *Abe* paused within the lock while the outer doors closed; then the inner doors opened and we crept forward into Broadway, Mousetrap's centerline tunnel, at ten miles per hour.

I'd been down Broadway before, but my jaw always drops. The *Abe*'s forward screen showed us drifting through a rotating, man-made tunnel that seemed bigger than the Grand Canyon, its walls shimmering with the crisscross Widmanstätten crystal pattern of meteoric nickel iron.

But most of North Broadway's walls were obscured by a whiskering of docks and shipyards. We cruised for miles past keels and skeletons of new cruisers, frigates, transports, even Scorpion fighters, gnatlike compared to the rest. Beyond the shipyards lay miles of repair yards, every slot filled by ranks of fleet operational ships in for refit. The whole array flickered with sparks sprayed by welders and was lit by spotlights played on scaffold-wrapped hulls.

Whenever I cruised North Broadway, I reflexively scanned the ranks of docked cruisers for the *Emerald River*. It wasn't the cruiser I hoped to see, but her skipper, the estimable and lovely Admiral Mimi Ozawa. But Mimi had been rotated Earthside, after leading the Second Fleet across T-FIP jump after T-FIP jump, in a futile search for the Slugs' homeworld. Sometimes with me aboard, mostly without. I sighed.

Broadway's middle miles were darker, pocked with adits and burrows that tapped pockets where raw materials, from aluminum to zinc, had concentrated within the moonlet's nickel-iron mass. Boxcar-sized ore cars beetled back and forth from the mines to the smelters, where the fabric of Mousetrap was being transmuted into the building blocks that defended the Human Union.

Farther on, South Broadway glittered, as windows of offices, training and living spaces spilled light into the vast tunnel.

The *Abe* eased up to her mooring, one of a dozen ringing the tunnel, from which vessels transferred passengers and cargo to and from the south eight miles of Broadway.

An hour later, Ord and I had separated. He signed us in to respective billets in the Officers and NCO's quarters, while I tubed upweight—that is, feet-first out toward the surface of Mousetrap—to level forty-eight. I exited the tube as an MP saluted me, still checked my ID as though I might be a disguised Slug, then smiled. "Welcome back to the Penthouse, General."

Level forty-eight was the outermost of Moosetrap's cylinders, all arranged concentric to Broadway. Level forty-eight was called the Penthouse, even though it was buried miles deep in Mousetrap's nickel-iron mass, because it was the top—bottom, actually—tube stop and because, as the outermost ring, it had the least-curved floors and ceilings and the most Earthlike rotational gravity in Mousetrap.

The Spooks monopolized the high-rent district because they were the ones who designed Mousetrap, but more importantly because they deserved the extra comfort. The Spooks didn't rotate home every twelve months like Mousetrap's GIs, civilian contract labor, and Space Force swabbies. Marginally nicer quarters were small compensation for the hardships of 'Trap Rat status.

"Jason!" The king of the 'Trap Rats strode down level forty-eight's main corridor toward me, arms wide. Like the rest of his geek subjects', Colonel Howard Hibble's uniform had wrinkles on its wrinkles. A smoker's wrinkled skin had hung on his slim bones when I met him, and the years hadn't smoothed or plumped anything.

I met Howard during the Blitz, in 2036, when I was an infantry trainee and he was a professor of extraterrestrial intelligence who had, therefore, been assigned by the army to military intelligence. Howard's rank decades later was only colonel, because he couldn't lead troops to free beer. But Howard was the most powerful man nobody ever heard of, by virtue of his intuition about what made the Slugs tick. He controlled the Spook budget, which was buried in Defense Department line items that nobody ever heard of. He succeeded first because he was a genius and second because he played Washington politics like the intel paranoid he had become. Hence the MP guarding the tube exit onto level forty-eight.

I raised my palms as high as I could without separating my sore breastbone. "No hug!"

Howard frowned as he sucked a nicotine lollipop. "I heard. But you're here." He smiled.

"Mind telling me why?"

He ushered me back to his office, a large part of Mousetrap's pressurized volume, which he kept as tidy as the inside of a trash compactor. He poked a pile of old paper books so that they toppled and revealed a chair. "Sit down, Jason."

He sat across from me and swiveled his desk screens away so we could see each other while we talked.

I said, "The word is that Silver Bullet's locked and loaded."

He narrowed his eyes. "Where did you hear that?"

"From the kid we rode up to the *Abe* with." I paused to watch him squirm, then said, "Howard, I'm C-in-C Off-world Forces. I see the Silver Bullet Weeklies before they get encrypted and sent to you."

He closed his eyes, then nodded. "Oh. Yeah."

No point mentioning what Wally had told me about what the Bren rumor mill was putting out. I shoved aside a sandwich wrapper, a dead frog floating in a specimen jar, and a chessboard that blocked my view across Howard's desk. "Is your summons about Silver Bullet?"

"Not exactly. Assuming Silver Bullet is operational, what would you say is the biggest remaining obstacle to winning the war?"

"Finding a target for it. Mimi Ozawa was so many light-years away for so long that I can't remember what it's like to be horny."

Howard wrinkled his brow. "Memory loss and diminished libido are natural results of aging."

"Howard, I was kidding."

"Oh." He shrugged. "Well, normally, one way to develop intelligence to solve a problem like locating the homeworld would be to interrogate prisoners."

"But Slug warriors have the independent intelligence of a white corpuscle."

"And we've never captured any more sophisticated part of the organism. In fact, we've never even seen one."

"But you have a plan?"

"I have an opportunity. I need you to make a plan."

It was my turn to narrow my eyes. "Am I going to like this opportunity?"

Howard plucked a rock paperweight off his desk and stared into it. "You never do."

SIX

HOWARD HELD THE ROCK between his thumb and forefinger, then turned it so the crystalline faces within its translucent mass reflected the compartment light. "Weichselan diamond."

I shrugged. "I hear they're so common there that the Weichselans used to throw them at rabbits." Weichselans were the Human Union's caveman country cousins, kidnapped from Earth by the Slugs thirty thousand years ago, then abandoned on a planet that looked like Earth during the Weichselan glaciation, complete with woolly mammoths. On many of the planets where the Slugs left humans behind, man had progressed and flourished. On Weichsel, man had just survived.

Howard nodded. "The Weichselans did use diamonds as throwing stones. But this one's a souvenir collected by an Earthling diamond miner."

"We reinhabited Weichsel?"

"Just a few diamond miners. We evacuated them back here eleven days ago."

Hair stood on my neck. "Evacuated?"

Howard nodded. "A precaution, as soon as the cruiser

group orbiting Weichsel detected the new Pseudocephalopod invasion force."

I closed my eyes, then opened them. "The maggots are back." I wasn't surprised *that* the Slugs were back. The Human Union's defense posture, so massive that it made the Cold War look like peewee football, was predicated on the assumption that they would return. I cocked my head at Howard. "But why Weichsel? Why a sideshow, and the same place where they feinted last time?"

Howard leaned back in his chair and stared up at the ceiling, and I leaned forward in my chair. The reason the army and the Congress and the UN put up with Howard and funded his clandestine programs was that his intuition about the Slugs had proven right so often over thirty years of off-and-on war.

He said, "The Pseudocephalopod knows we reacted to the first feint at Weichsel only by stationing cruisers there and fighting it to a draw, out in space. It infers—correctly—that we don't value Weichsel highly and that we defend it lightly."

"So?"

"So the Pseudocephalopod reasoned that it could slip in and plant a small force on Weichsel easily."

I turned my palms toward Howard. "Again. Why?"

"So we'll mount a counterattack from here in the Mousetrap and drive it off Weichsel."

"Another feint. To draw away our rapid-response forces, so the Slugs can attack us elsewhere." I nodded.

Howard said, "Not a feint. Feints are intended to mislead. The Pseudocephalopod is direct in its tactics."

"But we won't take the bait."

"Oh, yes, we will. Because it's excellent bait."

I stiffened. "Huh?"

Howard waved on a hologen in his compartment's corner, and it flickered as he scrolled to an overhead, visible-light image of a flat snow-and-rock landscape. I could tell it was Weichsel because a half-dozen rust-orange mammoths ambled at the image's far edge. At the image's center, snow drifted against one side of a bulbous Slug-metal blue disk. Based on the size of the mammoths, the disk was ninety feet in diameter and twenty feet high. Six snow-covered ridges stretched away from the disk like wheel spokes.

I leaned toward the image. "We've never seen a Slug instrumentality that small, except for individual Warrior weapons and those booby-trap footballs they leave around. What do you think it is?"

Howard nodded. "Our collective hunch is that you're looking at a hard-shell facility housing a control Ganglion, armored and with enough cognitive capacity to control operations on a planetary scale. A remote brain, if you will."

"There's no Troll?" Normally when the Slugs set up housekeeping on a planet, they dug in a transport ship as big as a small mountain, a "Troll" by United Nations phonetic designator. Trolls were purpose-built to incubate Slug Warriors by the millions.

Howard shook his head. "We've identified four Fire-witches orbiting Weichsel, and a force of fifty thousand Warriors, deployed in defensive positions around the Ganglion."

I shook my head. "When the war started—hell, any-time up until the last two years—that was scary. But the war fighting balance has shifted. Four Firewitches? Today one Scorpion squadron will eat them alive. Then we can stand off and brilliant bomb the maggots and their brain from orbit."

"But if we could capture the brain intact, we might be able to locate the Pseudocephalopod homeworld."

I raised my eyebrows. We had captured a few Slug ships over the years, but the little maggots were regular kamikazes. The thinking parts always self-destructed before we could examine them.

I pointed at the snow-covered-disk image. "What makes you think we could take this brain alive?"

"Two reasons. First, you can devise and execute a plan that will achieve tactical surprise. Second, the Pseudocephalopod fully expects that you will take the brain alive, as you put it."

"So it's a trap. By now, we've learned not to walk into Slug traps."

Howard pulled his chessboard back between us, then moved a white pawn, undefended, into a center square. "It's not a trap, it's a gambit. A sacrifice of valuable material offered to gain time and space." He slid a black bishop onto the center square and captured the white pawn.

I cocked my head. "What time are the Slugs after? What space?"

"Well, I don't know. But if you capture that brain intact, and if we can use it to develop the targeting intelligence we need, and if the fleet can deliver weaponized Cavorite on target, before the Pseudocephalopod completes its own plan, we win the war. Not win a battle every few years. Not wait until the technology pendulum swings back against us and toward the Pseudocephalopod Hegemony. We can win. Finally. Forever."

I sighed. "So human beings can get back to beating each other's brains in."

"I prefer to think in terms of a lasting peace."

"If we take the Slugs' gambit, but all of your 'ifs' don't come true, what happens?"

Howard shrugged. "Human extermination. The end of civilization. Stuff like that."

I smiled and shook my head. "Fortunately, your superiors aren't about to risk Armageddon to win some chess game." My smile froze, and my eyes widened. I frowned at my old friend. "Howard, you haven't sent this idea of yours up the line for approval yet. Have you?"

"No—"

I blew out a breath. Howard was a paranoid nerd, but he didn't deserve to have his career ended because he pushed one idiotic idea. "Good. Because if you did, they'd relieve you in about two minutes."

"It wasn't my idea. It was sent down the line to us, already. From Earth. We are to attack Weichsel with all deliberate speed." He pointed to an encrypted chip on the desk. "That's your copy of the order."

My eyebrows rose so far that the skin on top of my head wrinkled. "You're kidding."

I read the order. He wasn't.

SEVEN

TWENTY MINUTES LATER, Howard, Ord, and I had changed into Eternad armor, and we exited a tube downweight, at level six, the small-unit maneuver range. The range had a seventy-five-foot-high ceiling and a twenty-acre floor set with obstacles and targets that the range umpires could move to simulate varied tactical situations.

Holo training has its place, and Ready Brigade spent hours each week in the simulators. But there's no substitute for sweat, noise, chaos, and physical exhaustion.

As we arrived, platoons from Ready Brigade Mousetrap maneuvered, squads in full tactical Eternad armor advancing at a crouching run while others covered them, then leapfrogged past their buddies. Detonation simulators shook the floor; hot smoke confused visible and infrared images. Squad leaders suddenly found their radios cut off by the umpire, forcing them to pop their visors and shout commands over the chatter of blanks and the screams of "wounded."

The brigadier general who commanded Ready Brigade stood fifty yards from us. When he spotted us, he popped his helmet visor open, waved, then jogged toward us.

Howard said to me, "Jason, it would take us weeks to send objections back to Earth and get a response."

Ord, his own visor open, leaned toward me. "In the meantime, sir—"

I sighed. "An order is an order." From the first day I wised off as a trainee, I've bent plenty of rules. But even if I was now prepared to disobey a lawful order, my superiors would just relieve *me,* and my replacement would have to execute the order, but at the disadvantage of being new to the job. Which could get more GIs killed and increase the chance of failure. There would be time later to vent. For now, my job was to do the job I was sworn to do.

Ready Brigade's commander arrived, in Eternad armor, helmet tucked under one arm, sweating. He saluted. I returned it and smiled. "Keeping them busy, Rusty?"

He grinned back. "Keeping myself busy, too, sir. One thing about Mousetrap, there's not a lot else to do."

I motioned him to follow the three of us into a vacant umpire's blind, where the four of us leaned against the dark consoles. I was about to cure Ready Brigade's boredom, and the cure would be painful. I said to Rusty, "You've heard about the Weichsel incursion?"

He glanced at Howard, then said, "Unofficially, sir. Did Space Force grease the maggots yet?"

I glanced at Howard, myself, then said, "Not exactly."

EIGHT

RUSTY LEFT HIS EXECUTIVE OFFICER in charge of brigade training, and then he, Ord, Howard, and I reconvened our little war council back on Spook level forty-eight, huddled around a conference table in a neat and tidy compartment adjoining Howard's office.

I outlined the mission and my concept. It would have been unprofessional to betray my own reservations, and I don't think I did.

Rusty shook his head slowly and his brow wrinkled. "I don't know, sir."

"Big rewards justify big risks, Rusty. How soon can you embark Ready Brigade?"

"The preparedness standard for a Ready Brigade is wheels-up in fourteen hours, sir. Last drill we did it in twelve hours, thirty-nine minutes—"

Ord raised his eyebrows at me and almost smiled. Wheels-up hearkened back to a time when troops deployed in fixed-wing aircraft with retractable landing gear. At the turn of the century, a crack light division like the Eighty-second Airborne would have needed sixteen hours to embark.

I said to the brigadier, "Last time I was at the Pentagon, a Marine claimed that the Marine Ready Brigade at Camp Pendleton once went wheels-up in twelve hours flat."

Rusty smiled. "My command sergeant major gently suggested to the brigade after the last drill, sir, that twelve thirty-nine was a time even jarheads could beat. Ready Brigade will be embarked in eleven hours flat, if Space Force can warm up the bus that fast."

Ten hours later, I watched as Ready Brigade's three thousand troops crowded the hundred-foot-wide platform of South Forty D to which the *Abraham Lincoln* was moored. The soldiers shuffled toward the maglev-tunnel-sized aft hatch in the *Abe*'s flank. Gravity on Broadway, near Mousetrap's centerline, was low enough that the Eternad-armored soldiers easily carried individual loads of personal weapons, shelter, ammunition, rations, and unit- and mission-specific equipment in back and chest packs that made them look like cartoon Santas on Christmas Eve. On Weichsel, at ninety-eight percent Earth gravity, each soldier would cut down to a combat load within minutes after disembarkation but would still be loaded like an abused burro.

Into the *Abe*'s forward hatch slid the hovertanks of Ready Brigade's armored cavalry battalion, their engines whispering at idle in the light gravity.

I walked alongside a specialist fourth, his freckled face pale inside his open-visored helmet. He was combat-fit—they all were—but he breathed in staccato gulps. "First combat deployment, Specialist?"

He turned to me and his eyes widened. Then he said, "Sir! I deployed with the Eighty-second to Korea after the quake, General."

I nodded. Human Union Space-Mobile Division Mousetrap was this century's equivalent to the old-time gunslingers of the United States' Eighty-second Airborne Division, a razor-edged unit light on equipment, long on mobility, and ready to move anywhere within hours, improvising on the fly if necessary, whether the mission was disaster relief or stinging the scourge of the universe on the ankle. The 'Trap Rats were mostly volunteers seconded from crack Earth units like the Eighty-second, the Légion Étrangère, and even the Ghurka Rifles, with a sprinkling of offworld talent.

The kid asked me, "Is it true, sir? We really get to fight Slugs?"

Howard and the Spooks weren't going to brief the brigade until the *Abe* had buttoned up and cleared Mousetrap's south doors. But the fact was that after three decades of war, indications of Slug espionage or communication interception to discover human plans remained zero. The maggots didn't spy on us any more than we spied on the common cold virus. If we got in the Pseudocephalopod's way, it exterminated us, or fought to its last deployed Warrior trying. If we didn't get in its way, the Pseudocephalopod ignored us. I nodded to the kid.

He pumped his fist and grinned. "Outstanding!"

I sighed, and he shuffled on toward the *Abe*'s intake hatch. The bluster of esprit de corps sometimes carries troops to victory, like wind in sails. But only those who haven't seen war are fond of it.

All these kids were about to learn that lesson.

NINE

SIXTEEN HOURS OUT FROM MOUSETRAP, the whisper of my boots against ladder rungs echoed in the deserted vastness of one of the thirty-six launch bays that belted the *Abraham Lincoln*'s midsection. So did my rasping breath. The aft access platform perched between the launch rails, thirty feet above the launch bay deck plates, and heights terrify me.

I reached the platform and clung to its handholds. The open-hatched ship poised above me was a Scorpion, a ninety-foot-long ceramic teardrop of a single-seat fighter and the current game changer in this war. The Slugs invented Cavorite drive, and we stole it from them fair and square. Then we adapted it not only to behemoths based on the Slugs' own massive ships, like the *Abraham Lincoln,* but to the elegant gnat that was the Scorpion. Scorpions flitted and stung like no space vessel the Slugs had ever seen. That's a poor turn of phrase, because the maggots don't have eyes and are blind in the non-infrared spectrum. But to date, the Scorpion's confirmed ship-to-ship kill ratio against the Slug Firewitch stood at two hundred twelve to zero. Also, a Scorpion could maneuver as easily, though more slowly, in a planet's atmosphere as in a vacuum.

"Mind if I join you, sir?" I clutched a railing, then looked down. Ord stood on the deck below, looking up at me, hands on hips.

I had been reading inflections in Ord's voice and posture for three decades, and I knew this was the time he had chosen to discuss the incident with the private on Bren. I wasn't going to add to the unpleasantness by having the conversation thirty feet up. "I'll come down."

My boots thumped the deck, and I turned and looked back up at the Scorpion's stern, where the clamshell doors of the weapons pod stood open for loading, like the speed brakes on a conventional jet. A Scorpion in combat could hover dead still, but it could also fly faster than any rocket or bullet fired out of its front end. So Lockheed had designed it to drop "fire-and-forget" guided munitions out its back end, the way conventional jets ejected radar chaff and flares to confuse homing missiles. The Scorpion's internal weapons bay stinger was twenty feet long.

I pointed at it. "A squad in Eternads can pack in there. It's gravity cocooned, like the cockpit. Ten thousand miles per hour to zero in one thousand feet. And inside the squad will feel six G, tops."

Ord nodded and sighed. "I remember when I saw the holonews from the Paris Air Show. Captain Metzger and the Scorpion shocked the world that day, sir."

So this was why Ord had sought me out here, alone in this bay. So he could segue the conversation to my godson. To avoid taking the bait, I cocked my head. "What do you think of my tactical concept, Sergeant Major?"

He cocked his head back at me and wrinkled his forehead. "Potentially brilliant. High risk. If I may say so, sir, much like its creator."

Crap. There was no escaping the impending deluge. I sighed. "What's on your mind, Sergeant Major?"

One corner of Ord's lip twitched up, as close to a smile of recognition as he ever came. Then it faded into a frown of concern. Ord wore concern proudly.

"Sir, the general knows I have the highest regard for him as a soldier and as a human being."

Oboy. A senior NCO addressing an officer in the third person signaled an impending lecture, like a mother calling her kid by first, middle, and last names.

Ord cleared his throat. "But your life view has worried me since Congresswoman Metzger's death, sir."

Even after three years, to hear it said aloud that Munchkin was dead struck me like a slap. Munchkin and I, both orphaned by the Slug Blitz in 2036, had soldiered together as gunner and loader. We had both found and lost the great loves of our lives during the battle that followed, and I had delivered her son, my godson, in a cold cave on a moon of Jupiter. The army is a big family, but Munchkin had grown closer to me than a sister, and her son had grown up like my own.

I blinked, then cleared my throat. "My life view is fine, Sergeant Major."

Ord's gray eyes softened. "Have you heard from Captain Metzger, sir?"

I shrugged. "Since the embargo, nothing but propaganda gets out of Tressel. I read one that says he's the air vice marshall." Meaning no, my godson hadn't contacted me since his mother's death. Not so much as a happy-birthday holo chip.

"He must be quite busy, sir. The aircraft test ranges are remote. Perhaps he's been out of touch."

I snorted. "He must be out of touch if he's still working for those Nazis."

Tressel's civilization had evolved from slaves kidnapped from Earth by the Slugs to mine Cavorite thirty thousand years ago. Tressel resembled Earth, but stunted back in the mid-Paleozoic, and Tressel's humans lagged Earth technologically by a hundred fifty years. Socially, they could have passed for Germany in the last-century thirties.

The Slugs' Tressel mines had played out thirty thousand years ago, and Tressel didn't have anything else we wanted. Therefore, Earth's politicians could afford to be shocked—shocked!—at Tressen human-rights abuses, so they embargoed trade with Tressel.

Tressel remained a member of the union, and so an ally, "in the event of a clear and present threat from a common enemy," meaning if the Slugs came back.

Ord said, "Sir, I think Jude's loyalty is to General Planck, not to the party. Neither of them are Nazis. And I don't think Jude . . ."

I cocked my head. "Blames me for his mother's death?"

"Sir, he knows you literally gave your right arm attempting to save her."

I flexed my organic prosthetic. Guaranteed by the surgeon general to be better than original equipment or Uncle Sam gets his money back, and I get my stump back. "Then why are we having this discussion?"

"Sir, I think *you* blame you for her death."

"I spent six months in the special-needs ward at New

Bethesda listening to shrinks tell me not to blame myself, Sergeant Major. I'm past it."

Ord opened his mouth, then closed it, then said, "As you say, General."

I walked beneath the Scorpion's open stinger and squinted up into its shadowed interior. "You think we can anchor fast ropes to those weapons racks?"

"A mountaineering team's already working up a fast-rope descent technique in Bay Nine, sir." He paused. "Sir, how is Admiral Ozawa? If I may ask."

I sighed. Ord wasn't going to let go of my personal problems. Mimi Ozawa and I had met early in the war, and it had taken us only about twenty years to figure out that we had the hots for each other as badly as a het couple our age can. Fortunes of war being what they were, by the time we figured it out, we were constantly light-years apart.

I awaited eagerly the hard-copy letters Mimi wrote daily, which arrived in bunches aboard each jumped cruiser. I awaited even more eagerly the holos she sent. I will note that because these passed from a space force admiral to a general, they were uncensored. Beyond that, use your imagination.

"You may ask, Sergeant Major. She's chafing at a dirt-side assignment." Mimi was a fighter jock kicked upstairs to command cruisers, and she was generally regarded as the best—excepting only my godson—driver in the Human Union of any flying object in the human inventory. She was also too smart, too uniquely knowledgeable, and had hogged too many years of the shipboard command time that flag officers coveted. So Space Force had rotated her to Earth ten months before to serve as the first commandant of the Human Union Military Academy. I hadn't seen Mimi live for three years, and Ord's question made me ache.

"If I may say so, Admiral Ozawa is a fine officer and an even better woman, sir."

"No argument." We walked from the launch bay, our steps echoing in the vastness. "If I did have a problem, which I don't, Mimi would be part of the solution, wouldn't she?"

"Yes, sir. But an unmatured relationship may be a source of anxiety, rather than a source of strength."

I stopped, then turned to face Ord. If Ord weren't as much surrogate father to me as my command sergeant major, I would have told him he was getting into areas that were none of a subordinate's business. The potential trouble with my relationship with Mimi was the trouble with most service personnel's relationships. Contact was so infrequent that the person you left behind had grown into someone else by the time you returned to them. And so had you.

At best, the anxieties caused a tense blind date after every separation. At worst, one or the other of you couldn't stand the new person, or the stress of reacquaintance, or both, and the relationship crumbled.

"Sergeant Major, Admiral Ozawa and I aren't close enough for me to be anxious." Actually, I pined for Mimi every moment that I wasn't preoccupied by my job. But those idle moments were few, and Ord, by his nod, knew it.

We stepped out into the companionway, headed for a preliminary briefing. A couple of swabbies painting bulkheads straightened as we passed, and the extra sets of ears ended the discussion, for the time being.

One day later the *Abe* stood poised to jump through the Temporal Fabric Insertion Point that would pop us out three days of starship travel away from Weichsel.

In Launch Bay Fourteen, I stood alongside Ord, both of us armored up in the uniform of the day. We watched as Howard Hibble, nine of his Spooks, and a loadmaster who would handle their disembarkation on Weichsel stood in line on a makeshift steel-lattice access ramp that led into the poised Scorpion's wide-open stinger pod.

The Spooks, who were flabby or pencil-skinny in street clothes, lurched up the ramp looking like albino gorillas in Eternad winter-camo armor. Unlike the armored grunts now loading in the other bays, each Spook carried a fraction of an infantry soldier's basic load, just a sidearm and a mission-specific gear pack no bigger than a turn-of-the-century laptop bag.

Ord frowned. "I wish we weren't going in meteorologically blind, sir."

Ord always found something to frown about. It's in a sergeant major's genes. But I agreed with him. Weichsel was at the moment light-years away, across an impenetrable black hole. Even after we popped out, we would be committed to landing with little idea of current and impending weather conditions at our landing zone.

Weather is a greater peril for an attacker than a defender even in the best of circumstances. Weichsel was not the best of circumstances. It looked like Earth in winter, but the planet was prone to hurricane-force blizzards. Worse, the storms arose suddenly from nothing. Or at least nothing the weather weenies could identify in advance.

I shrugged. "Calculated risk." Well, actually, my exometeorology officer had thrown up his hands and said the risk was incalculable. He did note that the first two Earth survey parties to land on Weichsel had perished in flash blizzards.

Ord's finger bobbed as he counted Spooks. Then he flipped down his visor, checked his display, and frowned. "Odd. The intel landing party's one body short."

I said, "So it is."

Ord swiveled his head toward me, jaw slack.

TEN

ORD STARED AT ME as hydraulics hissed the upper ladder scaffold away from the Scorpion. "Sir, you aren't thinking of landing with the assault troops?"

"As a consultant. A resource. Not in the chain of command. The last thing the company commanders on the ground need is brass looking over their shoulders. That's why I'm not on the manifest."

Ord's mouth formed an "O" as his back straightened an additional half inch. "A theater commander in the first wave of a two-company raiding party? You could get killed! Sir. It's completely . . ."

Reckless. Immature. And so on. But history recorded that Churchill, one of Ord's favorite quote sources, tried to hitch a ride on a landing craft on D-day. Churchill got talked out of it at the last minute, but my situation wasn't comparable, because Churchill was a civilian, and also he had nothing to add to the battle.

"Sergeant Major, I was the first modern human being to see a Slug alive. Colonel Hibble and I are the only people left alive who've been inside a working Troll incubator ship. This is a hasty operation, with the war at stake.

This plan, more than most, won't survive contact with the enemy. Improvisation, based on intuitive knowledge of the Slugs, may decide the result. No human in this galaxy has fought more Slugs in more venues than I have. If I didn't apply my specialized expertise on the ground, where it could do some good, I'd fire myself." My chest puffed a bit. I doubt that Churchill made as good a speech when he argued his case.

Ord chewed his lip. Real-time battlefield communication had made leading from the front obsolete since Rommel, and we both knew it.

I pointed at the Spooks as they gawked and dawdled. "If Rusty's two best infantry companies can protect *that* bunch until the cav lands, they can sure protect me."

Ord crossed his arms, frowned, but nodded. "I want the general to know that I question the true rationale behind his decision."

"But it *is* my decision?" Generals don't need to persuade sergeants. Maybe I was really persuading myself.

"Indubitably, sir."

I nodded and harrumphed.

"Then may I accompany the general?"

"No. There isn't room, and you're too valuable here." Both reasons were more or less true.

I locked down my visor, then stepped toward the loading ramp.

"General?" Ord's voice crackled in my earpiece.

I turned back toward him as he saluted. "Keep the maggots off your ass, sir."

I returned his salute and smiled through my visor. "Always, Sergeant Major. This one should be easy."

ELEVEN

FOUR MINUTES LATER, I stood tail-end-Charlie on the ramp behind the Spooks as a medic plugged in to the meds catheter on each man's armored thigh, then handed the troop off to the loadmaster to be fitted into the Scorpion's weapons bay like a breathing log with Plasteel bark.

As only one of seven hundred fifty survivors from the Ganymede Expeditionary Force, I remembered how, during the Blitz at the start of the war, infantry got hauled through space for days, sedated and stacked inside de-mothballed space shuttles, to save space and conserve life-support systems. I also remembered being hauled off the battlefield of the First Battle of Mousetrap like a flour sack, in the emptied weapons bay of a Scorpion, which up until then nobody had ever ridden in.

Today, we had drugs that could knock a GI colder and revive him sharper.

I put two and two together and figured that we could convert the fastest, stealthiest single-seat fighters in the universe into squad-carrying landing craft. Nobody had tried it yet, but it seemed to me like a terrific way to surprise the maggots.

I gave myself a mental back pat for that particular application of my specialized expertise. Just one more example of why I should send myself in with the first wave. I stepped up to the medic.

He pointed at the cap of my catheter, his eyes on a sedative syrette while he unpeeled it. "Open up, newbie. This doesn't hurt."

It was actually easier for the medic to open the catheter cap from outside the suit, but forcing a newbie to reach around and unscrew it with his gauntleted fingers was a simple test to be sure the newbie had at least some fine-motor skills in armor.

I said, "You go ahead, doc. I've done this before."

He jerked his gaze up from the syrette, and his eyes widened when he saw the stars stenciled above my helmet visor. "General Wander?"

"Just along for the ride. What are you pouring, today, son?"

He unscrewed my catheter cap, then plugged in the syrette. "Uh—thousand milligrams of timed-release Neobarbitol with a delayed amphetamine and caffeine chaser. And a hematopoietin to enhance red blood cell growth. Thirty minutes from now, you'll drop out like you fell off a table, and when you wake up you'll be ready to scrimmage the Chicago Bears for forty-eight hours straight." He paused. "At least—"

"At least that's how it affects younger troops?"

"Yes, sir."

I hate drugs, but I hate missing a party worse. I patted his shoulder as he depressed the syrette's plunger. "I'll be fine, son."

The loadmaster also did a double take when he saw me

shuffle into the bay. He and I would be rearmost in the pod, and thus first from this ship to exit onto Weichsel. He harnessed me, then helped me pack in alongside three young Spooks and boots-on-helmet to the trio behind us. Most were already purring along in the low-metabolism sleep that would allow all of us to live together in this oversized sewer pipe for three days.

The loadmaster wriggled in alongside me. The medic dosed him, then toggled the ramp's controls and backed out on it. That left us all hanging in the bay, heads down, like bananas on a stalk, with the deck plates thirty feet below us.

I held my breath. Then the clamshell doors below whined closed and left us in absolute darkness. I exhaled. I don't mind tight spaces as much as I mind heights.

The way the first phase of this operation, the part I was about to sleep through, was supposed to work was that as soon as the two infantry companies and the Spooks were buttoned up inside their Scorpions, the *Abraham Lincoln* would make the jump from the Mousetrap and pop out three days' travel from Weichsel.

We didn't know what kind of sensing the Slugs used to detect a ship, but it seemed to work as well—and as poorly—as ours. That meant the Slugs occupying Weichsel would know immediately that a human cruiser had appeared three days away from them. The Slugs also knew that in three decades of war we had staged every landing we had attempted by bringing capital ships like the *Abraham Lincoln* within low-orbital distance. So, *Abraham Lincoln* would carve obvious, loitering figure eights just beyond the Temporal Fabric Insertion Point it had popped out of, posing no threat.

However, as soon as *Abraham Lincoln* popped out, she would launch all thirty-six Scorpions poised, like the one I hung within, on her launch rails. The Scorpions would make for Weichsel like scalded gnats, as invisible to the Slugs as Scorpions were to us, according to the Spooks.

Two days and twenty hours later, the infantry inside the Scorpions would waken. Two days and twenty-three hours later, all thirty-six Scorpions would form up in space a hundred miles up, directly above Howard's precious Slug brain. Then the Scorpions would dive straight down through Weichsel's atmosphere at ten thousand miles per hour, stop on the proverbial dime at an altitude of forty feet, turn their stinger ends down toward the ground, and open their bay doors. Scorpions were less gravity-shielded than cruisers, so the troops would endure six G and arrive bruised and nauseated, but that was a price any GI would gladly pay to avoid being shot at.

The Slugs, knowing that the *Abraham Lincoln* remained a safe three days' journey away, would be tactically astonished. At least, that was the assumption.

But if this first-wave landing went wrong, the Scorpions' bays were clogged with useless troops, not weapons to defend themselves ship-to-ship. The four Firewitches patrolling above Weichsel weren't nimble, but as soon as they realized they had company, they would swoop in. At best, the Scorpions would scatter like quail and sneak back to the *Abraham Lincoln,* and the operation would crater. At worst, pieces of these kids and of me would be scattered across the snow a hundred light-years from home.

In my earpiece, over the beeps and chirps of telemetry, the Scorpion pilot's intercom voice buzzed. "In a moment, our flight attendants will begin our beverage service for all of you back there in the main cabin. Correct change is always—"

I slept.

TWELVE

———

"—CONTACT WITH THE WEICHSEL stratosphere in forty seconds. Some heat will bleed through from the skin into the bay back there, but nothing your armor ventilators can't handle." The Scorpion's pilot was speaking again. The loadmaster's elbow jostled me as he checked static lines in the dark. I switched to the squad net and heard the Spooks all around me grumbling and puking into their helmet disposal tubes.

Evidently the younger Spooks had all been enjoying wakefulness longer than I had. Just as well. My head pounded between my temples, and risen bile seared my throat.

The pilot said, "Hang on back there. You must be taller than the mouse to board this ride." Inside my helmet, I rolled my eyes. If they held a comedy contest for Zoomies and drill sergeants, nobody would win.

We dropped like the mother of all roller coasters, and six G of deceleration stuffed my stomach into my socks. Somebody moaned over the squad net. The Scorpion, and presumably thirty-five others arrayed around it, slowed from speeds measured in thousands of miles per second to a ten-thousand-mile-per-hour crawl. The Scorpion's gravity cocoon kept us from being pulped like beefsteak tomatoes, but nobody was laughing.

Then we stopped.

A moment later, familiar, normal weight returned, then shifted as the Scorpion rotated until we hung in the darkness, inverted, like bats. Blood roared in my ears.

"Take care out there, guys." There was no hint of stand-up comic in the pilot's voice this time.

The loadmaster said, "First rank, prepare to down-rappel."

Then the clamshells whined open, and above my head, forty feet below, the snowdrifts of Weichsel burst so bright white that my armor's sensors darkened my visor to blast level.

The loadmaster said, "First rank out!"

I dangled from a synlon rappel line below the Scorpion's tail, one hand paying out line through the carabiner at my waist, while I muttered about whose bright idea it was for me to be here.

I arrived on Weichsel in an explosion of snow and sank past my knees. Then a Spook landed on top of me, and pushed me beltline-deep.

A half-dozen voices grunted and swore.

Somebody said, "Holy moly! Isn't this exciting?" That was Howard.

Somebody else said, "Goddamit, Howard! Get off me!" That was me.

I shoved Howard off into a drift, broomed snow off my visor with my gauntlet, and looked around. The infantry ringed us, galloping wide-legged atop the snow on the snowshoe webs that had jackknifed from their boot soles.

Each platoon net I listened in on rattled with necessary communication, with no word wasted. That indicated good training. There was also heavy breathing. That indicated that running in snowshoes isn't for the flabby.

Above us hovered all thirty-six Scorpions, only ours and one other still reeling in rappel lines and closing their pod doors. The air above each scorching-hot fuselage shimmered. Vulnerable as they dangled like monstrous hummingbirds, the Scorpions would remain above us only until the ground commander released them.

For a hundred-yard radius around us, the top yard of snow had been blown away by the downdraft of air pushed by thirty-six Scorpions, as they had screamed down through a hundred miles of atmosphere like hypersonic bulldozers.

One thing I noticed was what wasn't here. No blizzard. The sky was clear—not even a breeze stirred the snowflakes. I smiled.

Also, there were no Slugs. No mag-rail rifles fired, no masses of armored Warriors maneuvered to assault us. Complete surprise!

Unless we had landed in the wrong spot. My heart skipped.

Next to me, Howard jumped up and down, knee deep in snow.

"Goddamit, Howard! What are you doing?"

He grinned at me through his visor. "Jump yourself, Jason! We're standing right on top of the Ganglion!"

I jumped and was rewarded by a hollow bong as my boots struck metal. In all directions, the snow sloped away from the dome-shaped hummock we stood upon. A half-dozen drifts converged on the spot where Howard and I and the pile of flailing, armored arms and legs that was the Spook team stood.

I jumped again.

Bong.

"I'll be damned." I knew Rusty's troops and the *Abe*'s pilots were good, but they had crossed millions of miles of space in three days, then hit a target no bigger than a backyard swimming pool, all without our enemy being the wiser.

The Spooks, assisted by GIs with wide manual snow shovels, were already foxholing down to each of the six radiating ribs through which, according to Howard, the Ganglion sent and received communication to and from the Warriors under its command.

Once we severed the Ganglion's ability to communicate with its Warriors, the Slugs wouldn't drop like marionettes with cut strings, but they wouldn't fight and maneuver as units, either.

I waddled through the drifts to the nearest foxhole, then peered down at the Spook and GI below. They knelt on the hole's floor, a convex patch of blue Slug metal, as the Spook fitted a charge to a seam in the Ganglion's arm casing. Then they paddled up the snow and stood, the Spook fingering a black detonator while the GI called, "Fire in the hole" three times.

The charge flashed, hissed, and raised a steam cloud that hung in the frigid air. Within a fifty-yard radius, five more hisses sounded, and then five more steam clouds hung.

As we watched, the steam drifted together, coalesced into a single plume, and rose into the clear, still sky, past the hovering Scorpions. Beautiful. Perfect.

Howard said, "Uh-oh."

THIRTEEN

TWENTY MINUTES LATER, wind whipped our helmet antennae and swirled a snow fog so strong that, even with enhanced optics, visibility was down to forty feet.

Howard shouted, his voice booming in my earpiece, "It was the atmospheric disturbance created by the Scorpions' hypersonic passage. Now the storm's building on itself."

I winced. "Howard, we have radios. You don't have to scream."

Howard slapped at a rope that writhed in the growing gale as it dangled again from the Scorpions. "Jason, we can't abort this now."

Howard's Spooks, working through the gathering blizzard, had cut through the Ganglion's armored housing, and we had our first look at Slug royalty after three decades of war.

It was a blob as big as a two-seat urban electric and as green as snot. No evil eyes, flailing tendrils, or slobbery fangs. Just a blob with a half-dozen thigh-thick armored cables plugged in around its midsection. The cables, torched black by the Spooks' cutting charges, now led nowhere.

The exposed Ganglion, free of its armored housing, hovered above the snow on a disk, presumably held up by Cavorite.

I leaned into the wind, toward Howard. "It's mute and blind now?"

"I think so. But it could have—"

Zzeee.

Someone screamed.

I said, "Heavys!" The Slugs waged war more like Neanderthals than like a millennial master race. If something they didn't like got in their way, they threw an object at it. Slug Warriors' magnetic-rail rifles were just scaled-down versions of the Slug artillery piece, which tossed a projectile the size and weight of a wall safe.

Red fog spat at us, mixed among the snowflakes. The fog trailed back thirty feet from Howard and me, to the neck ring of a Spook kid's armor. A single heavy round, lobbed in here for ranging purposes, had decapitated him.

I said to Howard, "It called fire on its own position! We gotta get out of here."

A surrounded human soldier might call artillery fire down on his own position, to take the bad guys with him, and save his buddies or his mission. Slugs behaved the same, but the altruism was missing. In this case, it was simple logic for the Slugs. The Ganglion wanted its troops to kill it, lest we be allowed to capture it. Also, of course, it wanted to kill us.

The commander of the infantry was already moving his troops off the Ganglion hummock. Four Spooks had fastened ropes to the Ganglion's motility plate, so they could tow it away from this spot before the Slug heavy rounds began raining down on us.

Zzee. Zzeee. Zzee.

A battery volley of red-hot heavy rounds thudded around us.

Crump.

Above our heads, a heavy struck a Scorpion amidships. The Scorpion disappeared with a rumbling boom. It didn't explode. It didn't crash. It disappeared.

Howard said, "The round stripped the shielding off the Cavorite mass. The ship shot away from here at miles per second."

Crump. Another Scorpion disappeared.

Three of the Spooks who had been pulling the Ganglion out of harm's way lay dead alongside it.

In my earpiece, the Scorpion Squadron leader said, "Raiding party reembark! We'll get you out of here!" He would also get his own ships out of here, before more of them got creamed.

Another heavy volley rained in; a round struck a man, and he vanished.

The ground commander radioed Howard. "Colonel Hibble, we can't get a sling on your brain plate in time."

Howard said, "Get your troops out. The Ganglion weighs nothing. Two people can tow it out of the kill zone. You come back and pick us up after the storm."

I sighed. I knew who those two people were going to be.

Howard was a devious geek, but under fire he developed a heroic streak.

Zzee.

I flinched, though I had no idea where the incoming was bound, and something knocked me faceplate-down in the snow. I lay there and felt around my shoulder. A Slug heavy had lawn-mowered down my back, stripping away my pack and my armor's life-support systems. But except for a thump between my shoulder blades, I seemed to be unbroken.

I levered myself up to my knees and peered through the storm.

Troops snaked up ropes, back into the remaining Scorpions, as Slug rounds continued to pound our landing zone. Wounded were roped up before the able-bodied GIs, as, it appeared, were bodies. That would probably cost lives, but no Ready Brigade soldier was going to leave a buddy behind, even under an artillery barrage.

Howard and I grasped the tow ropes on the Ganglion and leaned forward as we towed it through howling snow and away from the zero point where the heavy rounds kept rattling down like hailstones.

The remaining Scorpions, barely visible through the driven snow, buttoned up, then disappeared.

The heavy rounds stopped. Silence, except for the wind, returned to Weichsel.

By my visor display, Howard, our green POW, and I had already moved four hundred yards north of the landing zone. My display also said straight-line winds were gusting to one hundred six miles per hour.

I toggled through my visor display to Systems Check, then swore. My armor's heater had quit. Actually, it hadn't quit, it had left the premises, sheared off by the Slug heavy's near miss. Already, despite my exertions, I shivered inside my armor.

According to our intel, two thousand yards from our landing zone, a perimeter defended by ten thousand Slug Warriors ringed the Ganglion hummock from which we fled with our kidnap victim.

If we could slip through that perimeter under cover of the storm, we might find a place to hole up. If we remained inside the perimeter, when the storm blew out we would be dead meat, and our prisoner would be rescued or killed by its own troops.

We slogged on, completely blind now and crawling to stay beneath the worst gusts, until my visor display predicted that the northern segment of the Slug perimeter, populated with its share of ten thousand unfriendly, man-sized, armed, and armored maggots, lay two hundred yards to our front.

Inside my armor, I shivered harder.

FOURTEEN

HOWARD AND I lay side by side in the snow while gusts now measuring one hundred thirty miles per hour rocketed snow above us, and the outside temperature remained two degrees below zero, Fahrenheit. The wind chill wasn't worth checking, though my armor would have calculated it. My armor had lost its heater, not its brains.

Therefore, I heard Howard perfectly when he whispered over the intercom, "We won't be able to shoot our way through the Pseudocephalopod lines."

Actually, with our M40s, the two of us, like any human infantry, could shoot our way through many times our weight in Slug Warriors. But once they realized where we were, the Slugs would pour onto our trail by the thousands, blizzard or no blizzard, brain-dead or not.

Stealth was our only option. I fingered the trench knife on my belt with numb fingers. "I know. On a normal Slug perimeter, the Warriors spread out twenty yards apart. I'll low-crawl up to the perimeter, take one out, then we'll tow the blob through the gap and disappear into the storm before they realize they're down a maggot."

Howard jerked a thumb back at our prisoner, wobbling

in the wind. "Even disconnected from the Ganglion, War-riors will react to the disturbance."

"They won't notice a disturbance. They see in the in-frared spectrum. They know human soldiers give off heat, and that's what they look for. My armor's stone-cold. And I'll knife the maggot, so there won't be any firearm heat flash."

"Then what?"

"Then we'll find shelter. When the storm breaks, they'll find us by our transponders."

Through his visor, Howard frowned. "What if your plan goes wrong?"

I shrugged inside my armor. Over the decades, I had salvaged more disasters than I had caused. However, in-cluding this fiasco, my track record with plans wasn't so great. "Then we'll do what we always do. Run like hell until we think of something. You have a better idea?"

"If we break through the perimeter, we'll be running through a blizzard for days. Our prisoner may not even survive. And your armor heater's broken. We're too old to try this, Jason."

"If we don't try this, we won't get older."

I cross-slung my rifle over my back, maxed my optics so I could see a yard in front of my face, and low-crawled through the snow.

Twenty minutes later, I paused, panting, behind a drift. My arm and leg muscles burned, my knee and elbow joints throbbed, and I sucked wind so hard that my visor's med readout flashed amber. According to the medic who had doped me before we landed, I was supposed to feel great. We *were* too old for this.

The wind swirled snow away from the area fifteen

yards to my front, and I glimpsed an angular black peak that rose a foot above the drifts. Hair stood on my neck. As expected, a Slug Warrior, faced away from me, was hunkered down in defense. Unlike GIs, Slug Warriors didn't share fighting positions with another soldier. Slug Warriors were more like sophisticated white corpuscles than individual soldiers, and they needed neither companionship nor a buddy to take watch while they slept.

I closed the gap between me and the Warrior to five yards, drew my knife, then chinned my comm bar. Behind me, Howard, presuming he hadn't fallen asleep, would see the "go" light in his visor display, feel the vibrate alarm on his cheek, and crawl forward with the Ganglion in tow.

I fingered my knife. There was no "book" on fighting *mano-a-maggot*. Few Earth troops had done it live, despite the Slug War's duration. Slug body armor was easily penetrated by a bullet or a broadsword swung by a six-foot-five Casuni. But a knife wielded by a guy so old that his joints creaked when he rode an exercise bike?

Slugs' armor ended in a skirt at ground level, because they traveled on one bare foot, though they didn't slime along like a true snail. There was an opening higher up in the armor through which the Warrior extruded a tentacle-like pseudopod to grasp its mag-rail rifle. And the armor was open at the anterior end so the Slug's infrared sensory patches, on what one might call its head, could "see."

The biggest knife target would be exposed by bulldogging the Slug over, like a roped calf, then stabbing its underbelly, but that would also create the biggest commotion. The pseudopod hatch at the armor's midriff was smaller than a saucer. The approach would have to be like cutting a sentry's throat from behind.

The Spooks say a Slug Warrior has no independent cognition, no sense of self, because it's simply part of a single, physically separated organism. The Slugs killed my mother, killed the great love of my life, killed more friends than I could count. So I should have been spoiling to gut this one like a trout.

Still, the knife tip trembled in my hand, neither from cold nor fear. My years had taught me how empty this universe was, and how unique life, any life, was within it. Even Slugs.

I stopped, drew a breath, and waited a heartbeat until my hand steadied. Another thing my years had taught me was not to wax philosophic during knife fights.

I paused again a yard behind the Warrior. It stood, the base of its armor buried in drifted snow, six feet long from armor crest to tapered tail, and five feet high. Its armor shone black in the storm's dimness, the transverse plates on its back overlapping like an armadillo's. Its pseudopod wrapped its rifle's peculiar grip. Peculiar to a human hand, at least.

The Warrior swayed, more than the wind required, as though listening to music.

I switched the knife to my natural hand, took a deep breath, then lunged.

FIFTEEN

My RIGHT ARM wrapped the Slug's midsection, where a human infantry soldier's breastplate would have been. The Warrior lurched, thrashed, and twisted the mag-rail rifle toward me. In a fight, a single maggot's no more effective than a ten-year-old throwing a tantrum.

My gloved fingers found the lip of the armor's anterior opening, and I stabbed the knife in with my opposite hand.

There was no need for accuracy, no slashing the windpipe or carotid artery, because Slugs had neither. When punctured, they gushed like squeezed grapes and dropped like sacks.

Howard panted up behind me, the Ganglion bouncing feathery in his wake, like a balloon on a string.

I stared down at the Slug, an armored banana against green-stained whiteness, and toed it. In these few seconds, the dead Warrior's lifeblood had jellied the snow.

Howard was already past me. I ran, caught up, and dug in the snow for the other rope trailing from the Ganglion's motility plate. The wind buffeted the floating saucer, but its own leveling systems whined, and kept it upright, as we towed it.

Zzee. Zzee.

I heard mag rifle fire behind us, over the wind. But nothing whizzed close.

Howard said, "The Warriors are reacting without coordination! We really did isolate them from command and control."

"They won't come after us, once the storm breaks?"

Howard waved his free hand as we pulled our prisoner through the snow. "They will. But in a disorganized way."

"Howard, twenty thousand against two don't have to be organized."

"It may not come to that."

"Why not?"

"We could freeze to death first."

I put both hands on my rope and picked up the pace.

Five hours later, the average wind speed had increased to one hundred thirty miles per hour, and we were reduced to crawling at, according to my 'Puter, a half mile per hour.

Howard's Eternads were keeping him warm and hydrated. "We" weren't going to freeze to death.

However, the heavy that had sheared my armor's back left me with only my 'Puters. The basic principle of Eternad technology hadn't changed since the start of the war. The energy of the wearer's movement charged batteries that ran the suits 'Puters, air-conditioning, heater, and miscellaneous life-support systems. I didn't miss the air-conditioning, and my exertions plus the armor's passive insulation kept me warm, though feeling in my fingers and toes had gone AWOL hours ago.

My biggest problem was the loss of those miscella-

neous life-support systems. The dry cold of a Weichselan blizzard sucked an exercising human dry like he was
crossing the Sahara. Scoops on Howard's boots sucked
snow in, melted it, ran it through his purifier, and stored
the resultant drinking water.

I had to stop periodically, pack snow into my helmet's
spare barf bag by hand, then tuck it inside my armor until
my body heat melted it. The worst of it was that a crate
full of Weichsel's extra-dry powder melted down to just
a glass of water.

I had knelt to scoop snow into my bag with ice-cubed
fingers. That left Howard, who flunked out of Cub Scouts,
on point. He plodded ahead, like a tin Saint Bernard.
While I scooped, I watched him, to gauge visibility. By
the time he got ten yards away from me, he had faded to
a shadow.

I panted into my mike, "Hold up, Howard. Don't get
too far—"

He vanished. The Slug on the saucer, tied to him, disappeared an eye blink later.

SIXTEEN

——

ONE MINUTE AFTERWARD, I paddled through the powder to the spot where Howard had disappeared so fast that I nearly went over the edge myself.

I jacked my optics and saw Howard, spread-eagled, face-down, fifteen feet below, at the base of a short cliff. The Slug saucer rested alongside him, bottom-up.

"Howard?"

Nothing.

"Howard?"

"I certainly didn't see that coming!" Howard's arms and legs flailed, scouring an inadvertent snow angel at the cliff's base.

"You okay?"

"I think so."

I picked my way over the cliff lip. Ten feet above Howard, the lip turned under altogether, and I slid off into a half-ass parachute-landing fall alongside Howard.

I righted the Slug saucer. Our friend shivered there on the vibrating plate, betraying no hostility and less inclination to flee. The cliff broke the wind down to a sixty-mile-per-hour swirl and stretched away to the limits of vision in both directions. Most significantly, in the cliff face directly behind us, over which Howard and I had tumbled, loomed a black opening twenty feet wide and ten high.

"Howard, you found a cave."

He pointed through the snowflakes. "Just resistant limestone above eroded shale. Probably hundreds like it along this outcrop. I doubt there's much depth to it."

I wrapped my rope around my glove again and pulled toward the cave mouth. "There's enough."

Ten feet under the overhang, the wind gave way to calm, and the twilight outside gave way to blackness deep enough that I paused to let my optics adjust. The ceiling even opened up a bit, rising to fifteen feet by my 'Puter. My visor's outside temp gauge shot up to a balmy thirty-four degrees Fahrenheit and continued to rise. I tugged off my gauntlets so I could rub circulation back into my fingers. Toes were next on my agenda. I popped my visor to enjoy the coziness.

I sniffed. I said to Howard, "Smells like—"

From the shadows, something rumbled.

I froze.

Howard said, "Uh-oh."

On further listening, the rumble was more a growl, but a very large growl. A boulder along the cave's back wall moved, then grew, as it resolved into something brown, furry, and grumpy.

The exobiologists had briefed us about Weichselan fauna, observed as well as anticipated. They noted that no analogue to the cave bear of Ice Age Europe had yet been observed on Weichsel, but the probability that such an analogue had evolved calculated at seventy-two percent.

The bear reared on hind legs and snarled at its uninvited

guests. The largest modern Earth Kodiak bear mounted out fourteen feet tall. Paleontologists estimated Earth cave bears could have been thirty percent larger than Kodiaks.

I can only report that the first observed Weichselan cave bear bumped its head on the fifteen-foot-high cave ceiling. This just made it grumpier.

I backed out of the cave as I unslung my rifle.

"Howard, bears eat berries and salmon, right?"

"Not cave bears. Their remains are high in Nitrogen-15."

"Meat eaters?"

"When available."

Any Weichselan two-legged hunter that this bear had encountered up until now would have been very available. The bear dropped down on all fours, lowered its head, and snarled.

I thumbed the selector switch on my rifle to three-round burst as we backed out, then tugged a smoke grenade from my thigh pouch. With personal transponders, smoke is obsolete as a position marker, and the cans are clunky to carry, but I carried them anyway. As Ord said, it was better to have and not need than to need and not have.

The bear stepped forward and bared its teeth.

I stepped backward as I popped the can and rolled it like hissing dice under the bear's nose.

When the can popped and hot crimson smoke billowed out, the beast yipped and jumped back into the shadows.

Howard and I ran like our hair was on fire.

An hour of exploring along the escarpment later, we probed another cave. This one wasn't as deep or as warm as the first one, nor was it as crowded.

We bundled our prisoner in a corner where the temperature measured thirty-six degrees Fahrenheit. There the blob seemed as comfortable as a blob can seem. Then Howard and I sat facing each other on the cold stone, while he uncoiled a hose that connected his scapular vent to my foot vents. His batteries were fully charged, and the barely warmed air he trickled over might stave off frost-bite for me, even though the throb of returning circulation made me grit my teeth.

Howard said, "You didn't shoot the bear."

I shrugged. "I didn't have to." I jerked my thumb at the Ganglion. "Will it survive?"

It was Howard's turn to shrug.

"If it does, how much can it tell us?"

"Ask me again after we get it to Earth alive."

I disconnected from Howard's armor and tugged my boots and gauntlets back on.

Howard said, "We could stay connected. That would be more comfortable for you."

I shook my head. "One of us needs to stay at the cave mouth, on watch. I'll take the first watch. While I'm warm." A relative term.

A half hour later, I sat at the cave mouth with my rifle across my thighs.

At two a.m. local, the sky cleared enough to show stars. Weichsel's version of the North Star sits in a constellation that looks like a bear.

At three a.m., the first dire wolf came sniffing around the cave, its eyes glowing red through the dark. A rifle shot would wake Howard. More important, it would flash a heat signature unlike anything natural on Weichsel. The Slug Warriors might be as disorganized as Howard thought, but why take chances?

I gathered a little pyramid of throwing stones, then

pegged one at the wolf. It bounced off his ribs, and he trotted into the darkness, more confused than hurt.

Later, I shook Howard awake, then turned in.

Blam-blam-blam.

The assault rifle's burst snapped me awake inside my armor, and the armor's heater motor, ineffectual but operating, teased me by prickles between the shoulder blades. The shots' reverberation shivered the cave's ceiling, and snow plopped through my open faceplate, onto my up-turned lips.

"Paugh!" The crystals on my lips tasted of cold and old bones. There was no cave bear in here at the moment, but there had been. I scrubbed my face with my glove. "God-damit, Howard!"

Fifty dark feet from me, silhouetted against the pale dawn that lit the cave's mouth, condensed breath ballooned out of Howard's open helmet. "There are dire wolves out here, Jason!"

"Don't make noise. They're just big hyenas."

"They're coming closer!"

"Throw rocks. That's what I did. It works." I rolled over, aching, on the stone floor and glanced at the time winking from my faceplate display. I just got wakened from my first hour's sleep after eight hours on watch.

I squinted over my shoulder, behind Howard and me, at our companion. It remained a hippo-sized, mucous-green octopus on a platter, humming a yard above the cave floor.

Sleepy or not, I had to get us three off this Ice Age rock unfrozen, unstarved, and undigested.

I groaned as my replaced parts awakened, more slowly than the rest of me.

"Jason!" Howard's voice quavered.

I stood, yawned, wished I could scratch myself through my armor, then shuffled to the cave mouth, juggling a baseball-sized rock from palm to palm. Last night, I had perfected a fastball that terrorized many a dire wolf.

As I stepped alongside Howard at the cave mouth, he lobbed an egg-sized stone with a motion like a girl in gym class. It landed twenty feet short of the biggest, nearest wolf. The monster sauntered up, sniffed the stone, then bared its teeth at us in a red-eyed growl. The wolf pack numbered eleven total, milling around behind the big one, all gaunt enough that we must have looked like walking pot roast to them.

The wolves couldn't eat us. A dire wolf could gnaw an Eternad forearm gauntlet for a week with no result but dull teeth.

I looked up at the clear dawn sky. The wolves were, however, bad advertising. The storm had wiped out all traces of our passing and, I hoped, would retard any search by the decapitated Slug Legion.

I planned for us to hide out in this hole until the good guys homed in on our transponders.

If any good guys survived. We might starve in this hole waiting for dead people.

I wound up, pegged my baseball-sized stone at the big wolf, and plinked him on the nose. I whooped. I couldn't duplicate that throw if I pitched nine innings' worth. The wolf yelped and trotted back fifty yards, whining but unhurt.

Howard shrugged. "The wolf pack doesn't necessarily give us away. We could just be a bear carcass or something in here."

I jerked my thumb back in the direction of the green blob in the cave. "Even if the Slugs don't know how to track us, do you think they can track the Ganglion?"

Disconnected or not, our prisoner could have been screaming for help in Slugese at that moment, for all we knew.

Howard shrugged again. "I don't think—"

The wolf pack, collectively, froze, noses upturned.

Howard said, "Uh-oh."

I tugged Howard deeper into the cave's shadows and whispered, "Whatever they smell, we can't see. The wind's coming from upslope, behind us."

Outside, the wolves retreated another fifty yards from the mouth of our cave as a shadow crossed it.

My heart pounded, and I squeezed off my rifle's grip safety.

Eeeeerr.

The shadow shuffled past the cave mouth. Another replaced it, then more. As they strode into the light, the shadows resolved into trumpeting, truck-sized furballs the color of rust.

Howard whispered, "Mammoth."

The herd bull strode toward the wolf pack, bellowing, head back to display great curved tusks. The wolves retreated again.

Howard said, "If we shot a mammoth out there, the carcass would explain the wolf pack. It could make an excellent distraction."

He was right. I raised my M40 and sighted on the nearest cow, but at this range I could have dropped her with a hip shot.

Then I paused. "The carcass might attract those big

cats." Weichsel's fauna paralleled Pleistocene Earth in many ways, but our Neolithic forefathers never saw saber-toothed snow leopards bigger than Bengal tigers.

Really, my concern with Howard's idea wasn't baiting leopards. Saber teeth can't scuff Eternads any more than wolf teeth can. I just didn't want to shoot a mammoth.

It sounded absurd. I couldn't count the Slugs that had died at my hand or on my orders in this war. And over my career I had taken human lives, too, when the United States in its collective wisdom had lawfully ordered me to.

It wasn't as though any species on Weichsel was endangered, except us humans, of course. The tundra teemed with life, a glacial menagerie. Weichsel wouldn't miss one mammoth.

So why did I rationalize against squeezing my trigger one more time?

I couldn't deny that war calloused a soldier to brutality. But as I grew older, I cherished the moments when I could choose not to kill.

I lowered my rifle. "Let's see what happens."

By midmorning, events mooted my dilemma. The wolves isolated a lame cow from the mammoth herd, brought her down two hundred yards from us, and began tearing meat from her woolly flanks like bleeding rugs. The mammoth herd stood off, alternately trumpeting in protest at the gore-smeared wolves, then bulldozing snow with their sinuous tusks to get at matted grass beneath. For both species, violence was another day at the office.

Howard and I withdrew inside the cave, to obscure our visual and infrared signatures, and sat opposite our prisoner.

The Ganglion just floated there, animated only by the vibrations of its motility plate. After thirty years of war, all I knew about the blob was that it was my enemy. I had no reason to think it knew me any differently. For humans and Slugs, like the mammoths and wolves, violence had become another day at the office.

Howard, this blob, and I were on the cusp of changing that. If I could get us off Weichsel alive. At the moment, getting out alive required me to freeze my butt off in a hole, contemplating upcoming misery and terror. After a lifetime in the infantry, I was used to that.

Zzee.

The sound came from somewhere behind the cave, and the mag rifle round struck a bull mammoth's flank. The herd stampeded away, to our front, and after a hundred yards, another volley of Slug rifle fire dropped a half dozen of them.

Slugs behind us. Slugs in front of us. It was coincidence. More likely, it was that they had picked up the signature of Howard's rifle shots.

I unsnapped my ammunition pouches, because when the maggots come, they come faster than a casual reload can bring them down.

Howard did the same, shaking his head and muttering under his breath, "Oboy."

SEVENTEEN

TWENTY MINUTES LATER, the first movement of Slugs showed in my optics, around the distant mammoth carcasses. I couldn't see the Slugs, but I saw curving, uplifted lines carving the snow like shark-fin wakes as the maggots tunneled closer.

The little bastards never tired of coming up with surprises for us.

"Bullfrog, this is Scorpion leader. Over." My heart skipped. The voice in my earpiece was faint but welcome. I glanced at Howard, and he nodded as he tapped his own earpiece.

I said into my helmet mike, "This is Bullfrog, Scorpion leader. You got a fix on our transponders? Over."

"No fix, Bullfrog. We've just been cruising and broadcasting. Can you say your position? Over."

Howard popped his visor and spoke to me. "Between the cave and the storm's atmospherics, they can't find us."

"I cannot provide my position, Scorpion leader. But can you see the Slugs to our front and rear? There must be thousands. Over."

"No visible Slugs, Bullfrog." Of course not. The pilots were looking for traditional Slug massed Warriors, in black armor. But the maggots were burrowing beneath the snow.

Zzee. Zzee. The second round cracked rock off the cave lip and shot it across the cave.

"Look harder! They're in our laps."

"Bullfrog, we can't see jack squat from up here. Our combat floor is now fifteen thousand. Except for pickup. We can't pick up what we can't find."

I swore into the mike. "How many did you lose to the heavys yesterday?"

"Six, Bullfrog. We gotta stay high or we won't do you or us any good at all."

Zoomies never changed. Late in the last century, before the Second Afghan, even before the First Afghan, the old Soviet empire's gunships had been chased back to altitudes that rendered them ineffective against ground targets by a few well-placed shoulder-fired missiles. Not that I blamed the Zoomies. Scorpions and their pilots were in short supply, especially to the pilots' loved ones.

I crawled to the cave mouth, raised my finger cam, and peeked. The burrows converging on us numbered in the hundreds, and the closest were a hundred yards away. And that was just in front of us. The noose was certainly drawing close on our flanks and rear, too.

I dug in my thigh pocket, jerked out my last smoke canister, and lobbed it out into the open. As purple smoke billowed in a widening cone, I said, "Scorpion leader, I have marked my position with smoke. Do you identify? Over."

"I haven't seen smoke since flight school, Bullfrog. Where the hell . . . Okay. I identify purple smoke. Over."

"I confirm. Purple smoke. Target is troops in the open. Under a foot of snow. What are you packing?"

The closest burrows were fifty yards away now.

"Antipersonnel CBUs. Where you want 'em? Over."

"Drop on smoke. I say again, drop on smoke."

"Bullfrog? I confirm we are prepared to deliver CBUs on purple smoke. Please say your position relative to smoke."

"Our position is danger close. I say again, danger close."

The first Slug popped out of the snow, ten feet away, mag rifle at the ready. I dropped it with an aimed shot. Then another came up behind it, and Howard peppered it with a three-round burst. There were a hundred more burrows just behind the first two. We couldn't play whack-a-mole very long. We had overhead cover and Eternads. Our prisoner, however, wore no armor.

Nobody is quick to fire on his own troops, even if his own troops tell him to.

I said, "We're being overrun! Bring the rain, Scorpion leader."

"Roger. Keep your head down, Bullfrog."

Howard and I scuttled as far back into our shallow cave as possible, then flipped our prisoner up on edge, belly out. The Ganglion's Slug metal motility plate shielded all three of us as we waited three heartbeats.

Scorpion leader's voice crackled in my earpiece. "On the way. God, I hope you're in a deep hole, Bullfrog."

If you believe, as certain outworld cultures do, that the ancestral human race of Earth is the spawn of Satan himself, the invention and widespread deployment over the last century of the cluster bomb unit may be the proof.

CBUs are cylindrical big bombs that split open to release a spray of a half-ton or more of little bombs, each of which explodes and spews hundreds of individual darts or fragments. If the bomber is particularly sociopathic, nerve gas capsules, radioactive pellets, incendiary pills, or germs can be substituted.

The worst of it, at least when used on humans, is that ten percent of the bomblets soft-land and don't detonate. They fester for years, as gratuitous land mines. To aid ordnance recovery personnel, the bomblet balls are painted bright colors. Worst of all, this color also attracts children.

However, at the moment, the morality of CBUs concerned me less than their considerable efficacy at blowing the crap out of maggots.

I curled my finger cam around the edge of our motility plate shield. A half-dozen Slug Warriors swayed, backlit by the dawn, in the cave mouth, like fat black cobras.

Inside my helmet, I muttered, "Come on. Come on!"

One warrior trained its rifle on the motility plate as twenty more darkened the cave mouth.

Ccrraacck.

The rock vibrated beneath my boot soles.

A one-ton CBU weighs the same as a one-ton bunker buster, but a CBU's concussion doesn't lift, then drop you, like a thud does.

The slugs in the cave mouth just went to pieces, chunks of armor and tissue splattering and ricocheting off the rock behind us, as well as off the Slug metal plate in front of us.

I pulled back my finger cam and shut my eyes.

Ccrraacck. Ccrraacck. Ccrraacck.

The smell of cordite leaked through my ventilator and filled my helmet.

The cave floor stopped vibrating. I counted to twenty, then peeked my finger cam out again.

Nothing moved.

"Bullfrog, this is Scorpion leader. Report fire mission effect, over."

I coughed at the smoke, wished my filters worked.

The voice came again, higher-pitched. "Bullfrog, do you copy?" There are worse fears in combat than the fear of blue-on-blue, of firing on your own troops. But none make you feel colder and sicker.

"We're fine, Scorpion leader. Wait one for damage assessment. Over."

Outside the cave, wisps of purple marking smoke mixed with gray explosive smoke and with the white steam of snow vaporized by red-hot metal shards.

The bombing had melted or blown back a foot of snow, and the black-armored carcasses of Slug Warriors, sprawled in pools of their own leaked green guts, dotted the remaining snow like boulders in a pasture. There were other carcasses, brown, in red pools. Dire wolves, mammoth, some razored beyond identity.

In my earpiece I heard, "Waiting." The voice croaked but was no longer shrill.

"Cease fire. Target destroyed. Over."

"Bullfrog, this is Scorpion leader. You and the package ready for extraction?"

I turned. Howard had already towed our prisoner, none the worse for wear, into the sunlight.

I said, "Bullfrog ready for extraction. Send down the sling."

Only then did I realize how successful this fiasco had been. We had captured Howard's first useful POW, mission one hundred percent accomplished. Our little raiding party had expected to take casualties for three days, holding off legions of Slug Warriors, until the rest of Ready Brigade could deploy from the *Abraham Lincoln,* then land in the Slugs' rear and decimate them. In fact, we had taken minimal casualties, and most of Ready Brigade hadn't even had to get its feet cold on Weichsel.

I paused and swore at myself. Had my life numbed me to the point that I defined a minimal casualty as one I didn't know personally?

The Zoomies radioed, "Bet you're glad to see the last of Weichsel."

I stared at a dead dire wolf and a cub-sized corpse, disemboweled beside it. Unexploded bomblets dotted the snow in the distance like spilled candy. "I'm sure the feeling's mutual."

The *Abraham Lincoln*'s return voyage from Weichsel to Mousetrap was uneventful. Ready Brigade would disembark, mourning its casualties yet feeling a bit surly over a fight most of the brigade spoiled for but never got. Then the *Abe* would haul Howard and its precious cargo back to Earth. I would part company with the *Abe* and return to my post at my headquarters on Bren.

I was in my cabin, packing my duffel to transship from the *Abe* to the next available transportation from Mousetrap to my headquarters when Howard rapped on my hatch frame, then stepped through, anyway.

He asked, "Jason, why are you doing that?"

"I packed my duffel when I was a spec 4. I haven't gotten that old or that special since." My rank entitled me to an orderly, my ego entitled me to refuse one.

"I mean why are you packing at all?"

"*Thermopylae*'s outbound to Bren ninety minutes after we dock." As C-in-C, I could make them hold her for me, but delaying a cruiser for one VIP would cost taxpayers the price of Thanksgiving turkey for a battalion. Besides, it would make me feel and look like a prima ballerina.

"I thought you were going on to Earth, to deliver the prisoner, with us."

I pointed with a handful of GI socks, in a general direction that I assumed was away from Earth. "Earth's the *last* place I should go. You said yourself that the Slugs' incursion on Weichsel was bait. My place is at my headquarters."

"Your headquarters operates fine without you. It's operating fine without you right now. And you've been away from Earth a long time."

Howard was right, of course, about my staff. In a profession where unexpected death was part of the job description, only bad officers made themselves indispensable. He was wrong about the other. "I have fewer ties to Earth than a Weichselan. And I've spent thirty years trying to forget the Blitz, not remember it. That's why I declined the *Ganymede* invitation."

Mankind's first interplanetary capital ships had been the chemical-fueled, cobbled-together sister ships *Hope* and *Excalibur*. I had watched the war destroy both, *Hope* in the victory at the Battle of Ganymede, *Excalibur* tilting at the windmill that had been the Slug Armada.

The first generation of starships followed, hybrids, propelled between planets by antimatter drive and between stars by Cavorite drive we pinched from the Slugs. This next class of cruisers was named for fallen human heroes, like the *Abraham Lincoln*. Not least among those heroes was my best friend, and father of my godson, the hero of Ganymede, for whom the *Metzger* class was named.

The third-generation, all-Cavorite-drive cruisers were the *Bastogne* class, named for historic battles, like the *Yorktown* and the *Tehran*. The first cruiser named for a battle of the Slug War was the *Emerald River*. The second would be the *Ganymede*. As the then-breveted commander of the Ganymede Expeditionary Force, I had been asked to christen the ship that would memorialize the first human victory of the Pseudocephalopod War.

"You know I think you should have accepted. Not for yourself. For all of us." Howard's eyes softened between his old-fashioned glasses. We were both among the seven hundred of ten thousand who survived the Battle of Ganymede.

A lump swelled my throat. "Exactly. Any of you would be qualified to christen the ship. I don't need the pomp and circumstance. I don't need the pain of remembering."

Howard rested a hand on my shoulder. "Jason, your pain goes deeper than what you lost at Ganymede. Come back with me. Come back with us. Not to christen the ship. But you should be there."

I blinked. "Why?"

Howard slipped out his microreader, punched up an entry on its screen, and turned it toward me. "They've decided on a replacement for you at the ceremony, someone else to christen the ship."

I read what glowed on the screen, which was a program for the ceremony.

I stiffened. Then I stopped packing. "Why don't you give me back those two packages I gave you? I'll deliver them myself."

Howard nodded. "Good." Then he narrowed his eyes. "Exactly when did you last spend time on Earth?"

I stared at the ceiling, then ticked off on my fingers. "Not counting Pentagon meetings, hospitalization, and one academy speech . . ." None of which got one out on the economy. "Thirteen years." I shrugged. "I doubt things have changed that much."

Howard frowned. "Maybe. But neither have you."

EIGHTEEN

WE DEPARTED THE *ABE* IN EARTH ORBIT, and our shuttle landed at Reagan, inside Greater Washington, but on the military side of the field. We arrived a day ahead of schedule, on purpose, so the receiving personnel weren't expecting us. Howard wore civvies and insisted I do the same, also, so no one would notice our arrival with the most important POW in human history. Howard had a tarp stretched over the Ganglion, stenciled "rock samples," so no one would notice. Maybe they wouldn't, but they probably noticed the twenty plainclothes, assault-rifle-toting security Spooks that surrounded the "rock samples," and the chain-gun equipped tilt-wing that hovered above them.

A Spook convoy met Howard and our prisoner and hustled them off to Fort Meade, so the interrogation could begin. I had my own agenda.

The Space Force staff sergeant at the disembarkation desk said, "We didn't expect you, General. But I can call up a pool car and driver in a couple minutes." I smiled at her. My first stop back here on Earth was personal, so I wasn't entitled to a car at taxpayer expense, though VIPs in Washington rarely observed the demarcation. Besides, any infantryman who couldn't carry his own duffel one lousy mile down a paved road might as well be a Squid. Or too old. I pointed out the window at the blue sky. "No, thanks. I've been away a long time. Looks like a nice day for an old infantryman to get reacquainted with home."

Outside, the day was Potomac-July steamy, a welcome change from the "Nuclear Winter" that the Slug Blitz had brought, so long ago. Beyond the port's fence, pure electrics, sleeker and silenter than the hybrids I coveted as a teenager, whooshed silently along the guideway. Behind the nose-to-tail, ninety-mile-per-hour river of autodrivers, trees had leafed out greener even than I remembered from childhood. The air smelled of deciduous forest in summer and triggered my childhood memories like Proust's madeleine. I squinted against the sun, and my chest swelled. It was good to reacquaint with home.

Ten sweaty minutes down the perimeter road later, my duffel had gained twenty pounds. I was so reacquainted that I thumbed down an airfield-maintenance Elektruk. I tossed my duffel into the 'truk's open back, climbed in alongside it, and got a dusty, windy lift across Reagan to the civilian terminal.

The Elektruk stopped in front of the car rental pavilion. I waved to the Trukker, then hopped over the tailgate. When I brushed dust off my sport jacket, the twenty-year-old sleeve split from the shoulder at the seam. I stood alongside my duffel, sweating and muttering on the sidewalk outside the civilian terminal, wiping sweat off my upturned hat's inner band.

A middle-aged woman in a business suit clicked by in heels, toward the entrance. Her makeup was the color of new chalk, and her hair spiked like a turn-of-the-century goth. As she passed me, she tossed two coins into my hat.

I sighed and stared down at my vintage civvies. They looked fine to *me*.

I stepped into the terminal's cool and was ten feet from the first of a dozen Hertz kiosks when the holotendant popped on and smiled. "Welcome, new Hertz customer! Please—"

"I've had an account for years."

The holotendant turned a palm toward the thumbreader. "—Identify yourself."

I pressed my sweaty thumb against the reader's platen.

The holotendant's smile replicated. "Welcome, new Hertz customer."

"Yeah. I guess it's been a while." I commanded, "Create new account."

Pause. She flickered as she smiled. "Your identity does not appear in the TWD. You must be in the TWD to create an account."

I rolled my eyes. "What's the TWD?"

The holo flickered into a professor wearing a Hertz-yellow mortarboard. "To register for the Tracking Waiver Database, please contact your local law-enforcement agency. Thank you for visiting Hertz."

Professor Mortarboard vanished, and the kiosk darkened. I stepped back four paces, then forward. The kiosk flashed alive again and ran me through the same routine. I said, "I have to be in Pennsylvania by dinnertime. Look, I'm a lieutenant general—"

The kiosk winked dark again.

Behind the middle of the kiosk row was one single kiosk. The attendant seated there was either live or a theater-quality holo.

I walked to her, hat in hand, dropped my cloth duffel off my shoulder. Sweat dripped off the tip of my nose, and I panted. "Can you help me get to Pennsylvania?"

She was probably nineteen, as chalky and spiky as the businesswoman had been, and her eyes were downcast at a flatscreen from which canned laughter rippled. She looked me up and down, her eyes narrowed, and she pointed at the public-announcements flatscreen above baggage claim.

A message scrolled across the screen: "To assure a pleasant experience for Reagan InterUnion's travelers, solicitation is prohibited on the terminal grounds."

I tugged my torn jacket sleeve back up to my shoulder. "I'm not panhandling. I just haven't rented a car in a long time."

She eyed my dusty shoes. "Apparently." But she flipped up a keyboard and poised her fingers above it. "Home address?"

"I don't have one. At the moment. On Earth."

"Somehow, I'm not surprised." She flipped the keyboard back down and whispered into the bud mike on her lapel.

Forty seconds later, a cop stepped alongside us. He cocked his head and read the name and rank stenciled on the duffel at my feet.

He turned to the girl as he pointed at me. "This is your vagrant?"

She shrugged, rolled her eyes, and waved her sitcom back up on her flatscreen.

The cop said to me, "How can I help you, General?"

"I need to rent a car. Personal business. But I'm not in this TWD thing, apparently."

He nodded. "For a citizen to drive on a guideway, he

has to waive his Thirty-eighth Amendment right of free-dom from satellite tracking."

I snorted. "What idiot would waive that right?" Even tracking off-duty soldiers' dog-tag chips had been cur-tailed years ago.

He shrugged. "Every idiot who wants autodrive com-muting. Which is all of us. Anyway, no waiver, no rental. And it takes a day to register in the database, sir."

I sighed. If you sell poison cheap enough, democracy will find suicide an irresistible bargain. "I have to be in Pennsylvania tonight."

The Hertz girl looked up. "I'm allowed to rent you a manual drive with no tracker. But you can only drive back roads. And the mobile recharge coverage costs extra, be-cause nobody knows where you are."

I smiled. "Actually, I'd prefer that." But looking old and shabby didn't make me an easy mark. "And I'll de-cline the extra coverage."

Her jaw dropped. "Nobody declines the mobile re-charge coverage."

"I do."

She pointed at my wrist 'Puter. "If that's not registered, I'm required to offer to rent you a temporary, so you can access the net."

"And the temporary has a tracker?" I shook my head. "Just the car, thanks."

She shrugged, then sighed, and a contract form ap-peared on her flatscreen. "Thumb here, here, and here."

Four hours later, I sat behind the wheel of my rental car as it rolled to a silent stop on a dirt road somewhere in southeastern Pennsylvania.

The car slightly changed the whine it had been reciting

for the past twenty miles. "My motive batteries are now fully depleted, except for emergency flasher power. If you have not already arrived at a charging station, mobile recharge is on the way. If you do not have prepaid mobile recharge service, you may purchase it on the net. Thank you for choosing Hertz." The car shut down, and its flashing dash light turned from amber to red but kept winking.

I slammed my palms against the wheel, then exhaled and eyed the unconnected 'Puter on my wrist. I slid the door back manually, stepped out into the road, and surveyed my situation, hands on hips.

The country I could see was forested and silent but for insect drone. The only hints of the hand of man beyond the road itself were weathered, cut stumps amid the second-growth trees. I kicked a tire, cursed the car, cursed 2067 Earth, cursed the Hertz girl, and, finally and most appropriately, cursed my own stubborn stupidity.

According to the Navex, before it went Benedict Arnold on me with the rest of the car, the backside of my destination was just over the rise to my front, two hundred yards away. I stripped off my sport jacket, rolled up my shirtsleeves, lifted the first of my packages out of my duffel, then locked my duffel in the car.

Then I sighed and hiked up and over the rise. As predicted, a hundred yards past the rise's crest, dull in the late slant of early-evening sun, I came to a locked metal farm gate astride the road, flanked by three-strand wire fencing. A metal sign on the gate read "National Historic Site. Authorized access only."

I sighed, stepped to the gate, and swung a leg over.

A shadow flickered across my shoulders and forearms, then a tin voice above me said, "Halt and be recognized."

NINETEEN

I FROZE ASTRIDE THE GATE.

A surveillance 'bot whirred around to face me, a dragonfly with a six-foot Plasteel wingspan.

Unlike a county-mountie surveillance 'bot, the turret on this one, which followed my every twitch, in unison with the 'bot's optic sensors, mounted a six-barrel microgun in place of a nonlethal dazer.

A voice boomed from the 'bot's speaker. "Get off the fence, raise your hands, then back away twenty feet."

I did.

"Why are you here?"

"I'm invited for dinner."

Pause.

"Why didn't you come to the front gate?"

"I had to rent a manual-drive car, so I couldn't use the guideway. The car ran out of juice back over the hill." I jerked my thumb back down the road. "You can check."

"Who are you?"

"Lieutenant General Jason Wander. My ID's in the car."

Pause.

It seemed neighborly to fill the silence. "I declined the mobile recharge coverage."

The 'bot's turret whined, and I heard the microgun's safety click off. "Nobody declines the mobile recharge coverage."

The 'bot hovered, I sweated, and my upraised arms grew heavy.

During the pause, I could hear my interrogator breathe through his open mike, and his voice came through faintly. "Yes, ma'am. That's who he claims to be. The car checks out, a rental . . . completely discharged."

Pause.

"He says he declined it, ma'am."

Another pause.

"Yes, ma'am. Only an idiot."

My interrogator sighed, more loudly, then spoke to me. "She says it can only be you, General." The 'bot's safety clicked back on. "Sit tight, sir. A tilt-wing will be out to pick you up in three minutes. We'll tow your vehicle in and charge it. Welcome to Eisenhower Farm."

TWENTY

ON THE APPROACH TO EISENHOWER FARM, the tilt-wing overflew the pastoral hills that had once run with the blood of the Battle of Gettysburg. Eisenhower bought the farm during his presidency, as a retirement place, because he had been a soldier and the land overlooked the ghosts of Lee's lines along Seminary Ridge. The Eisenhowers passed the farm to the National Park Service in 1967, a century ago, and ten acres had been retransferred a few years back, by act of Congress, to the two least likely co-habiting VIPs on Earth.

Margaret Irons and Nat Cobb stood arm in arm, heads down against the tilt-wing's downwash, as I ran to them, stooped beneath the thumping props. The tilt-wing lifted, returning to whatever secret place the Secret Service kept it in, and the gale and roar faded.

Maggie was the first of them I got to, slender as wire, no taller than my shoulder, with hair that clung in ermine ringlets against her mahogany skin. She hugged me, and only gingerly did I hug back, keeping one eye on her Secret Service detail. A former president is a former president, after all.

Nat Cobb, my boss since before the Battle of Ganymede, was as thin as Maggie and as pale as the snows of his Maine birthplace. His sparse hair was clipped in a retired four-star's brush, as white as his female companion's. He patted my back. "Good to see you, Jason."

Like many people who saw through Virtulenses, Nat said that to remind new acquaintances that *blind* was a relative term. He made the remark to me from reflex. Nat Cobb had breveted me to succeed him in command in battle when a Slug heavy splinter took his natural sight, and I had long since thereafter learned that he saw what was going on in Washington better through Virtulenses than others saw it twenty-twenty.

I stood back from the second U.S. president to resign her office and the longest-serving U.S. Army four-star.

It warmed me that the only two Washington survivors I knew well enough to admire chose to spend their retirement in each other's company. Though the physical aspect was creepier than visualizing my parents having sex.

Nat said to me, "How you feeling, son?"

President Irons and General Cobb *were* old enough for me to be their son. But "old" has been a moving target, lockstepped to medical progress, throughout human history. Alexander the Great died of disease or boredom with life at thirty-two. Even in Eisenhower's day, a century ago, people still aged so rapidly that the government paid them to retire at age sixty-five, so they could rest a few months before they croaked.

I shrugged. "Pretty good. You two?"

It was Nat's turn to shrug. "We'll be better if Howard's POW spills some beans."

Neither Nat nor Maggie had ever been much for small

talk. I smiled as I shook my head. Howard's secrecy about the Ganglion's capture was impenetrable, except by Maggie and Nat's back-channel network.

The two of them toured me around their place before dinner. I walked, as, at a discreet distance, did Maggie's Secret Service minders. Maggie and Nat rode little scooters that floated six inches off the ground. They were Cavorite-powered prototypes, in effect parallel machines to the saucer we dragged the Ganglion around on. Spin-off technology no more justified war than full employment for cops justified burglary. But plenty of swords had been beaten into better plowshares for centuries.

Nat's voice graveled as he pointed out landmarks of the great battle that had forever marked this place. Maggie remarked about her predecessor, Lincoln, his few words at Gettysburg, and the great battle for civil rights that he began, which historians said didn't fully end until she was elected president. I told them about the outworlds, in particular about the recent dustup on Weichsel.

After a dinner punctuated with old war stories and new Beltway gossip, the three of us creaked in wooden rockers, on a porch lit by the flicker of oil lanterns, as distant frogs sang.

I pulled out the package I had brought and presented it to Nat. "Sorry I missed your Relief and Retirement ceremony."

Nat waved his hand. "Penguin-suit hoo-hah."

Margaret Irons raised her chin. "It was lovely and dignified, Nathan. You looked very distinguished."

Nat lifted my retirement gift to him from its case, and the Cavorite stones on its scabbard glowed with their own crimson light.

I said, "From Ord and me. He says a Marinus-forged broadsword's finer than the best Japanese *koto*."

Nat smiled as he drew the blade and turned it so it flashed in the lantern light. "You might want to borrow this when you meet your new boss."

Nat's commission, as well as his retirement date, had been extended six times by act of Congress. I had been commanded by—and protected against my own inexperience and blundering by—the same mentor for decades.

I grimaced. "So I hear. We powwow tomorrow, after the christening."

War stories and gossip had been exhausted, and only the tyrannosaur in the corner, which I knew was the real reason I had been invited, was left to discuss. Ice rang against crystal as Margaret Irons sipped her bourbon. "You can go see him tonight, you know, Jason. The tilt-wing can land you in New York in an hour. The staff will take care of your rental car."

I furrowed my brow in the dark. Maggie wasn't talking about my new commanding officer, but my estranged godson.

Nat leaned on the arm of his rocker closest to me. "Jude arrived from Tressel with the rest of the Tressen delegation at Luna Base. They're coming down from Luna aboard the *Ganymede*. She lands at midnight. Bringing her down in daylight would've stolen the visual thunder for tomorrow."

Since the Blitz, human ships of the line had been fabricated in lunar orbit, then lived and died in vacuum. With Mousetrap's shipyards now humming, *Ganymede* would be the end of her line. She was the last starship scheduled to be built within the Solar System, as production shifted to a nickel-iron asteroid captured as a moonlet by a planet light-years away. In that, *Ganymede was* like a tyranno-saur just before the Chixulub Impact, the mightiest of her kind, a race about to be extincted by a lump of interstellar trash.

Yet none of the billions of humans who never left Earth, whose taxes and sweat had built the great ships for all the decades of the war against the Pseudocephalopod Hegemony, had ever seen a cruiser in its mile-long, Plas-teel flesh.

So the politicians had decided to christen the *Ganymede* in New York.

"He's the right person to do it, you know." I swallowed. "But what about the blockade?"

Tressel, home to my godson since his altruistic enlist-ment there, had also become the most repressive society in the Human Union. The Human Union had accordingly severed ties with Tressel to punish its leadership.

Maggie snorted. "The blockade blocks emigration and trade, not diplomatic contact. Democracies talk to dicta-torships because talk sells better to voters than war."

"That's a bad thing, Madame President?"

She frowned. Not at my "youthful" impertinence, but because she had been instructing me to call her just plain Maggie for years. She said, "Sometimes. Our diplomats were talking to the Japanese when they bombed Pearl Harbor."

Nat Cobb rocked forward, then touched my thigh with a bony hand. "Jason, we didn't ask you out here to de-bate politics. You've never been spit for politics, anyway. You've been an unhappy boy."

I stiffened. "I haven't been a boy since the Blitz, sir."

General Cobb had also tried to get me to stop calling him sir.

"You know what I mean. You never thought like conventional military, even as a trainee. In an unconventional war, your temperament had its place. You matured on Bren, during the Expulsion. By First Mousetrap, people thought your judgment was catching up to your experience and ingenuity. But since Second Mousetrap, people think you've changed. I hear."

"People" meant Ord. Ord and Nat Cobb had nursed me up since infantry basic. Ord had ratted me out, as usual.

I sighed. "If I hadn't landed with the Spooks, the Weichsel raid might have failed."

Nat raised his palm. "We didn't ask you here to debate strategy and tactics, either. Jason, it's time for you to become a whole human being."

I flexed my prosthetic arm, drew breath into my regrown lungs, and rubbed my Plasteel-femured thighs. "Too late for that."

It was Maggie's turn to lean forward and touch me, on my shoulder. "No. You need to resolve the issues between yourself and Jude. And you can. If not for your own sake, for the sake of your troops. A depressed commander can be a bad commander."

"Why do you think I'm here for the ceremony? As soon as I saw Jude was going to christen the *Ganymede,* I came." Jude was the closest thing I had to a son, and I was the closest thing he had to a father. But it was the unavoidable curse of the military parent to be an occasional visitor to one's children.

Nat nodded. "It will be a start. But awkward."

Maggie said, "Mimi Ozawa joined us for dinner, too,

just after she took over at the academy. Were you planning to look her up while you were here?"

I rolled my eyes. "She's invited me to address the Cadet Corps during Commandant's Time, two days after the christening. I'm taking a day's leave in between, to see her. Okay?" I braced myself for one of them to ask me whether I needed to borrow the family car, so I could take that nice Ozawa girl out to the drive-in for a milk shake, like some flatscreen situation comedy the two of them had grown up with.

Nat looked at Maggie, then back at me. "One more thing."

I sighed. I was too old for lectures, but also too old to argue with people even older.

Nat leaned forward on his elbows. "I'm not your shrink. I'm not your commanding officer anymore. But I am your friend. Jason, you're disconnected from the people you love. Worse, you're uncertain whether they love you back."

I spread my palms. "Jude's been behind the new Iron Curtain. Mimi's duty stations and mine have been light-years apart, and the human race is at war for its survival. What did you expect me to do, desert?"

Nat said, "No. But maybe you could add a functional relationship to soothe the pain of the dysfunctional ones."

A female orderly, blonde and smiling, stepped onto the porch with a decanter and refilled our glasses.

I watched her walk away. "You mean proposition cocktail waitresses half my age?"

"I'm serious. There's plenty you can do. Socialize more."

"Away from Earth I outrank my potential buddies by a couple of stars, sir." I turned to President Irons. "You know the problem. You can't even get people you've known for years to stop calling you Madame President. Poker's no fun when the other guys let you win. And Ord's idea of guys' night out is ironing his battle dress uniforms."

A dachshund, Fritz the Fourth, if I remembered the press releases, waddled onto the porch and got scooped onto the former presidential lap. Maggie scratched her dog's ear. "Animal companion holistic therapy's been accepted practice for decades. Centuries, really."

I rolled my eyes. "A pet? There are no pugs in space. The poop issues alone—"

Nat said softly, "You mothballed Jeeb after Second Mousetrap, didn't you?"

My chest softened inside. "He's so old that maintenance cost would have been prohibitive, outworld."

Jeeb was a four-decade-old, J-series Tactical Observation Transport, a turkey-sized, six-legged mechanical flying cockroach. Nobody remembers brain-linked spy TOTs like Jeeb for two reasons. First, faster, smaller, stealthier, cheaper Autonomous Mechanicals obsoleted them by 2050. Second, the Department of Defense quietly swept everything about brain-link technology under the rug a decade after that.

The combat intel value of brain-linking had been that instructions passed from wrangler to 'bot, and intercepted communications and images passed back from 'bot to wrangler, immune to interception and jamming, and at least as fast as the speed of light.

The mutual link was so strong and transparent that TOTs, though the cyberneticists deny it to this day, permanently imprinted the personalities of their wranglers. But if combat or, for that matter, a bus wreck killed the wrangler or destroyed the TOT, the surviving partner effectively experienced its own death. The few wranglers who didn't suicide lived out their days as vegetative guests of the Veterans Administration. Surviving TOTs just got scrapped.

So, by dint of a Department of Defense salvage title, I "adopted" Jeeb when he was orphaned by the death of his wrangler, and my friend, at the Battle of Ganymede.

Nat snorted into his bourbon until it bubbled. "Expense, my ass. All you do is bank your paycheck, anyway. Dust the little rascal off and take him with you."

I frowned. "If I agree to do this, can I finish my bourbon?" It wasn't really a question. A former president and a former four-star were accustomed to having their "suggestions" followed. Besides, I missed the little roach.

Maggie actually had the tilt-wing make an intermediate stop on its way to deliver me to New York, at the storage unit complex where I kept my Earthside worldly goods. The night 'bot didn't know what to make of a visitor who didn't enter through the main gate, but my ID checked out. Twenty minutes later, the 'bot tracked the tilt-wing as it took off, now laden with the crate within which nestled the night 'bot's elderly, distant relative, plus spares and diagnostic 'Puter.

I sat in the tilt-wing's presidential-purple upholstered passenger compartment, staring at the crate. My reunion with Jeeb would require no more than unpacking baggage.

I stared into the darkness as the tilt-wing bore me north. The reunion that awaited me in an hour, and the baggage, would be more complex.

TWENTY-ONE

IN MY LIFE, I've flown into many cities at night. Into Lhasa glowing under a Himalayan full moon. Into Marinus, its weapons forges painting drifting clouds red, in a two-mooned sky. Into Paris, sprawled like a glittering tapestry across the Seine. There are bigger cities. There are prettier cities. There are certainly friendlier cities. But no city in this galaxy quickens my heart like the boil of lights that is New York.

The tilt-wing banked above the East River's silver ribbon, then feathered down onto the pad atop the shoreward tower of the United Nations–Human Union complex.

The old UN Tower's bustle made it glow like a Wheaties box, but the Human Union Tower stood dark, except for marker lights flashing on its roof pad. A young woman in a powder blue uniform met the tilt-wing and escorted me to ground level.

I scuffed the elevator floor as we rode down. "Carpet's like new."

She smiled. "Only the bottom three floors of this tower are occupied."

The Human Union Tower replicated its United Nations twin in size and in antique, Atomic Age slab architecture.

It sounded inadequate that the diplomatic center of four-teen planets could be as small as the diplomatic center of just one. But most of the union's populations, descended from Earthborn humans discarded by the Slugs, were preindustrial at best and Neolithic at worst. Earth sugar-daddyed the baby union the way the United States had the United Nations a century ago.

My guide led me across the Human Union Tower's lobby, our footsteps echoing on marble, and out onto the plaza that overlooked the East River. Traffic rumbled be-neath and around me, and beyond the police barricades that ringed the plaza, crowds buzzed.

My guide pointed at the full moon as a shadow eclipsed it. "You see the holos, but . . ."

Maybe *Ganymede* had been brought in at midnight to preserve its visual impact for the next day's ceremony, but the buzz of the crowds beyond the barricades built like the roar of the monsoon cascading off the Tressel Barrens rainforest. New Yorkers have seen it all, but when they haven't, they turn out like kids for a circus parade.

I stared up, where my guide pointed, and let my jaw drop. Seeing a cruiser in space provides no sense of scale. *Ganymede*'s royal drift to Earth marked the first time a cruiser had ever tested its structural strength against Earth-normal gravity, though the shipwrights and physicists had insisted for years that a vessel shielded and strong enough to transit a Temporal Fabric Insertion Point could cer-tainly withstand one puny planet's gravity.

When *Ganymede*'s hull fully eclipsed the moon, the as-sembled thousands gasped. When she dropped below the moon and settled noiselessly above the river, like a reeled-in parade balloon on Thanksgiving morning, they cheered.

Ganymede was a blindingly white cylinder that hovered, oblivious to gravity, like a spidery, disaerodynamic dirigible, so close above the East River's chop that water splashed her hull. Yet the observation blister on her nose's centerline nearly touched the top of the ancient iron suspension tower of the Fifty-ninth Street Bridge, three hundred fifty feet above the waves. A New Yorker who wanted to travel from *Ganymede*'s tip to view the Cavorite baffles on her tail booms would have to walk a mile, twenty blocks, from Fifty-ninth Street south to Thirty-ninth Street.

My guide's mouth hung open. "My. God."

"Your tax dollars had more to do with it than He did." According to Maggie Irons, one reason for this extravaganza was to show the public what it had been paying for. And also to demonstrate that moving production to Mousetrap would free up unimaginably large manufacturing capacity on Earth, capacity that could be reconfigured to produce necessities like sports electrics and beach hoverboards.

A City of New York fireboat, spraying water from its nozzles in hundred-foot arcs, skittered out to *Ganymede* like a roach chasing a bus. *Ganymede* rolled silently around her axis, until the door of Bay Six out of thirty-six midship bays stabilized ten feet above the river, and then its hatch rolled back up into the hull. An ant jumped from the hundred-foot-wide hatch opening to the fireboat's deck; then the hatch closed.

My guide asked, "Is that the guy you're meeting?"

I nodded.

"I hear he's from Tressel. I've never seen a Tressen."

"He's not Tressen. He's Jude Metzger."

She wrinkled her brow. "I've heard that name someplace."

I sighed. Jude's father had died saving the human race. Thirty years later, his mother had, too. But to this generation, they might as well have been Millard Fillmore and Clara Barton.

The fireboat glided alongside the riverbank, and Jude jumped to the quay, then climbed the stairs to the moonlit table of the plaza. He was twenty-six now. As lanky as his father, Jude had strawberry-blond hair and his mother's olive Egyptian complexion.

He stepped onto the plaza in Tressen Class-A uniform, black and tailored.

When he saw me, his eyes widened. "I was expecting to see General Cobb. When they invited me, they said you wouldn't christen the ship."

"I wouldn't. I came to see you."

Amid the crowd noise, a silence swelled in the space between my godson and me.

My guide swallowed. "Do you need anything else, General?"

I kept staring at Jude. "No, thanks."

She left the two of us.

I shrugged, said to my godson, "You eat on the way down?"

He shook his head. "But I'm okay."

"Join me, then?"

He opened his mouth, then closed it.

I stood in the middle of a city of twenty-eight million, as alone as I've ever felt.

Then he shrugged back. "Sure."

I turned and led him to a cab rank beyond the barricades. "We have a lot to talk about."

TWENTY-TWO

EVEN IN NEW YORK, a stormtrooper outfit draws stares in a deli at one a.m.

I sipped coffee. "You transshipped from the *Powell* to the *Ganymede* out at Luna?"

Jude bit a dill pickle spear that he held between thumb and forefinger, then smiled. Tressel's plant life was mired back in the pre-angiosperm mid-Paleozoic. "You always liked pickles. Been a long time?"

He nodded. "I'm staying at the Tressen consulate. The rest of the delegation's bunking aboard *Ganymede*. Captain's guests."

Ganymede wouldn't be in service for months, but her captain had been assigned to watch over her, and get to know her, since her keel was laid. He would know every rivet and plate in her, know her better than a father knew his daughter.

"Your father didn't get command of *Hope* until two weeks before we embarked for Ganymede."

"Poor war planning."

"We didn't plan on this war."

"It's been thirty years. Does anyone have a plan to end it?"

I bit my corned beef on rye, chewed, then swallowed. Jude was my godson. He was also an officer in the armed services of a nation that was not precisely an ally. "Maybe." I changed the subject. "I hear you're building an air force."

He grinned. "Someday. Tressel's materials technology is still stretching canvas across wood fuselages to make air mail carriers. It's amazing how far we've come, so fast. I feel like a Wright brother."

Maybe he really didn't know how efficiently the bastards for whom he was speeding up the mail were quietly exterminating half of Tressel. Or maybe the rumors I had heard about the camps were false. But I couldn't force myself to begin the debate.

We talked sports, and about our common acquaintances, and about New York, until the deli closed. Then I walked with him to his billet at the Tressen consulate, which was near my hotel, according to Navex.

The moon had set while sparse traffic trickled down the deserted streets.

Jude turned his collar up against the chill as our footsteps echoed off the brownstones that flanked us. "You think I blame you, don't you, Jason?"

Like his mother, he said what he thought. "Do you?" I asked.

"Nobody told me! I was right there, and nobody even told me she was still alive."

"Jude, you know the Slugs were jamming the radios. And there was nothing you could have done."

He stuffed his hands in his uniform jacket pockets as we walked. "I was mad at the world. And you were part of the world."

"I was doped up for weeks," I said.

He eyed my regrown arm. "I'm sorry that you lost your arm. But they did a nice job on this one."

I shrugged. "I didn't even know about the blockade for months."

"I should've gotten in touch with you. I could've snuck a chip offworld through the consulate."

I stopped and faced him beside trash cans lined up beside a front stoop. We could talk past each other for another ten blocks, or we could communicate. "The last thing she said—" My throat constricted as the moment flooded back. I blinked, took a breath. "The last thing she asked was that I take care of you. Take care of her baby, she said."

Jude blinked back tears, nodded. "You always have."

I shook my head.

"Jason, just because we didn't walk down to the fishing hole together every afternoon doesn't mean you weren't there for me."

Bong.

A guy sat up between two trash cans, grimy and smelling like old wine. "You two wanna keep it down?" Then he cocked his head. "Spare any change?"

Jude shifted his feet, and the man's eyes widened at Jude's uniformed silhouette. The man extended his arms, palms waving. "Not for booze! A loan. To get me home."

I fished in my trouser pockets until I assembled a wad of bills, and I tucked them into his breast pocket and patted it. "Don't decline the mobile recharge coverage."

He wrinkled his face, then smiled at Jude while pointing at me. "This here's a good fella."

Jude said, "I know."

SleepExpress was the only alternative in midtown

Manhattan that flashed up when I had narrowed my booking search to government per diem or less. It turned out to be a century-old parking structure redivided into cubicles the size of an embarked division commander's cruiser stateroom, meaning a bed, Sanolet, and desk, with room left over to stand a frozen pizza on edge. At SleepExpress the stateroom desk was replaced by a pay-per-view porn hologen, a bonus I was too tired and too old to appreciate. But I've slept in places that made SleepExpress feel like the Waldorf Astoria. I suppose I could have withdrawn cash and supplemented my per diem card out of pocket, but Nat Cobb had taught me by example that a commander shouldn't live better than he expects his kids to live.

Morning dawned clear and cool. After years in places where pork and maple trees lay in the evolutionary future, I went looking to sit down and breakfast on pancakes, real maple syrup, and bacon. After six blocks of menu reading, I realized that the balance remaining on my per diem chip would cover only coffee in a therm cup and a doughnut eaten standing up at a counter.

At *Ganymede*'s christening I greeted old comrades, all of whom, unlike me, of course, had turned older, fatter, and grayer. Jude's speech would have made his mother and father proud. Then the starship circled above Manhattan like a thunderhead, or more accurately, like an advertising dirigible, for the rest of the morning, while pedestrians craned their necks.

After the ceremony, I caught a cab to 100 East Fiftieth Street, the address where I was to meet my new boss, who had traveled up from Washington to meet me. Despite Nat Cobb's advice, I didn't take along a sword.

TWENTY-THREE

WHEN THE CAB DROPPED ME OFF, it said, "We have arrived at 100 East Fiftieth Street. Welcome to your destination . . ."

The cab paused, then clicked.

"The Waldorf Towers." General Galen Pinchon was toughing it out in the discreet and separately addressed part of the Waldorf-Astoria that served those for whom the Waldorf offered insufficient exclusivity.

According to a hallway plaque outside Pinchon's suite, Douglas MacArthur had occupied the suite for years after he retired.

Pinchon's aide met me at the door and steered me around a room-service trolley, its linens upturned to shroud the remains of what smelled like bacon and real maple syrup.

The aide swung a hand around at the silk-papered walls as he rolled his eyes. "Thank heavens general officers are exempt from per diem!"

"They are?"

He flapped his hand at me. "You know *that*, General! If you tried to live on per diem in Manhattan, you'd probably have to sleep in a garage and eat stale doughnuts."

"Probably."

Pinchon sat reading a holoscreen, behind a marble-topped desk that would have looked at home in the Summer Palace of Marin.

I had finished my own reading about Pinchon aboard Maggie's tilt-wing on the way to New York. Pinchon had gone straight from ROTC to the Pentagon and, they said, never left. His commission was in the Adjutant General's Corps. AG's most vital role, to the average GI, was mail delivery. AG's other roles included administration of military bands, awarding medals, and personnel matters. AG's roles did not include shooting, nor getting shot at.

Nonetheless, Pinchon had been chosen to succeed Nat Cobb as commander of all of the army's unconventional ground forces. Unconventional forces, which encompassed both Earthbound snake eaters and everything offworld, had done most of the army's shooting and getting shot during the near-century that had passed since the Cold War ended.

Pinchon looked up at me. He looked ten years older than I was, with sunken cheeks and lips that puckered like he had sucked a lemon and never recovered.

He smiled and waved me to a chair across from him. "Glad to be home?"

I could still smell the bacon. "Some things are hard to get used to, General."

He smiled again. "Me being one of those things, I suppose. You probably wonder why someone with a non-combat, personnel background got Nat Cobb's slot."

Pinchon was going to tell me why, even if I said I *didn't* wonder, so I sat mute.

He stared into his palms, then looked up. "The war's been coasting downhill for a couple of years now."

"I've been pedaling the bike too hard to notice, sir."

He nodded, smiled again. "I understand. If propulsion-grade Cavorite wasn't flowing from Bren, if Mousetrap wasn't secure, if Bren wasn't providing a stable staging area for Silver Bullet, and, most recently, if the Weichsel raid hadn't yielded the last puzzle piece we need to exterminate the Slugs, the existence of mankind would still hang in the balance."

"Aren't you starting the victory party a little early, sir?"

"Like you said, you've been busy pedaling the bike. Mankind's best minds think we entered the war's end game months ago. We just have to play it out."

I squirmed in my chair. "That's great. I intend to play it out. So it doesn't get screwed up. Sir."

He pressed his lips together. "Jason, your contributions have been extraordinary, and so have your sacrifices. Do you feel that you've done enough?"

Hair rose on the back of my neck. "When we know the Slugs are gone, I'll feel like I've done enough. Sir, what are you trying to say?"

"The end game—Silver Bullet—is a Space Force show. Basically it's a reconnaissance to locate a target, followed by a bombing mission to deliver a single, outcome-determinative device."

I straightened in my chair. "Every time we've thought we had the Slugs on the ropes since I've been in this war—and I've been in it from the beginning—we've been wrong, General Pinchon. Maybe Silver Bullet's Hiroshima, maybe it isn't."

He nodded. "We have been wrong. And if it hadn't been for people like you and Nat Cobb bailing us out, we wouldn't stand today on the threshold of final victory, ready to move to new challenges."

Stale doughnut congealed in my stomach. "Is this my golden handshake?"

Pinchon frowned. "Jason, by statute, the U.S. military is authorized three hundred twenty active-duty generals at a time. The math works out that there are currently slots for only a dozen army three-stars, like you."

The numbers fluctuated, but even I knew that the brass ceiling had been the law since before the Cold War. It meant that just as perfectly competent senior general officers figured out how to do their jobs, they got squeezed out of the top of the officer corps, like used toothpaste out of a tube, so junior generals could move up.

I said, "Nat never got pushed out."

"The war was different then. And Nat was different. He knew how to watch his own back in Washington."

I smiled, even as my heart sank in my chest. "He watched mine, too."

Pinchon sighed. "Frankly, Jason, given your record, Nat's the only reason you got far enough that we're having this conversation."

I couldn't argue. The army had been trying to fire me since basic training, and for good reasons. I was no MacArthur, no Eisenhower. I had stumbled through a career doing the wrong things for the right reasons, then scratching and clawing back from the brink of disaster only by the grace and intervention of people like Ord and Nat Cobb. That didn't make the shock of this moment less electric.

"What about my command? My kids."

"Our outworld presence will be reconfigured. We

won't need and can't afford a ground army forward-deployed to meet a threat that's about to disappear. Most of your command will be safely redeployed home with the gratitude of their respective nations. Any commander should be delighted with that outcome."

Maybe so, but shock gave way to heat that flushed up from my gut. My fists balled at my sides. "That's it? You think I'm going to go quietly?"

"Jason, there's nobody here to protect you this time. Nat's gone. And you'll be retired on a four-star's pension. The defense industry will snap you up as a consultant, if the holo nets don't hire you as an expert first. This isn't a punishment, it's a reward."

"How long have I got?"

Pinchon smiled, as gently as I suppose he knew how. "You make retirement sound like a tumor." He waved the holo screen so it faced me. "Before you leave, I'll print out your retirement forms for you. They become effective when you sign them. Meantime, let's run through your ongoing benefits and privileges . . ."

He talked for, as my 'Puter read later, forty-four more minutes. I didn't hear one word.

Finally, I found myself standing beside the elevator, with a breast pocket full of army paper, in silence broken only by hollow ringing in my ears, as though an eight-inch howitzer shell had detonated alongside me. I stared back at the MacArthur plaque on the hallway wall. There was a quote, from MacArthur's address to a joint session of Congress, after Truman rightly canned him for trying to start World War III in Korea. MacArthur had quoted a barracks ballad: "Old soldiers never die; they just fade away."

I stared at the quote for a long time before I pressed the down button.

At a kiosk down in the Waldorf's lobby, I rented another manual drive, including mobile recharge coverage.

Five minutes later the car whispered up to the curb, and as I pressed a bill into the live doorman's white-gloved hand, I said to him, "Fade away, my ass!"

Then I slipped the renter out, between the yellow nose of one cab and the tail of another, and told my car to give me directions to Maryland.

TWENTY-FOUR

FORT MEADE, MARYLAND, wasn't the only place Howard's Spooks infested, but it was the place where they had for years maintained facilities to hold a Slug smart enough to tell them anything—if, like a dog that chased cars, they ever caught one.

Howard buzzed me in through the doors of a three-story black glass cube with a sign out front that read "International Communicable Disease Research Center. Protective clothing required beyond this point."

He was wearing slacks, sandals, and a T-shirt that announced "On my planet, I'm normal." The most military thing about him was an old-style ID badge he wore on a lanyard around his chicken-wattle neck. The army had long ago come to terms with the need to let Howard run his Spooks the way he wanted to. The honeymoon had lasted because his methods allowed him to recruit persons who thought outside the box. Way outside.

We stepped into the elevator, and Howard poked his badge into a slot for a subbasement level five stories down. Alongside the slot, someone had taped a hand-printed sign that read "Dungeon. Quiet please! Torture in progress."

The elevator opened to a desk labeled "Security," behind which sat a girl wearing farmer's bib jeans over bare shoulders, with corporal's chevrons pinned to the strap of an empty leather shoulder holster. She made one of those waves where the hand remains still while the fingers wiggle. "Hi, Howard. Who's your friend?"

I sighed. Ord's head would have exploded.

We passed by her, then through a set of double doors. Howard said, "Her IQ is one ninety-five."

"One would hope."

The room we entered was big enough to garage three buses, and at its center floated my green traveling companion from Weichsel, under a cone of soft blue overhead light. A cable thicket ran from plates taped to the Ganglion's hide to consoles along all four walls, behind which sat a hundred Spooks.

I pointed at the cables and frowned. "Is that how you make it talk? Electric shock?"

Howard's eyes widened. "The sign in the elevator was a joke!"

"I got that, Howard."

"Jason, the Pseudocephalopod has no concept of withholding information from another because it's never known another. It's the only one of its kind. There's no need to coerce anything, any more than you coerce a book to let you read it. We simply had to synthesize an algorithm that translated the information stored in this Ganglion."

"Had. You've already done it?"

"We've been preparing for this moment for years."

"Did it know where it came from?" I had come to see Howard from curiosity, but after Pinchon made me walk the plank, a half-hope had formed in a selfish corner of my mind. If Howard's prisoner didn't possess the navigational information we needed, we couldn't end the war soon. If the war wasn't ending, Pinchon might not send me to the glue factory. Perversely, during the entire drive down from New York, I had hoped the Ganglion would prove to be a bust.

Howard grinned. "Absolutely! Last night we deciphered a sequence of twenty-six jumps that lead from Weichsel to the homeworld system. Simple, really. We're just tidying up now."

"Great." It was. In fact, it was the greatest news of the war. Somehow, I couldn't get as excited as I should have been.

Behind Howard, Spooks had lined up to get their pictures taken standing in front of the Ganglion. Some hammed it up, holding a magazineless pistol, presumably borrowed from the corporal in coveralls, and snarling. Most smiled, whooped, and pumped fists overhead.

Howard said, "Want to get your picture taken with the Ganglion? Before the war ends?"

I shook my head. "I've got another stop to make."

Fort Meade, like many military reservations, is big enough, and has enough excess, mothballed, built-out space, that it hosts activities in addition to those connected with its primary mission. Often, those activities are temporary, pending completion of permanent facilities.

The temporary location of the three-year-old Human Union Military Academy was in a sixty-year-old complex four miles from Spook Castle.

HUMA's commandant lived in a government-provided house on the temporary academy grounds, like a university president. I parked at the curb, lifted a package the size of a Kleenex cube off the seat beside me, then carried it to the front door and rang the bell. As I waited, I looked around. The place was more bungalow than house, walled in peeling stucco, with a roof of cracked red tile and a dropcloth-sized lawn baked to steel wool by summer.

I thought it was the most beautiful home I had ever seen.

Clack.

The door's deadbolt rattled, then the door swung inward, squealing on unoiled hinges.

TWENTY-FIVE

MIMI'S MOUTH DROPPED OPEN, and her brown eyes widened in her perfect face. A towel turbaned her head, and she stood barefooted in a gray sweatsuit. "I thought you were flying down. Tonight."

"Pinchon finished with me early. Evidently my 'Puter's not connected to the net, or I would have let you know."

Her breath hissed out. "You can rent a temporary for five bucks, Jason." She shook her head while she fiddled with the towel that wrapped it. "You're an inconsiderate child."

After three years, this wasn't how I had imagined this moment.

It was hot on her front step. "Can I come in?"

She stared at me, then stood aside. "Yeah. I'm sorry. I love being commandant. But a cadet got caught cheating on an exam today. Another one broke her back on the obstacle course. And we're over budget for the quarter."

She closed the door behind us and walked me into her living room. Framed citations and flat photographs of uniformed crews and long-mothballed vessels cluttered the walls, along with the kinds of parquet-framed mirrors and gilt-threaded tapestries that look memorable in port

bazaar stalls but tawdry forever after. Amid a career's flot-
sam, a worn green sofa angled in front of the dark hologen. She flopped on the sofa, then tugged the sweatpants
on her thighs like they were mainsails. "And look at this.
I wanted to look beautiful for you. But no, you—" Her
officerial lip quivered.

I sat beside her and lifted her chin with my finger. "I've
never seen anything more beautiful in my life."

Her eyes widened as she blinked back tears. "You're
serious. You're such an idiot."

I set the wooden box in her lap.

"What is it?"

I shrugged.

She raised the lid, plucked out a translucent snowball
of a rock, and turned it in her fingers, so the facets inside caught the light. She squinted and frowned. "Is this a
Weichselan diamond?"

"Blue white, with a one-hundred-six-carat perfect core,
if it's cut right, they tell me. You could say I picked it up
cheap, but the freight was murder."

She smiled. Then her face creased into panic and she
stiffened.

I threw my palm up. "The jewelers said it's suitable
to be set as a pendant. A major piece suitable for evening
wear." The jewelers had also said it was too big for a ring,
but clarifying it that way would have made the moment
even more awkward.

Mimi relaxed and held the diamond near her throat as
she turned her head left, then right, and watched her re-
flection in the mirror on the far wall.

She returned the jewel to its box, smiling at me. "You
might not be an idiot."

Mimi unwrapped the towel from around her head, then curled around until she faced me, on her knees on the sofa, and leaned toward me and breathed in my ear. "I missed you, Jason."

A diamond may be a girl's best friend, but it is also a boon companion to a man who might not be an idiot.

Four hours later, I lay on my back, staring up at the ceiling of Mimi's bedroom. Her head lay on my bare chest, and her finger traced the scar-tissue line where my regrown arm joined my shoulder. "Your arm works fine. Everything works fine."

Military homecomings are blisteringly awkward in so many ways. But once physical contact occurs, mutual hormonal autodrive kicks in for a while. I kissed her hair and knew that the right thing to do was to savor the moment, to say nothing.

Therefore, I said, "Pinchon fired me."

Her finger continued to trace across my chest as she whispered, "Huh? It sounded like you said—"

"I did. My Relief and Retirement ceremony's in ninety days."

She sat up straight and shook her head, which made everything else shake delightfully. "No. Doesn't that idiot know there's a war on?"

"Not for long, there isn't. Howard's already got a fix on the homeworld. The weaponized-Cavorite project is down to just troubleshooting."

"You're going to fight the retirement mandate."

"I was, I guess." I shook my head. "But I dunno. You're here. I could be here."

The panic crossed her face again, and she looked toward her kitchen. "I was gonna do a rack of lamb, but . . . I could scramble some eggs. I input for a guest, so the house ordered extra."

"Sure. That would be fine."

Twenty minutes later we sat at her kitchen table, me in underwear and Mimi in a silk robe. I pushed eggs around my plate with a fork.

She leaned forward. "Are they all right? I don't cook much."

"They're great. It's the chives. I'm allergic."

"I didn't know."

She ate one bite, then said, "Jason, I put in for a command."

"Another ship? That would take years."

"Not a keel-up command. I told them I'd take any rust bucket that opened up."

"You just said you loved this job. And in your letters you said that you loved—"

"I do. I think." She turned away as she stabbed her finger back at my plate. "But, hell, I can't even make eggs for you right!"

"That's a small thing. The kind of thing people in love learn about each other when they spend time together."

"Oh, really? What about the big things? When you take the retirement gut-punch, I'm there for you. But they put me out to pasture as a schoolmaster and you don't give a shit! All you do is complain about my cooking!"

My jaw dropped, and I spread my palms. "I never—you said . . ." For once, I shut up before I made it worse. How can you know a person you see at three-year intervals?

We sat and stared into the tabletop.

Mimi said, "Jason, I'm not ready to sit in rocking chairs playing Nat and Maggie."

"Neither am I. Earth hasn't changed for the better while I've been gone. Or I've changed for the worse. So what do we do?"

She stood up, carried both our plates to the sink, and scraped the eggs down the drain. "I don't know. Can we talk about it tomorrow? After your speech?"

We reloaded the dishes in the Sanaid, then sat on her couch in the dark, her head on my shoulder, without speaking, until I heard her breath turn heavy as she slept.

I stared into the dark, at our reflections in her mirror. They touched, but they were dark silhouettes that I couldn't make out.

I tried to sleep, too, but wound up thinking about the speech I had to give in four hours.

TWENTY-SIX

THE NEXT MORNING I stood at parade rest on the academy's lecture-hall stage and stared out across three thousand young faces, all eyes staring up at me. The cadets' uniforms were gray, impeccable, and indistinguishable one from another. The faces, however, were brown, white, yellow, male, and female. Tattoos curled around some faces; jewels dangled from others. They were badges of their human homeworlds, each spawned by, and once ruled by, the Pseudocephalopod Hegemony. Some of those worlds I had fought to free from the hegemony. Some I had fought to keep in the union. The names of some I could barely pronounce.

Mimi stood to my right, then gave me a wink.

She gripped the podium, and her words to her cadets echoed off the arched 'lume ceiling. "I'll keep the intro brief. I know you don't want the assembly to run long. That could shorten morning PT."

Three thousand throats boomed a chuckle off the ceiling. Then silence returned.

The ceiling 'lume dimmed, and a quote faded in on the flatscreen wall behind the commandant. Mimi turned, then read aloud:

"'Terracentric it may be to refer to "The Pseudocephalopod War," much less to date its onset from "2037." However, all history pivoted on those events in the Spiral Arm, as undeniably as conventional space folds around every ultradwarf at every Temporal Fabric Insertion Point. Students of that time and place will find no truer account than in the warrior's-eye view of Jason Wander.'
—*Chronicles of the Galaxy*, Volume XXIII"

That was I. That was me. A historical footnote.

The commandant turned back to her Corps of Cadets. "Today's topic is a retrospective on the campaign for the liberation of Bren." Mimi took a seat in the audience, leaving me alone center stage.

I stepped alongside the chair placed there for me. My legs ached, as they always did in the mornings. So did every other part that the Slugs and the calendar had forced the army to rebuild.

But I frowned down at the chair and said to the audience, "Everybody provides one of these for me, these days. Deference to rank, or age, I suppose. But infantry doesn't sit."

Whoops and pumped fists erupted from the back rows, where the lousy students stood. When the first graduating class came to draw postgrad assignments in a few months, the top students would snatch the glam slots, like flight school and astrogation. The back row would become infantry lieutenants. It was natural selection. Infantry gets the sharp, dirty end of the stick from the beginning, so it learns to laugh about it.

I smiled and pumped my fist back at them. Where they were going, whatever the war, they would need their sense of humor.

I cleared my throat.

PalmTalkers swiveled up alongside whispering lips. Personal 'Puter keyboards unfolded in hands. A few kids snatched pterosaur-quill pens and sheets of flat paper from hiding places beneath stiff shirtfronts. Different cultures, different study habits.

I waved the devices away. "No notes. You get enough logistics and tactics at the puzzle factory next door."

Laughter.

I said, "Bren wasn't liberated by so-called military genius."

A kid in back raised his hand. "Then why do our chips teach the Bren campaign, sir?" He knew the answer. Every kid in the union knew it. He was just stretching the lecture.

But I answered like they didn't know. "Because it turned the tide of this war. We flew the transport we captured back to Earth, used that ship's power plant for a template, used Bren's Cavorite for fuel, and built the fleets that liberated, then unified, the planets of the union. My meaning was that wars are won by soldiers sacrificing for other soldiers. And by trial and blunder. And by which side got stuck in the mud least. And by commanders who learned to lead effectively while engulfed by chaos, and lunacy, and their own heartbreak."

Twenty minutes later, I took questions. The kids knew

that Mimi wanted cadets who spoke their minds. I pointed at the raised hand of a shaved-headed kid with indigo-dyed eyebrows.

She stood as straight and as hard as a Casuni broadsword and asked, "Sir, our poli-sci chips say the real liberation of Bren depends on Bassin the First."

I nodded. "They're right. The uncivil 'peace' among the clans that's followed the expulsion of the Pseudocephalopod Hegemony has killed more Marini, Casuni, and Tassini than the Slugs did."

With those indigo eyebrows, she was clearly Tassini. Probably second-generation emancipated. I guessed she was asking a rhetorical question, designed to educate classmates to whom slavery was just a word. If it hadn't been for the changes that started on Bren with the Expulsion of the Slugs, she'd be bending over some landowner's plow or washtub, like her grandparents did. Thanks to emancipation, she had traveled to the stars, here to the motherworld, where she had learned things like astrogation and comparative lit.

She asked, "You agree with the chips that say the war was wrong, then?"

"Creating freedom for people can't be wrong. Even if some people create wrong out of freedom."

She half-smiled at the kid next to her.

I pointed at his raised hand, and he said, "Maybe the war was right for Bren. And for the union. But on a galactic scale, since the Expulsion we haven't seen the end of war. Soldiers are still dying."

He didn't know that the end of this long and inglorious— is there any other kind?—war was imminent, and I couldn't tell him.

So I said, "'Only the dead have seen the end of war.' The chips attribute that quote to Plato. It's still true twenty-five hundred years after Plato died. The lesson you're here to learn is, never waste the life of any soldier you command."

He nodded.

I said, "Even if you learn that lesson, you'll hate it. Command is an orphan's journey."

The kids milked question time for twenty minutes more, then the applause from the infantry gonna-bes in the back rows shook the Omnifoam floor tiles.

As I stepped offstage, someone in Space Force blue grasped my elbow and steered me toward an exit.

It was Jude.

I stopped like I had walked into a Glasstic door. "What are you doing here?"

"I hear you gave the same speech last year. They still applaud."

"They applaud because I talk so long that the commandant cancels PT. What's going on?"

Jude slid back his uniform sleeve, which was now Zoomie blue, not Tressen Nazi black, to show me the red-flashing screen on his wrist 'Puter. "Orders. We lift on next hour's fleet orbital."

I frowned. The only thing that could transfer a Tressen officer into the service of the Human Union was clear and present danger from the common enemy.

Jude said, "You won't believe what the Slugs just did. Want to hear where we go next?"

I shook my head. "Just so we go together."

After Mimi dismissed the corps, she stepped backstage, widened her eyes when she saw Jude, then hugged him.

Then she frowned at both of us, hands on hips. "What the hell's going on?"

Jude said, "Nobody exactly knows. Something big on Bren."

I held Mimi at arm's length, shrugged. "To be continued."

She touched my cheek, and her eyes glistened. "Someday."

TWENTY-SEVEN

FORT MEADE IS A SHORT DRIVE FROM REAGAN, but a tilt-wing picked up Jude, Howard, and me, sped us above the guideway traffic, then delivered us to the tarmac fifty feet from where the hourly fleet orbital lingered, just for us.

Also fifty feet from us a staff-driven pool car had parked. Pinchon stood, feet planted, arms crossed, in front of the shuttle's extended belly ladder. His cheeks were more sunken, his lips more tightly drawn, than when I had met him at the Waldorf. I paused in front of him, and he cleared his throat.

Before he could speak, I said, "I've got the retirement papers with me. Effective on my signature, you said? Because it may take me a while to get around to signing them. If that's okay, General?"

For a moment, he stiffened. Then he stood aside. "Godspeed, General."

I laid my hand on the belly ladder's rail and climbed aboard the shuttle.

As we strapped in, Jude asked, "Who was puckerface?"

"My new boss."

"So he doesn't know much about your job yet?"

"He knows when to get out of the way."

Ninety minutes later, Jude, Howard, and I stepped out of the shuttle onto the arrival platform in a launch bay aboard the *Tehran*.

The *Tehran* had been held in orbit for us, delaying its long-scheduled departure to Mousetrap for refit. *Tehran*'s refit had also been pushed back, so she could barrel straight through the Mousetrap, jump again, then deliver us to Bren a couple of days faster. Normally priority-transport procedures would have cost a couple of days while we changed to a fresh outbound cruiser at Mousetrap.

Tiny in the vast bay, between us and the exit hatch from the bay into the ship proper, stood *Tehran*'s skipper.

His chin thrust out, his feet were planted, and his arms were crossed, in a pose like the one Pinchon had assumed when we met in front of the up-shuttle's ladder. But it was clear that the skipper wasn't about to get out of the way.

TWENTY-EIGHT

THE *TEHRAN*'S CAPTAIN was actually a rear admiral, so I ranked him, but barely. Red-faced Boston Irish, he had, therefore, proven a competent drinking companion. Eddie Duffy stabbed a finger at my chest. "This bettah be good, Jason!"

As the *Ganymede*'s christening had recently proved, cruisers were built stronger these days, but the swabbie book still called for them to refit after enduring the stress of a T-FIP jump like the one the *Tehran* would make to deliver us into the Mousetrap. But Eddie Duffy had just been ordered to jump his baby, his only child, the ship he had nursed since it was a set of blueprints, back-to-back into Mousetrap and then out the other side, to get us to Bren sooner. He didn't like it.

I jerked my thumb over my shoulder at Howard. "This guy'll explain it all, Eddie."

Howard forced his eyes wide. "Why do you think I know, Jason?"

"Because you always do." The branch insignia pinned crooked on Howard's lapel was military intelligence, the people who renamed paranoia "need-to-know." So, professorial geek though he was, Howard tossed information around like anvils.

Ten minutes later, we sat in Captain Eddie's wardroom while Howard briefed us.

Neither Jude nor Eddie knew about the facts that underlay Silver Bullet. I didn't know what had just happened, but I knew that Silver Bullet had to be at its heart. Therefore, if mankind was going to put things right, Silver Bullet could no longer be the Spooks' little secret.

Howard, as was his wont anyway, began at the beginning.

A Threedie schematic of Bren from space was the first visual up on the holo. Around the blue planet's equator orbited the White Moon of Bren, an atmosphereless rock, crater-pocked a billion years ago, much like Earth's single moon. From north to south over Bren's poles orbited the Red Moon of Bren, smaller, faster moving, and as unmarked as a baby's cheek.

Howard pointed at the Red Moon's image as it circled Bren. "The Red Moon is an astronomic peculiarity. It orbits Bren north–south. Ordinary moons orbit roughly east–west, around their captor's equator. That's because ordinary moons and their planets coalesce from a disc of material spinning around their star, so a planetary system is shaped like marbles rotating on a tray."

I nodded. "The plane of the ecliptic." I'd heard this part of the lecture before, therefore I showed off before Howard went rocket science.

Howard said, "So we knew from the get-go that the Red Moon was a rarity. An interstellar wanderer, captured by Bren's gravity, when the Red Moon penetrated the Bren system, at a right angle to the plane of the ecliptic."

Howard waved up the holo's magnification, and the Red Moon's image swelled until it filled the holotank, like a red porcelain basketball. He rotated his hands around the image's circumference. "The Red Moon's second peculiarity is that, though it's too small to trap a protective atmosphere, it isn't pocked by impact craters, like its sibling, and like most ordinary moons. The Red Moon's third peculiarity is observable indirectly. Unlike an ordinary moon, the Red Moon doesn't measurably affect Bren's tides, like an ordinary moon its size would."

The captain shifted in his chair, nodding and spinning his hands like he was winding twine. "In the beginning, the Earth was without form. Please. I got deteriorating stores to deal with, Colonel."

I turned to him and raised my palm. "Patience, Eddie. This is all connected." Howard's detective work had been impressive enough to deserve a hearing. Besides, "deteriorating stores" were simply munitions that got swapped out for newer ones, a throwback to the days when explosives became unstable over time. As a covert adviser I had spent a career thankful for every muddy case of plausibly deniable, sweating dynamite, so my sympathy was limited. Eddie, like Squids generally, wasn't nearly as busy as he thought.

My godson squirmed, too, the way I did when the topic was the Slugs. They had cost Jude friends, and nearly his own life.

Howard frowned back at Eddie. "This is already an oversimplified presentation. Bren is very Earthlike. But Bren's fauna avoided the mass extinctions that punctuated Earth's natural history. Why?"

Eddie shot me a glance that said he didn't care why.

Howard raised his index finger. "Because the periodic cosmic bolide strikes that have punctuated Earth's prehistory missed Bren."

"Cosmic bolides." Eddie looked around like he was searching for a yardarm to hoist somebody from.

I raised my palm to cut Howard off, then gave Eddie the CliffsNotes version. "Comets and asteroids missed Bren because its gravity didn't suck them in. Bren's gravity didn't suck them in because something near it affected its gravity. Eddie, the Red Moon is solid Cavorite. It barely stays in orbit around Bren, and it eats gravity, like the *Tehran*'s Cavorite impellers do."

Eddie was impatient, not dumb. His eyebrows rose, and he whistled. "Cavorite's poison to the Slugs. If we could package enough Cavorite, we could end the war."

Howard nodded. "Which is the threshold upon which we stood, until four days ago." He waved up a new holo. This one showed the Red Moon, too, but it was a visible-light telescopic image, not a Threedie simulation.

The Red Moon looked grayer, as though obscured by fog.

Howard waved up the magnification, and I shuddered.

It wasn't fog, it was Slug ships, each Firewitch as big as a domed stadium, each Troll as big as Mount Rushmore. The cordon the maggots had thrown around the Red Moon looked more like a mosquito swarm.

I asked, "Where did they come from?"

Howard shrugged. "Not through the Mousetrap."

Eddie said, "So much for the strategic crossroad theory."

Howard shook his head. "Nobody ever said the Mousetrap was the only way to reach the union planets, just the most efficient. We have no idea how many jumps this new armada had to cross to come in the back door. I suspect this was a Long March for the Pseudocephalopod Hegemony."

"Armada" was what history had come to call the last Slug invasion fleet to threaten a human-inhabited planet. The Armada of 2043 had destroyed virtually Earth's entire defensive capability at that time, and the Armada had numbered "only" one hundred twenty-one Firewitches and a single Troll incubator ship.

It was unclear that our acceptance of the Slug's Weichsel gambit had helped them sneak up on Bren. But the timing convinced me that the Slugs had coordinated their Weichsel feint with this much larger move. The maggots had snookered us again, not by deceiving us but by laying their cards on the table and allowing us to misplay ours. Would we ever learn? I rested my forehead against my palm and closed my eyes. "How many this time, Howard?"

"The force visible in this image comprises two thousand four Firewitches and sixteen Trolls."

Jude, Eddie, and I rocked back as one. My own eyes' evidence notwithstanding, I shook my head. The Human Union, fully mobilized on a war footing for decades, had finally built up its strength to levels that made the forces of the Warsaw Pact look like a Brownie troop. Yet our cruisers plus far-more-numerous Scorpion fighters, even projected out two more years, totaled less than seven hundred. "Howard, that's impossible."

"Jason, we have no idea how long the Pseudocephalopod has exerted hegemony over this galaxy, or even whether its reach is confined to this galaxy. We know Cavorite originates at the boundary of this universe. For all we know, the Pseudocephalopod's reach extends that far.

This manifestation, which seems massive to us, could be a tiny part of its strength."

Eddie shook his head. "I don't buy it. The Red Moon's the biggest threat we've ever posed to them. This is the maggots' last hurrah. They just threw in the kitchen sink, because it's all they've got left."

Jude wrinkled his brow, then asked a fighter pilot's question. "Howard, you said there are two thousand Firewitches visible in this image. We must've had cruisers on station around Bren. How many did their Scorpions destroy ship-to-ship?"

"Plenty. Our kill ratio of Firewitches by Scorpions remains prohibitively high, by our standards."

Eddie asked, "What intelligence do you make of that information, Colonel Hibble?"

In intel-speak, "information" is raw data. The picture the Spooks weave from information is "intelligence." George Washington said that "the necessity of procuring good intelligence is apparent & need not be further urged." When it came to the Slugs, nobody in the decades of this war had ever woven more good intelligence pictures than Howard Hibble.

Howard cocked his head. "The Pseudocephalopod has a history of solving problems with force, rather than guile. No new tactics or weapons. Just more of them here."

I nodded. So far as we knew, for all their longevity and omniscience, Slugs hadn't even invented the wheel. Why bother if you can beat gravity in another way? Based on what we were seeing now, we had encountered every type of ship the Slugs had during the war's early years.

There were the Troll and Firewitch, and the interplanetary Projectile. There was a fourth type, a small, hypervelocity version of the Projectile that was so rare that we had never really seen one, just the streaks it left and the damage it did.

Howard said to Eddie Duffy, "The bad news is that I disagree with your interpretation of this incursion, Admiral Duffy. This force isn't the kitchen sink. The Pseudocephalopod probably has much more where that came from. Still, it could be worse."

Eddie stared at the wall of enemy warships that now quarantined mankind from the weapons project that was supposed to win the war, and he cradled his chin in his upturned palm. "Two thousand ships isn't the kitchen sink? Christ on a crutch, Colonel! It is worse."

Despite Eddie's other misgivings, the *Tehran* transited the two jumps across the Mousetrap without so much as a popped rivet and, with a screen of Scorpions deployed and spoiling for a fight, set up in an orbit around Bren that kept the planet always between it and the Slug fleet.

That, arguably, was overcautious.

We arrived two weeks after the Slugs did, but the Slugs still hadn't attacked our bases on Bren. They hadn't attacked the Stone Hills Cavorite mines. They hadn't attacked our vessels, except any outnumbered Scorpions that attacked them first.

The Slugs' only hostile action, other than crashing our party uninvited, had come upon arrival. The old cruiser that had orbited the Red Moon, serving as Silver Bullet's base, was now a debris field in a loose and deteriorating orbit. Basically, the Slugs ignored us while they did the industrious little maggot things they always did.

All of this mystified everybody.

Except Howard.

TWENTY-NINE

THE NEXT DAY'S DAWN shrouded the River Marin's delta in icy drizzle, so Howard stood gripping a temporary lectern set up in the Spook hangar at Human Union Camp Bren, outside the old city of Marinus. Behind him the prototype Scorpions that had been modified to deliver Silver Bullet perched like pearlescent roaches on their landing gear. On rowed Marini benches in front of Howard sat the three hundred members of the Scorpion ground crews and pilots, who were his command's only survivors, by the chance of being dirtside when the Slugs arrived.

Representing Earth's host and ally, Bassin the First, absolute monarch of Marin and nominal ruler of the fractious commonwealth plains nations of Bren, sat behind Howard, to one side. Bassin wore the simple brown uniform of a colonel of combat engineers. Alongside him, set back a pace per Marini protocol, sat Ord, Jude, and me.

As an infantry commander, I've presided over too many memorial services. As head Spook, this was Howard Hibble's first.

A tombstone-sized flatscreen set up on an easel next to

Howard scrolled a numbered list of names of the missing in action, as he read them aloud.

With telescopic optics, from drones sent to recon the Red Moon, we could make out frozen human bodies, limbs splayed like DaVinci's Vitruvian Man. The kids cartwheeled amid the hull plates and mattresses of the destroyed Spook laboratory ship, eccentrically orbiting the Red Moon, barely held by its peculiar gravity. Officially, Howard's kids weren't even dead, just absent, a cruelty of war accentuated in space engagements. We lost eight Scorpions trying to get in and recover bodies before the effort was halted, though not for lack of pilots begging to try.

The name alongside missing soldier number one was "Applebite, R.," the kid that Ord and I had ridden up with back before Weichsel, back when the best minds said the war was nearly won. When the last name, "Wyvern, A.," scrolled by, the number alongside had swollen to 1,372.

Howard's shoulders sagged, and he clung to the podium sides as he stared at the hangar floor.

Ord wore his Class-A topcoat over his uniform, more, I suspected, to insulate himself from sentiment than the chill. The first time I saw him, he had been strutting through a Pennsylvania winter in starched cotton drill sergeant's fatigues while us trainees had shivered inside our civilian winter coats.

Howard stood mute and numb. His kids' war had always been a holo arcade game, with the bleeding and dying done by other kids on the sharp point of the stick. He cleared his throat, then said, "They never expected this. I never expected this."

Howard's remarks were less than Churchillian, but they were honest, which mattered.

Alongside me, Ord wiped his nose and whispered to me, "Expect the worst from the gods of war and they will seldom disappoint you."

I whispered back, "Did Churchill say that?"

"Why, no, sir. You did."

"Really?"

Whatever else Howard had planned to say, it was apparent he wasn't going to make it through. Bassin watched, then inclined his head toward the back of the hangar.

A lone Marini bandsman marched from the rear of the hangar, with exaggerated arm swings, spun an about-face, then stood alongside Howard. The bandsman's black hat, bigger than a watermelon, could have passed for a British foot guard's bearskin, though the skin was proto feathered dinosaur. Marini infantry were still piped to battle by skrillers. A skrill resembles a bagpipe, except its pipes are carved from the hollow bones of pterosaurs.

The bandsman unfolded a yellowed paper music sheet, fastened it to a wooden clip on the blowpipe, then played "Amazing Grace" like he had known it all his life.

It was the first time I saw Ord cry. Everybody cried.

It was the kind of day to go home, draw the blinds, and drink alone. But we couldn't do that.

THIRTY

———

AN HOUR LATER, my staff officers, plus Howard, Ord, Jude, and me, sat in my conference room. Hail ricocheted off the windowpanes like shrapnel while we tried to paddle through the muck that the gods of war had ladled onto us.

I said, "Howard, what the hell are the Slugs doing? If they have enough of an alternate Cavorite source that they can drop two thousand Firewitches and sixteen Trolls on us, they don't need to mine the Red Moon."

Howard stared at a box of stationery on the corner of my desk. He had too many hard-copy letters to write. "The Red Moon is useless to them for that, anyway."

I straightened in my chair. "What?"

"Cavorite is fragments—not really matter, as we think of it in this universe—that 'rubbed off' the boundary between this universe and the next one. Cavorite is antithetic to this universe, especially to one of this universe's fundamental forces, gravity."

"Which is why it's useful."

Howard nodded. "This universe reacts to this foreign material the way your finger reacts to a splinter. It cocoons Cavorite fragments at the interuniversal boundary, so they drift through this universe insulated, until something like us or the Pseudocephalopod gets hold of them."

"Little Cavorite meteors fell on Bren. One big one orbits around it."

Howard nodded. "The big one, the Red Moon, is too much of a good thing. Cavorite stones are toxic to the Pseudocephalopod, but not as toxic as the sort of Cavorite that makes up the Red Moon. That's why, I suspect, the Pseudocephalopod bypassed the Red Moon originally and chose to use human miners to excavate the less toxic Cavorite fall in the Stone Hills. The Red Moon's not the only place where we've seen the Pseudocephalopod bypass concentrated Cavorite. Besides, the Red Moon's Cavorite is too powerful to harness. An impeller loaded with Stone Hills Cavorite can hurl a starship through space. But the sort of power locked up in the Red Moon could knock a whole planet out of orbit."

"They're going to knock Bren out of orbit?"

Howard shook his head. "No need. The Pseudocephalopod is perfectly capable of destroying a planet without help from a Cavorite bolide."

I stared up at the ceiling. Every nine hours, the Red Moon, with its thousands of Slug outriders, passed north to south above some part of the Marini commonwealth, then, nine hours later, south to north above another part. Between the Slugs and us ghosted a defensive screen of Scorpions, but everybody knew that if the Slugs chose to, our defenders couldn't prevent the maggots from raining destruction on this planet the way they had Earth during the Blitz in 2036. "So what the hell are they doing up there, Howard?"

"This." Howard waved up a holo, visible-light drone imagery. It showed low-angle, high-resolution images from a skimmer that had flashed across the Red Moon, transmitted images, and then, no doubt, been shot down by the Slugs.

The image showed lumpy, asymmetric, wheelless machines gliding back and forth across a glassy red plain. Atop each machine bulged a leaden sphere. As we watched, one machine plucked off a sphere from its sibling, then replaced it with another.

Howard pointed at the discarded sphere. "Even with extensive shielding, the Pseudocephalopod workers operating this machinery don't last long."

Jude said, "Isn't it obvious? They knew that we were about to destroy them. They took over the Red Moon to stop Silver Bullet."

Howard shook his head. "The Pseudocephalopod is economical in its actions. It could more easily have stopped Silver Bullet by destroying our ground facilities, or the entire civilization of Bren. Or it could have simply stood off and bombarded the Red Moon with slow Projectiles or with fast Vipers, until it broke the Red Moon into vagrant fragments."

I frowned. "Howard, you know plenty about what the Slugs aren't doing. What *are* they doing?"

"I don't know. But Silver Bullet is stalled until we stop them from continuing to do it."

"How do we stop them?"

My Space Force liaison major shook her head. "We can't win a fleet-against-fleet battle."

Howard raised his index finger. "But if we stop them from doing whatever they're doing on the Red Moon's surface . . ."

Jude pointed at the holo image, which had cut off after just seconds. "That drone lasted two seconds once it pulled up. Even Scorpions can't stay close enough long enough to smart-bomb them."

Howard said, "And saturation bombing would leave the Red Moon useless to us."

I closed my eyes and rubbed them with my fingers. "Okay. Howard, if we modified a bunch of Scorpions the way you modified yours for Silver Bullet, they could carry more, right?"

He nodded.

"So we could use them to land infantry on the Red Moon. Not just a raiding party. A force that could take the ground and hold it. Then we could keep the Scorpions down there, so they wouldn't be exposed to fire."

Ord raised his eyebrows. "Sir, light infantry taking and holding unfamiliar ground when the enemy enjoys air supremacy?"

I pointed at my Space Force liaison. "You can't whip their fleet. But can you keep their fleet from ganging up on an exposed ground force?"

She frowned. "Maybe."

"No maybe. Do it."

There was more stone in the faces around my conference table than on Mount Rushmore. "I'm open to other options. Who's got some?"

Even Ord looked pale. Nobody said anything.

I slapped my palms against the tabletop. "Tomorrow. Same time. Please present me a plan consistent with this concept for your respective areas of responsibility."

Chairs pushed back amid thick silence.

"Ladies and gentlemen, this is an opportunity. Please present it to your respective staffs as such, rather than as a problem." I sounded so optimistic that I almost believed myself.

THIRTY-ONE

THREE WEEKS LATER, I sat in my office at sunrise, in the chair I had occupied the previous night and most of the other nights since I had set my army on this course. Action items choked my calendar flatscreen's inbox, and paper reports related to the onworld aspects of the operation overflowed a wire basket on my desk corner, like a last-century cartoon.

Jude rapped on my open office door's jamb, then stepped in without waiting for me to ask him. "You look like crap." He dropped into a chair across from me, then propped his crossed ankles on the far edge of my desk.

I rubbed my chin. "I'm gonna shave in a minute."

He eyed the tight-blanketed cot I had staff set up in my office's corner. "How long since you slept?"

"I take catnaps. Edison took catnaps."

"Edison was deaf, too. It didn't make him better at his job. Ord's not babysitting you like he should."

"I'm too old for a babysitter. And Ord's too old to babysit."

Jude jerked his thumb at my outer office. "Tell me about it. When I saw him yesterday, he looked like he'd aged ten years in three weeks. You don't look much better."

"So make me better. Tell me you've got the first modified Scorpion into flyable condition."

He grinned. "Why do you think I came by?"

I stood, arched my back as I rubbed it with my palms, and groaned.

He grinned again.

I said, "The replacement parts work fine. It's the original equipment that wakes up slow."

His grin disappeared, and he stood. "I'll give you a hand."

I pushed his hand away. "I'm fine."

He said, "Come on over to the hangar with me. You need a break. I'll make it worth your while."

THIRTY-TWO

A SHAVE, SHOWER, and uniform change later, Jude's footsteps and mine echoed in the Spook hangar, nearly lost in a din of metal against metal.

The space had become more factory floor than aircraft hangar, with a dozen Scorpions in various stages of conversion, each one's belly tile floating three feet off the floor. Each giant watermelon seed of a craft, bigger than an old fixed-wing fighter-bomber, got pushed from station to station by two enlisted ratings as easily as if they were rolling an oversized shopping cart.

The only reason Scorpions even had landing gear was so they could be shut down completely to switch out peripheral systems or to conserve peripheral system batteries. Cavorite never got tired.

Jude led me to a shut-down Scorpion resting on landing gear just inside the hangar's rolled-back main doors.

Modifying a single-seat Scorpion fighter to operate as a Silver Bullet bomber, or as our field-expedient troop carrier, essentially involved cannibalizing another Scorpion, then piggybacking the extra fuselage onto the existing one, with the nose of the cargo-passenger space faired in aft of the original ship's cockpit. The overall look was not only graceless but indecent.

No paint in existence could withstand the skin temperatures a Scorpion generated while operating in atmosphere. So the nose art, which consisted of two angry eyes and a shark-tooth mouth, was merely temporary chalk. The slogan below the teeth read "The humping cockroaches. Payback is job one."

Jude helped me negotiate the low-angled access ladder that bridged the Scorpion's flank, then we dropped through the upturned clamshell canopy into the side-by-side couches for pilot and systems operator.

The rating at the ladder's base cracked off a salute that Jude returned, then lifted the ladder away.

I turned to Jude. "What are you doing?"

He toggled a switch, the canopy clamped shut, then the visual screens that wallpapered the canopy lit, so that the opaque ceramic seemed transparent. "Taking her out for a spin. You'll like it."

"No, I—"

Jude powered the Scorpion on. There was no sensation of motion inside, but the scene outside bounced up and down as the landing gear retracted, leaving the Scorpion floating. The feeling was like playing a pre-holo video game, where the player sat in a chair watching the two-dimensional world ahead of him fly by.

Not that the old-style video experience bored me.

Jude nosed the ship out of the hangar at a walk, then drifted it above the city, left, right, canopy to the sky, canopy to the ground. Nose over, corkscrew, stall. I whiteknuckled my couch arms, not because of what my gut felt, but because of what my eyes saw. And unlike a video game, I knew that what my eyes saw was true.

Jude glanced down at my death grips on my couch. "Just go with it, Jason."

"Can we go straight?"

"You're on."

Marinus and the delta disappeared as we blistered along twenty feet above the Sea of Hunters. Jude sat back, smiling, hands off the paddles. "Just as stable as the original configuration."

"How fast are we going?"

"It's okay. We're over the sea."

"How fast?"

"Eight hundred."

I death gripped the couch again. "Eight hundred miles per hour?"

"No."

"Good."

"Per second."

We flashed across the opposite seacoast, and Jude nosed us up. The sky went black in a blink. "We can go faster now, Jason. No atmosphere."

I craned my neck. "Where are the Slugs?"

"In an orbit a hundred thousand miles above us. And, at the moment, on the other side of the world." Jude had inherited his father's piloting aptitude and daring, his mother's brains and marksmanship skills, and the bonus of having been the first person conceived and carried to term in space, where a stray ion had cut the right DNA strand and gifted him with the fastest reflexes in human history. He took us down, hovered the humping cockroach above the summit of Mons Marinus, the tallest peak on

Bren, and on the other side of the world from where we began. Ahead of us the sun rose, spreading as a luminous crescent across the continent. Jude tugged a flask and two pewter cups from his pocket and unscrewed the cap.

My eyes widened. "Booze?"

"It's five o'clock somewhere." He poked my side. "Jason! It's fruit juice." He revolved the Scorpion so its canopy was two feet from the peak's snow, then passed me the cups. "When I slip the canopy back, reach out and scoop snow with the cups. Be fast. The hull's so hot the snow'll melt before you can blink."

I did, and we drank a toast to the sunrise with Marini pear nectar cooled by snow from the top of the world.

I said, "That's something your father would have thought of. And something your mother would have loved."

He smiled at me. "It's only through you that I know that, Jason. I can ask you anything. Tell you anything."

I turned my cup in my fingers and stared at it. "Then tell me which side of the fence you're on. I mean between the union and Tressen."

He stiffened. "What brought that up?"

"I didn't tell you all of the last things your mother said to me. But I should. She asked me whether you were one of them. I told her no. Was I right?"

He rocked from side to side in his couch as the sun flooded into the cockpit and the screens darkened. "I don't know how to answer that. If the Republican Socialists are doing what the camp rumors, the ones you believe, say, then, no. I'd never be one of them. But Aud Planck's one-third of the chancellery. He'd never allow it."

"If he knew. You're spending all your time buried out

on some aircraft test range. I hear Aud's buried out paci-
fying the frontier."

Jude squirmed. "I'd know if something that bad was
going on. So would Aud."

"You think it's the kind of thing a propaganda ministry
advertises?"

Jude stabbed his finger at me. "Look, I've made my
stand for the union and against the Slugs, here and now.
Tressen's at the end of a jumpline, with no more Cavorite.
Tressen politics couldn't be less relevant to the problem
at hand, which is kicking the Slugs off the Red Moon."

I sighed, then nodded. "Fair enough. Which means I
need to get back to work. Take me home."

Jude sat still. "You drive."

"What?"

He pointed at a set of paddles folded beneath the electronic countermeasures console. "The Wizzo's got a re-
dundant control set."

"It's idiotic. This thing costs more than Costa Rica."

He snorted. "It'll be the most fun you've had with your
clothes on. You would have done it if my dad had asked
you when you were teenagers. And I'm right here to over-
ride if you overcook it."

I would have. He was. And my godson was also right
about the fun.

When we got back, a total of one hour and fifteen minutes after I left my office, Jude parked the Scorpion out on
the field, belly tiles high enough off the ground to avoid a
prairie fire. A tech with a chipboard met us.

Jude reverted from godson to test pilot, speaking to
the tech as we walked to the hangar through the early-
morning cool. "It handles fundamentally identical to the

original. No observable hull expansion problems with temperature variation. Well, I noticed a creak starboard rear, at the fairing."

I left my godson to his Zoomie duties and walked back to my headquarters with a bounce in my step.

We were planning a high-risk operation, but the reward demanded it. I might end up defeated like Lee at Gettysburg as easily as victorious like MacArthur at Inchon. And the people who surrounded me would make it work, just like they had made so many other things work over the course of this decades-long trip through this now-brightening tunnel.

I stepped through the door to my offices at zero eight hundred, smiling. We had been open for business since zero seven hundred, and the aroma of strong Tassini coffee mixed with the smell of ink on the ribbons of Marini clerks clacking away on steel typing machines. An Earthling staff sergeant looked up from Ord's desk. "Morning, General."

As I passed him, I looked left and right, into adjacent, unoccupied cubicles and file aisles. "Where's the sergeant major, Tierney?" Ord late for work was as improbable as the moons of Bren failing to rise at night.

I pushed open my office door as the staff sergeant shrugged. "Not here, sir. Put himself on sick call."

I froze with my palm against the rough wood. In thirty years Ord had never put himself on sick call. "Tierney, reset my morning schedule. I'll be out of the office for an indeterminate period."

He cocked his head. "What's up, General?"

"I've got a case of scotch to deliver."

THIRTY-THREE

I CHASED DOWN Hippocrates Wallace in an infirmary corridor between maternity and pathology. He glanced over his shoulder when I called, then turned and faced me with his rounds chipboard in one cocoa-colored hand.

I said, "There's a case of Glenmorangie in the footwell under your desk. Don't drink it all in one place, Colonel."

He grunted. "Took you long enough."

"I brought it all the way from Earth. And I've been busy."

"So I've heard." He stared at me for two heartbeats. Then he said, "You didn't come over here to deliver scotch."

I shook my head.

He pointed at an empty double room across the hall, ushered me in, then closed the door behind us.

My heart pounded. "I hear Ord put himself on sick call this morning."

"DeArthur stopped by downstairs, two weeks before you got back here from Earth. Complained of persistent sniffles. Got loaded up with the usual complement of patent meds and a download advising rest and clear fluids."

"You've known Ord long enough to know he'd never visit the infirmary over sniffles."

"I have. But he didn't come to me, just saw a duty nurse."

"And?"

"The next visit, which was just after you got back from Earth, he did come to me. I observed visible weight loss. He complained of flulike symptoms that persisted too long. I ordered some tests."

I closed my eyes.

I heard Wally draw a deep breath.

I said, "Pneumonia?"

"Jason, we can't beat all the bugs on Earth, much less the pathogens on fourteen alien planets."

I opened my eyes. "I don't understand."

Wally pulled up two chairs, sat me in one, then sat down across from me and laid a hand on my knee. "We've seen this bug infect Earthborns on Bren before. Mostly picked up in the Highlands, maybe waterborne. Ord was out in the boonies a couple days while you were gone. The locals are resistant. In Earthborns, it mimics cold and flu, while it digs in."

"Digs in. Where?"

"Jason, it's a total bastard. Once it gets going, it fragments erythrocytes faster than we can transfuse the patient."

"It's eating his blood?"

"The red cells."

"You have antibiotics."

Wally shook his head. "In a few years, maybe."

"The medic shot me up with a blood booster before the Weichsel raid. That would replace the red cells."

Wally shook his head again.

"You can transplant bone marrow."

Wally sighed. "That's cancer. Cancer would be easier."

I shook my head back at him. "No. Not Ord. No bug would dare—"

"DeArthur's a tough customer. But he doesn't have a younger man's immune system, Jason."

"Wally, listen up! I'm a fucking lieutenant general. I said no! Doesn't that count for something?"

I walked to the window, shaking my head. Troops drilled in the sunlight, and in the distance, aircraft floated into the cloudless sky. I said into the windowpane, "No, no, no!"

Blood roared in my ears, and finally I knew that my rank and my rage counted for nothing. Ord was dying. Not cut down in combat like a soldier. Murdered by some fucking Mesozoic bacteria. I grasped the windowsill, then pounded my fists on it. I spun and pointed at Wally. "God-damit! You call yourself a fucking doctor? I want the nurse who sent him home with two aspirin in my office in an hour! With her lawyer!"

"She could have shot him home to the Mayo Clinic on a cruiser and the result would be the same, Jason."

I pounded the wall again, until my fists were sore, while Wally stood by, silent.

Finally I turned to him. "How long?"

"Art's in remarkable shape for his age. And we can transfuse the hell out of him."

I blinked back tears. "How long?"

"Three weeks. Two quality."

I stepped back until I steadied myself against the windowsill, then whispered, "Does he know?"

Wally nodded.

I wiped my eyes with the heel of my hand, then straightened my gig line. "Where is he?"

"I'll take you to him."

THIRTY-FOUR

WALLY LEFT ME IN THE HALL outside Ord's room to suck it up. I got my game face on and stepped toward the door.

Dialogue I recognized, from a remastered holo of the last reel of a century-old flatscreen, trickled through the open door, out into the hallway. It was an Ord favorite. John Wayne, who played a U.S. Marine sergeant, was saying something about never feeling better in his life. As I recall, he said this during a lull in battle, while lighting up a cigarette, which shows you how times change. *Bang*. There was a shot, and the sergeant was dead. The end. Maybe times didn't change.

I froze, then sagged against the doorjamb and recomposed myself, while I listened to music play over the end credits.

Silence.

I rapped on the doorjamb. "Sergeant Major?"

"Come! And close the door behind you, trainee!" It was an exchange Ord and I had shared decades ago, when I was the worst trainee he ever had, and he was to me, well, what he had been for as long as I had known him.

I stepped into the room, around the gauzy screen that shielded the rest of the hospital from his wrath.

Ord lay on top of his sheets, cranked up to the angle of a poolside chaise. His arms and legs toothpicked out of a hospital smock, without his uniform the pale and fragile limbs of an old man.

He smiled at me as midmorning sun angled across his torso. Now that I knew, the hollows in his cheeks seemed so obvious. He said, "Thought I might enjoy a vacation at taxpayer expense, sir!"

I nodded. "About time, Sergeant Major. Mind if I join you?"

He wrinkled his forehead. "Sir, our paperwork—"

"Is being handled by Staff Sergeant Tierney and Brigadier Hawkins. You have a problem with either of those gentlemen's capacity?"

He stiffened. "Certainly not, sir."

Lunch was better than Meals, Utility, Dessicated. Barely. We watched *Sands of Iwo Jima* again, together. By the time the sergeant died again, late-afternoon shadows shrouded the room.

I said, "I talked to Colonel Wallace."

"I presumed as much, sir. If the general needs anything over the next week or two, I should still be able—"

I raised my palm. "What I need, Sergeant Major, is to come back again for the day, tomorrow. Maybe every day for a while. You okay with that?"

He tucked his chin against his chest. "If the general can spare the time."

"I can lay my hands on *Sergeant York* by tomorrow. Not colorized. Vintage."

He smiled. "I'd enjoy that, sir."

I got up at three to handle morning reports, met staff an hour earlier than usual, and arrived in Ord's hospital room before lunch. By that time, Wally's vampires had him tubed up, so he was sucking whole blood like Bela Lugosi.

After *Sergeant York,* he cleared his throat. "Sir, Adjutant General's Corps stopped by today before you got here. For my DR-663 CONUS Option Interview."

I shook my head. "English, Sergeant Major?"

"Disposal of remains, sir. Next of kin of personnel deceased outside the Continental United States have the option of repatriation of remains to CONUS at government expense by first available transport."

I pressed my lips together. "Damn generous of the government, isn't it, Sergeant Major?"

"Sir, I identified you as next of kin—"

I shook my head. "I—"

"—and if it's all the same to you, sir, I'd as soon not make the trip."

I blinked, swallowed, then stretched a smile. "Always trying to save the taxpayers a buck, Sergeant Major?"

"Sir, it's more that I'd like you to be there. And I'm told the Marini do military funerals up quite nicely."

I mumbled, "Anything. Anything you want."

"My will's in my footlocker, upper right corner of the pull-up shelf. It's up-to-date. Everything goes to the Noncommissioned Officers' Orphan's Fund." He slid folded papers across his nightstand toward me. "GI life-insurance policy. Enough to get me buried, buy a round for everybody at the NCO Club, and—"

I hid my forehead behind my palm, then ran my hand across my hair. "Stop!"

Silence.

"Please. Sergeant Major, you don't need to worry about that stuff. It will be taken care of. I swear." I breathed deep. "Do you want to talk about—I dunno—anything?"

He nodded. "There is something. One item of personalty I want to pass outside the will." He rolled on his side, then reached into his nightstand's drawer. He drew out a leather-holstered pistol.

I smiled. "Ah. The forty-five." Weapons had always been a busman's holiday for Ord, the only "personalty" he valued that hadn't been issued to him by the government.

The pistol he cradled, in a hand that seemed to have withered even since the preceding day, was his own M1911 Colt automatic. The design was pushing two centuries old. Too heavy, too hard to fire accurately, but Ord wasn't the only careerist who continued to carry a service .45 into combat as his sidearm. Ord's was an aftermarket blue steel version that he had souped up with custom-carved grips and hand balancing. And one unique modification made the pistol worth what it cost—a scratch along the receiver where the steel of Ord's .45 had stopped a bullet bound for his heart.

He drew the pistol from its holster and turned it in his hands. "Saw me through the Second Afghan, sir. Saw *you* through the Armada business."

I bowed as I sat, diplomat style. "A loan I was honored to receive. And lucky to repay."

He gazed at the ceiling, then closed his eyes, nodding as he recited postings and battles. "The Relief of Ganymede. Sudan. Kazakhstan. Peru. Tibet. Headwaters of the Marin. Emerald River. The Tressen Barrens Offensive. Second Mousetrap . . ."

I eyed the insurance policy flimsy on the nightstand, and a coal-black, ancient trough of a scar on his forearm, a badge of some forgotten heroics, then sighed. "You didn't get much for that life, Sergeant Major."

Ord opened his eyes and smiled. "On the contrary, sir. Churchill said all we make by what we get is a living. We make a life by what we give."

By delegating things I shouldn't have, cutting out catnaps, and pounding 'Phets like I hadn't since I was a teenager during finals, I managed to spend most of Ord's waking hours with him. Our blood matched, so I gave him a pint, then lied to a different nurse about it so that she took another pint a day later. I wheedled a medic for precombat blood boosters, to fool my body into making more red cells, so I could be transfused again, though the medic told me they wouldn't grow until it was too late.

No matter. Over the next nine days, the bug silently ate Ord alive, from the inside out.

On the tenth day, I sat with him for the last time.

His eyes had sunk into pits in his face. He dragged fingers across gray stubble on hollow cheeks and croaked. "They won't shave me, sir. It's driving me crazy."

In thirty years, Ord had never admitted discomfort to a living soul, so far as I knew.

"I'll speak to the nurse." A lie. If he bled out one nick's worth, there would be nothing left.

He said, "You're going to outlive me."

My throat swelled so I couldn't speak. I waved my hand. "Ahhh."

"I'm glad. No man should bury his son."

He had slipped away from reality. I whispered, "Sergeant Major, I'm not—"

"Yes. The way Jude is yours. I'm as proud of you as you are of him."

"Proud? I never got things right."

"But you always tried."

I laid my hand on his arm.

His lips moved. "You're on your own now, Jason."

Six minutes later, his skin was cold beneath my fingers.

THIRTY-FIVE

THE CLANS OF BREN cremate their dead on pyramidal pyres of gathered wood, and the time of Ord's funeral was dictated by the hour at which a pyre of a size appropriate to the departed's station was completed.

Bassin the First, himself, as a comrade in arms of the departed, would place the last log on Ord's pyre.

Bassin ruled a kingdom divided against itself, plains hunters and desert nomads against the worldly Marini, and, within Marin itself, abolitionists against slave holders. And none of the clans were crazy about having us neocolonial motherworlders on their soil. But Ord had fought shoulder to shoulder with them all when we had all made common cause and expelled the Slugs from Bren after thirty thousand years.

Therefore, over the next three days, Tassini Scouts carried janga wood from the Tassin desert, Casuni warriors brought scrub oak from the Stone Hills, and Bassin dispatched his royal barge upriver to gather magnolia from the base of the Falls of the Marin. Only when all that had been completed did Ord's funeral begin, on a clear, cold night in the center of our landing field.

The full White Moon lit the field so that the moon's light reflected off Earth troops' Eternad armor. It also reflected off the breastplates of mounted Casuni warriors on reined-in duckbills and off the delicate swords of Tassini Scouts mounted on twitching, ostrichlike wobbleheads. Crowds of civilian freemen and freewomen gathered, too, attracted by the spectacle.

Meanwhile, preparations to retake the Red Moon from the Slugs advanced. I had slept three hours each of the last three nights. I could have slept longer. My staff, the Marini, the Zoomies, and most of all the landing troops had forged and practiced a plan that I believed would succeed. We would retake the Red Moon, we would seek out the Slugs' home, and we would win the war. Ord had seemed to think that we would, and Ord had never been wrong.

The Red Moon rose above the horizon and silhouetted the fifty-foot-high pyramid that Bassin now climbed. After Bassin placed the last log, actually a ceremonial stick, Ord's catafalque was borne to the pyramid's top by a joint honor guard, then set ablaze.

I stood alongside Jude, both of us left of, and a pace behind, Bassin. A Marini band piped a dirge.

Jude whispered, "How are you doing, Jason?"

I shrugged. "I spent these last few days with him. Soldiers don't usually get to see death coming. I thought we'd talk about things that mattered. Things we hadn't said. But mostly we watched war movies and told stories. Sometimes we laughed." I shook my head. "I don't know."

The Red Moon, still befogged by the Slug fleet that kept us from it, had risen so high now that its disk intersected the roiling smoke plume that had been Ord.

In the civilian crowd, a murmur rose.

I shot Bassin a glance.

He leaned toward Jude and me and whispered, "It's nothing. If a warrior's smoke crosses his enemy's path before battle, it's bad luck."

I whispered, "Sure. It means he's already dead."

The dirge ended.

Jude said, "Huh?"

I stared where my godson was staring, up at the Red Moon, which seemed smaller.

The Red Moon shrank in the sky, from basketball-size to melon-size.

The murmur spread to the Casuni and Tassini ranks, then to the more worldly Marini soldiers, and finally to my troops.

Overhead, the Red Moon, our key to victory, had become as tiny as a crimson pea.

Then it winked out altogether.

Now the Tassini and Casuni pointed and shouted. Their mounts pranced and snorted.

Within the old city, miles from us, an alarm bell sounded, then another, then more, until the night echoed with them.

Bassin muttered, "This is impossible."

I shook my head slowly as I stared at the night sky of Bren, which for the first time in human experience held only one moon. "Expect the worst from the gods of war and they will seldom disappoint you."

THIRTY-SIX

ORD'S FUNERAL PYRE had burned out by the time the White Moon set and the sun rose. Recent events considered, a wagering man could have cleaned up last night simply by betting that the sun would rise.

Bassin had returned to the Summer Palace in the old city to show the flag of stability and, I supposed, to figure out how to explain the disappearance of the moon—disappearance of the moon!—to his subjects, before his enemies blamed it on him.

As commander in chief, the last thing I could do under the circumstances was act like the sky had fallen, even though it had, in reverse. So I sat at the head of my conference table in my conference room, with my staff plus Howard and Jude, and conducted my daily staff meeting.

When we arrived at new business, I turned to Howard. "What happened?"

He removed his old-fashioned glasses and rubbed his eyes. "It took us years to figure out how to achieve a controlled breach in the containment of the Red Moon's Cavorite. The difficulty and scope of the task was more complex to us at this state of human knowledge than the

Manhattan Project, to develop nuclear fission bombs, was last century. It could have taken the Pseudocephalopod far longer to develop the process, for all we know. What we do know is that the Pseudocephalopod implemented the process within weeks of its occupation of the Red Moon."

Tierney, whom I had brevet promoted to sergeant major, asked, "Did they blow the Red Moon up?"

Howard shook his head. "The Pseudocephalopod achieved a controlled breach of the Red Moon's Cavorite. It harnessed the moon's own ability to be pulled in one direction by the gravity of half of this universe. In effect, it made the Red Moon into a starship, a hot-rod engine of planetary proportions."

Somebody said, "Then the Slugs drove the hot rod off the lot at two-thirds the speed of light."

Tierney said, "The frigging moon just disappeared, Colonel Hibble. Why are things still so normal?"

Howard said, "If Earth lost its moon overnight, the tidal consequences alone would be catastrophic. But the very property, disobedience to the so-called law of gravity, that makes the Red Moon able to act as its own power plant renders its departure an astrophysical nonevent."

I said, "No problems for Bren?"

Howard shook his head. "Physically, no. Without the Red Moon to reflect sunlight, nights on Bren will be a little darker from now on. That's about it."

My indigenous population liaison officer said, "But socioeconomically, it's a handful. Bassin's still a brand-new king, by Bren standards, and the first male monarch in six hundred years. His enemies are saying the moon's disappearance is a bad omen. That abolition and personal freedom and toadying to us motherworlders are bringing Armageddon."

I set my jaw. "Without us, Bren would still be part of the Pseudocephalopod Hegemony, and their kids would still be dying of smallpox."

"Sir, we hear that Bassin's cabinet is advising him to crack down on his dissenters. And they want us to do the dirty work. And take the blame."

I nodded. "He asked me to meet him at the palace in an hour. Let's see what he wants." I turned to Howard, again. "Okay. Let's address our new situation. Obviously, we can't retake the Red Moon the way we planned. Can we chase it down?"

Howard shook his head. "With a head start, and a screen of protective spacecraft, all of which it's willing to expend to keep us from following, the Red Moon's effectively gotten away clean."

"To where?"

"I dunno."

"What are the Slugs gonna do with it?"

"I dunno."

"But the Red Moon could be used to reverse the course of the war, against us?"

Howard shrugged. "By sabotaging Silver Bullet, it already has. But you mean, could the Pseudocephalopod use the Red Moon offensively? In some unimagined capacity? Yes, it could."

"Howard, are we out of options?"

"Only the good ones."

THIRTY-SEVEN

THE STREETS OF MARINUS usually resemble Paris with friendlier drivers. Earth electrics like the staff car that carried me to the Summer Palace, via the boulevards and crooked alleys of the old city, usually elicited smiles and waves from hack drivers and kids on the sidewalks. Silent electrics didn't spook draft duckbill teams pulling wagons, the way Earth horseless carriages did at the beginning of the last century.

But the day after the Red Moon was kidnapped, drivers in the streets were surly with one another and with me, and crowds picketed outside the palace gates.

Picketing, or more specifically affording citizens the right to assemble freely and petition the government for redress of grievances, was a concept that had rubbed off on Bassin from translated history chipbooks I had given him. At the moment, he probably wanted to give them back.

A sergeant of the Household Guard, plumed and armored and as stiff as his sword, led me to Bassin the First. I recognized him. He had been a platoon sergeant during the Expulsion—in fact I had decorated him myself.

As we clattered up stone stairs, I asked, "What do you make of recent developments, Sergeant?"

He snorted into his gray mustache. "If I may be blunt, General?"

"One soldier to another, Sarge."

"This old world's still turning today, ain't she? If His Majesty would say the word, I'd drop a boiling oil cauldron on them bellyachers. We still got the old cauldrons in the gatehouse. That's what the queen, may paradise spare her from allies, would have done already."

"Yep. That's how we treat dissidents where I come from, Sarge."

He raised his eyebrows. "Really, sir?" Then he smiled and nodded. He leaned back toward me and covered his mouth with his hand as he whispered, "I suggested it to His Majesty. Perhaps you could put in a word, as well?"

I sighed. "If it comes up."

Bassin received me on a terrace outside his apartments, overlooking the distant crowds. We stood staring down, our hands on the terrace rail. Bassin smiled, his lips tight. "In my grandmother's day—in my *mother*'s day—no one would have dared assemble to express dissatisfaction with monarchial stewardship."

I smiled back. "Second thoughts about reform?"

"Daily. My grandmothers and my mother would be appalled at the state of the nation. The aristocrats and the western tribes are."

"Maybe even some of your household staff."

He smiled again. "Ah, yes. The boiling oil."

"You *could* go back to doing things the way your family always did them. Even that. You *are* the king."

The absolute monarch of Bren, who had lost a leg and an eye as a maverick crown prince opposed to slavery, crossed his arms. "I'd sooner be hanged and disemboweled by a mob."

I eyed the protestors beyond the gates. "Be careful what you wish for. I hear your advisers want us to pour the oil for you."

"They do. But I *am* king. Jason, if I resort to force at the first disagreement . . ." He shook his head. "We'll stay the course of civil resolution here. We'll assist the motherworld any way we can with the wider war, but you're the ones with the starships."

"If you weren't going to ask me to have my troops break some heads, then why did you ask me here?"

"Not to ask anything of you, my friend. To ask how you're managing. Ord was more to you than an exceptional noncommissioned officer."

I stared out across the city, at the slow-flowing River Marin. "I don't know. How did you manage when your mother died?"

"Badly at first. But they say a son isn't fully realized until his last parent is gone. I suppose that's literally true for an heir to a throne. You lost your last parent long ago, but the sergeant major, I think, stepped into that role for you since. Now, Jason, we're both orphans. There's no one to point the way for us. Now it's our job to point the way for others, and the only compass we have is within us."

Howard was waiting in my office when I got back from the Summer Palace.

He looked up, a nicotine gum stick between his fingers. "Did Bassin need help?"

I cocked my head. "No, I don't think so. But he gave me some. What're you doing here?"

"You asked about options."

I narrowed my eyes. "Howard, what haven't you been telling me this time?"

He scrunched up his face. "Can I just show you?"

THIRTY-EIGHT

———

HOWARD WALKED ME BACK TO HIS OFFICE, two flights down. He pointed at an ancient black-and-white photograph, framed on his wall. A man in a wide-brimmed hat and broad-lapelled suit that accentuated his thinness stood staring at the camera, alongside a beefier, mustached man in the last-century uniform of a U.S. Army two-star. The caption set in the mat around the photo read "Oppenheimer with Groves. Los Alamos, 1944."

I tapped the glass over the picture, a copy of which hung in every office I'd ever known Howard to make a mess of. "Your patron saints."

Howard stood beside me, arms crossed, staring into the gray and long-dead faces. "Silver Bullet is this century's Manhattan Project, Jason."

If the Slugs hadn't demonstrated the ability to neutralize our nukes from the get-go, the Manhattan Project could have been the Manhattan Project of this century.

Howard always understated his case about Silver Bullet's scope and importance. He did so less from modesty than from his Spook reflex to conceal the project and its cost. The concealment was more from the people who paid for it than from the Slugs, who really seemed to care less about us.

Compared to Silver Bullet, the Manhattan Project had been the technological equivalent of plumbing. The Manhattan Project had also been cheaper to the society that funded it. Cheaper by the degree that a cheeseburger is cheaper than an ocean liner, and the Manhattan Project had produced not one but two atom bombs within three years. Howard's Spooks had labored for three decades and counting without success.

I said, "At least."

"You know, at first Oppenheimer's physicists weren't sure they could manufacture enough enriched uranium to make a working bomb. And the manufacturing facilities would consume one-sixth of the total amount of electricity generated in the United States. An alternate design used plutonium, which was easier to come by but toxic and dangerous to work with. General Groves chose additional expense over the risk of failure and developed both designs in parallel." Howard stepped behind his desk, drew a grapefruit-sized object from a drawer, and tossed it to me.

It was a rock, but with the apparent weight of a balloon.

I whistled. "This is the biggest Cavorite stone in the history of Bren."

"Not only bigger, but as toxic to the Pseudocephalopod as the Red Moon's Cavorite. Weapons-grade Cavorite, if you will. I told you we had discovered other Cavorite falls. Places where the Pseudocephalopod had bypassed meteorites of greater toxicity to it, in favor of the placer deposits in the Stone Hills."

My eyes bugged, and I pointed toward the empty sky

beyond the ceiling. "Howard, you enlarged the national debt mining weapons-grade Cavorite in space. But you had it right here on Bren?"

"I didn't say that meteorite you're holding was from Bren. If the Red Moon was our expensive uranium bomb alternative, this sample represents our dangerous plutonium bomb alternative."

"I thought Cavorite wasn't dangerous to humans."

"In that form it isn't. But the alternative was backburnered in favor of the Red Moon due to political considerations."

"Meaning what?"

"Meaning the Human Union refused to do sensitive business with Neo-Nazis."

I rolled my eyes. "Howard, the only Neo-Nazis I know are the Tressens."

He pointed at the rock in my hand. "That specimen was collected when we surveyed a fall of meteoric Cavorite forty miles long and twenty miles wide on our first pass over Tressel."

Howard, Spook to his core, didn't say *where* on Tressel the Cavorite lay. I could have browbeaten it out of him, but something else chapped me more. "That's why we changed the course of the war on Tressel? To get the Cavorite?"

"Officially, to plant the seeds of peaceful democracy. Unfortunately, we didn't control the political outcome very well."

Not even Earth's politicians could stomach the junta that had taken over Tressel. The planet was cut off and stewing in its own totalitarian juices. If Jude hadn't had the pedigree he did, son of two heroes, with a skill we sorely needed, his ties to Tressel would have disqualified him from so much as setting foot on any other planet in the union.

"Besides, Jason, we had a source of weapons-grade Cavorite on Bren. Well, above Bren. And it was controlled by a progressive monarch whom the human-rights activists loved."

I sighed. "Now alternative two is the only one we have left. We have to make a deal with the devil to save our skin."

Howard sat in front of his screens while he decrypted a set of orders, then spun the screens so I could read them. They were addressed to me. "Not 'we,' Jason. You've saved Chancellor Planck's life, fought alongside him. Your godson is his protégé. Your peculiar brand of personal diplomacy succeeded with Audace Planck in the past. The one who has to make a deal with the devil, with Jude's help, is you."

THIRTY-NINE

"SLOW DOWN!" I death gripped the grab bar ahead of my seat as Jude, piloting alongside me, skimmed a two-seat Wall Crawler along the nickel and iron wall of Mousetrap's Broadway.

The quickest way to travel from Mousetrap's Bachelor Officers' Quarters to the shipyards of North Broadway is by Wall Crawler, a subsonic aerial go-kart custom-designed for quick, unscheduled people-moving around Mousetrap. With a test pilot at the controls, a Wall Crawler's more terrifying than quick.

Howard, Jude, and I had embarked for Tressel the day after I got my orders, laying over at Mousetrap while the *Tehran* put in for her overdue refit.

"Jason, relax." Jude serpentined the Wall Crawler through the lumpy iron hummocks of Broadway's mining midsection, then slowed as we picked our way amid the scaffold skyscrapers and half-completed cruisers of North Broadway. Jude slipped the Wall Crawler into a parking spot alongside a tubular hangar one-tenth the size of a cruiser dry dock.

Inside, a dozen bulge-bodied Scorpion variants floated three feet off the hangar's deck.

Jude ran his hand along one Scorpion's flank while he and a tech walked alongside the ship. I followed.

Jude said to the tech, "This one made a jump and back?"

The tech swung his chipboard to point at all dozen Scorpions. "They all have, sir. Every one came back solid, and none of the pilots got so much as a nosebleed."

For once, we were trying not to refight the last war, but to win the next one. We had surprised the Slugs on Weichsel by jumping a cruiser, then launching undetectable Scorpions while the cruiser stayed put, and the tactic had worked.

But we couldn't count on it to work again. The Scorpions now in the Spook hangar we had left back on Bren had been enlarged so that they could deliver a planet-killing dose of weaponized Cavorite. Otherwise, they were "stock," meaning they could shield their cargo—including humans—from G-forces of maneuver at extreme hypersonic speeds. But if they tried to jump through a Temporal Fabric Insertion Point outside the belly of a gravity-cocooned cruiser, they would be squashed into particles smaller than dandruff.

These new Scorpions were shielded like cruisers, a nanotechnologic triumph that had been impossible even in the comparatively recent days when new cruisers like the *Tehran* came off the ways. That meant that if—if—we could shake the Tressens down for weapons-grade Cavorite, and if—if—Howard's Spooks really had pinpointed the portal jump that would bring human ships within striking distance of the Slug homeworld, then we wouldn't even have to send cruisers in harm's way, or lose tactical surprise, by jumping them.

The tech asked Jude, "Sir, couldn't we just send these in fire-and-forget? Like the old cruise missiles?"

The debate about the need for manned aircraft and spacecraft had raged since the turn of the century, when U.S. remotely piloted aerial 'bots had started whacking terrorists.

Jude shook his head. "Remote communication travels at light speed. A joysticker can dogfight on Earth, but at space distances what he sees lags a second, and so does his input."

"I hear this won't be a dogfight, sir. Just fly straight at a planet-sized target, then pull the trigger. With respect, sir, aren't piloted aircraft just toys for generals who like to fly?"

Jude raised one finger. "When that trigger gets pulled, the only other intelligent species in the universe goes extinct. Would you trust that to a preset 'bot?"

The tech shrugged. "I suppose not."

We had taken human decision making out of war more and more over the last century. We could've taken humans out of even more cockpits, and out of more tank hulls, and even off infantry point walking decades ago, in favor of 'bots. War would have been cheaper if we had just eliminated the option to be human. But I saw value in keeping human life at issue. As Robert E. Lee said, "It is well that war is so terrible, lest we grow too fond of it."

The tech nodded, then said to Jude, "I guess you'll be flying lead, then, sir?"

Jude shrugged. "Like you said, it's not dogfighting.

Anybody who can handle a Scorpion can fly straight at a planet, then pull the trigger."

I stiffened at Jude's answer but held my tongue in front of the tech.

On the way back to the BOQ, we passed level twenty. It was sealed off, had been since the Second Battle of Mousetrap. Five thousand missing in action were entombed there, unrecoverable except at unacceptable risk to the excavators and to the fabric of Mousetrap. Jude's mother was among them.

I pointed at the fused iron wall and the plaque inscribed with five thousand names. "Jude, your mother, and before her your father, gave their lives to this war! You're going to let someone else pull the trigger that ends it?"

He stopped the Crawler, and he looked over at me as we hung there in Broadway's vastness. "They did. And you've given most of yours to it, too, Jason. Ending this war may define their lives. It may define yours. But my life will be defined by something else, something out in my future. Something you found but I'm still looking for."

I shook my head.

Jude leaned on the center console. "You can't dictate what I make from my life, any more than Ord could dictate what you made of yours, Jason."

"No. But I learned from him that I should do the right thing."

"And I've learned that from you."

"I hope so."

Nevertheless, three days later we reboarded the *Tehran,* outbound for Tressel, where we both fully intended to make a deal with the devil.

FORTY

I SAT WITH A PLASTEEL CRATE IN MY LAP, on my bunk in my double-wide stateroom aboard the *Tehran,* outbound for Tressel. *Tehran'*s accommodations were more generous than older cruisers', some already mothballed relics like me.

"They don't make 'em like they used to." Howard leaned against my stateroom's bulkhead and pointed at the object in the crate.

Jeeb stretched his ultratanium limbs like a waking, six-legged Siamese. A vintage Tactical Observation Transport looks like a turkey-sized metal cockroach, coated in radar-absorbent fuzz, with dual forward-directed optics that pass for eyes. Compared to cold, sleek modern surveillance 'bots, a TOT passes for cute.

Jeeb rolled onto his back and flailed all six legs like a newborn. According to the engineering texts, the machine was running through its joint-flexibility test program. According to me, and the other diehards who believed that TOTs imprinted their human wranglers' personalities, he was glad to see me and begging for a belly scratch.

I said to Jeeb, "You're fine. Knock it off."

He kept wriggling.

I added, "Please." He quit.

It's ridiculous to program precatory language into commands to a mere machine. But Jeeb's not a mere machine to me.

Howard sighed. "At least we won't need him to translate."

Like so much of what had once made Jeeb useful, translation of human language, on or off Earth, was now handled by personal clip-ons no bigger than an Oreo. Old TOTs like Jeeb, in their day, not only observed the battlefield, they intercepted and deciphered communication. A TOT could even teach a code or a language it had monitored, and then decrypted or learned, overnight.

"Howard, my worry isn't that the Tressens won't understand us. My worry is that they will."

"The Pseudocephalopod threatens them as much as it threatens the rest of the human race."

"Which won't make them less pricks."

"Aud Planck always struck me as a decent sort."

"Aud's only a third of the Chancellery. And his opinion probably counts for even less than a third because he *is* decent."

Jeeb sat up, telescoped out his wings, then tested them by fluttering across my cabin and perching on Howard's shoulder.

Howard scratched Jeeb behind his optics. "You have flexibility. Your orders are to secure permissions to prospect for and extract Cavorite. The price is open."

"Howard, I'm the last person I'd give a blank check to."

"No, the last person would be either of Aud Planck's colleagues. Just do what you can. Talk it out with them."

"What if I make a deal? How long until the prospecting starts?"

"I think we could start within a month."

"Shouldn't I know where the stuff is?"

"Of course. When negotiations reach the stage where you need to know."

Frankly, Howard was right. I've never had a poker face, and if I betrayed the location of the deposits with a twitch, it could cost us if we ended up having to go in and take it.

Jude rapped on the hatch frame, then stepped through. He had changed back into his neo-Gestapo Tressen black. Nonetheless, Jeeb's optics whined as they widened, and then he hopped from Howard onto the shoulder of another old friend.

Jude tickled Jeeb alongside the underside of the 'bot's carapace. After years in a box, Jeeb was getting spoiled rotten. "Downship leaves from Bay Twenty-two in an hour."

I set Jeeb's Plasteel cage on the deckplates. "I'll be dressed in twenty minutes."

Jude smiled at Jeeb as the 'bot preened his antennae for the first time in three years. "In spite of everything, you must be looking forward to seeing Aud Planck, just like Jeeb. Old friends are old friends."

We landed in the capital, Tressia, in a fern-grass town-center park tricked out with a yellow windsock that snapped in the breeze to aid our landing. Also snapping were two hundred Republican Socialist flags. The flags all flew at half-staff.

FORTY-ONE

THE TRESSENS GREETED US with one black-uniformed honor guard company, one chancellor, one military band, and one multilingual soloist.

The band maestro jerked his baton, and the band played the Human Union Anthem, which was actually "O Canada" expanded to include a verse for each planet of the Human Union, in the planet's principal language. French, Russian, and Chinese stood in for planets like Weichsel that hadn't developed a principal language. If you think standing through two anthems before an international soccer game is long, try fourteen verses of the same song.

Jude stood to my right, in Tressen dress blacks. Howard and I wore our own Class-A's, and our host wore his, while he stood facing us at attention as his nation's band played.

However, Berbek Zeit's black jodphur-pants uniform differed from the ground up. I had studied a Spook intel report during the trip to Tressel, a few weeks old and prepared by the Spook who fronted as Human Union cultural attaché in Tressia. Chancellor Zeit's black jackboots were custom-made to add three inches to his five-foot, six-inch height. How the Spooks got into Zeit's closet I didn't need to know. The Spooks also reported that the decorations on Chancellor Zeit's chest were phony, except for one he got for taking an enemy position in a one-room school. The position was defended by an old man armed with a cane and two dozen children. The defenders perished after the school doors were sealed from the outside and a fire accidentally broke out. In nine places simultaneously.

The Spook report concluded that Zeit "suffers from megalomania and multiple latent antisocial pathologies, exacerbated by adolescent trauma, presently manifested in authoritarian behaviors and trappings."

In other words, he was a sadistic runt who in high school got more wedgies than handjobs and was now getting even with the world.

The Republican Socialists had emerged from Tressen's postwar chaos to rule through a troika of chancellors. My comrade-in-arms, Audace Planck, was chosen as one chancellor because he was a hero people trusted, not because he knew politics. Zeit was chancellor for interior affairs, which had encompassed everything from rebuilding shelled-out hospitals to restoring calm on the streets. According to the Republican Socialists, Zeit was doing a great job of both.

According to our Spooks, however, Zeit was restoring calm by shipping everybody who disagreed with the RS to "pioneer" settlement camps above the Tressen Arctic Circle. The camps would "push back the frontier" and allow "those with pioneer spirit to be free."

History credits the Nazis as "efficient," but Zeit rendered them amateur. Poison gas and crematories were so much more complex and expensive than quietly hauling dissenters north, then herding the survivors of the journey into windswept, barbed-wire pens in the snow until they froze into ranks of meat. The operation took place out of sight, because the only way to Tressel's Arctic was by government transport. And the RS didn't have to dispose of the bodies. They just left them there until the snow covered them, then moved the fences and guard barracks and opened a new "pioneer settlement."

"O Canada," part fourteen, faded to welcome silence. The bolts of one hundred Tressen rifles crackled, then the honor guard boomed a salute that echoed off the old city's stones.

Zeit stepped forward to greet me, and I saluted first. His complexion resembled unbaked dough, cheeks peened by acne or smallpox. His eyes, as black and frigid as the orbit of Pluto, hid behind steel-rimmed bottle-bottom spectacles.

Zeit clicked his elevator heels as he returned my salute and nodded toward Jude. "My most profound condolences, General and Vice Marshall. I know both of you and Chancellor Planck were close."

The Spooks' recent update had reached us only as we boarded the downship. Ten days earlier, Iridian separatists had detonated an enormous roadside bomb that had obliterated the limousine in which two-thirds of the Chancellery had been riding. Among the two chancellors, one hundred bystanders, and security troops affected, only Chancellor Audace Planck had survived, although gravely wounded. He was now clinging to life in an undisclosed location. A massive manhunt throughout Tressen would soon bring the cowardly perpetrators to justice.

Spook translation, estimated with a probability of ninety-one percent: Zeit's Interior Chancellery goons had literally frozen the Iridian insurgency in its tracks months earlier. Therefore the Resistance no longer had the military capacity to steal a second grader's lunch money, much less coordinate a massive car-bomb, ambush. Planck's staff had finally snooped uncomfortably close to the genocidal truth about Zeit's Arctic new frontier. Therefore, Zeit had bombed the rivals with whom he shared power, and blamed the Iridians. But Aud Planck had survived the bomb, wounded, had figured out who was behind it, and had gone to ground. Zeit couldn't risk declaring Aud dead just yet, lest he pop up. So Zeit was ransacking his nation for his rival, under the handy cover of the search for the assassins.

"Thank you, Chancellor." I raised my eyebrows. "But I understood Aud Planck was alive."

"Yes, by God's grace. But his injuries . . ." He removed his spectacles, drew a hankie from his gold-braided sleeve, then wiped his eyes. The hankie came away dry.

"How soon can I visit my old friend?"

Zeit sighed as deep as a deflating tire while he retucked his hankie and shook his head. "I'm afraid his attending physicians believe any disturbance could be fatal."

I smiled. "To whom?"

Zeit stared at me.

I smiled again. "Aud's a hard man to keep down. I'm sure he's been making his physicians' lives miserable."

Zeit pressed his lips together in a smile and nodded. "My first experience with your sense of humor, General. A soldier salvages a light remark in the darkest moments, hey?"

I stared back at Zeit. "The dark moments lie ahead for whoever tried to kill him."

Zeit turned his eyes down while he tugged a pocket watch on a chain from his waistcoat and read it. "Of course. Well, I assume you will wish to rest after your voyage."

"You're very understanding. But let's do lunch. My diplomats will call your diplomats."

Our motorcade through Tressia rolled from the old quarter onto boulevards scrubbed as white as bone by Republican Socialism. Jude sat with clenched fists, staring out the chugging limousine's window as new stone buildings flashed by us, as identical as marble boxcars on a train bound in the opposite direction. "Zeit's always been cold. But I never believed . . ."

Honest people believe what they're told. I drew a deep breath. "Is he cold enough to bargain with?"

Jude spun away from the window. "You're not serious? We can't deal with—"

"You didn't have a problem dealing with the RS until now. Aud's a sand grain compared to what your RS has done to the rest of Tressen."

He shook his head. "The RS you think you see—"

"Finally, you see it, too."

"I don't. A power play by Zeit doesn't prove all that stuff about the camps. The RS you think you see could never be my RS."

I stared out the window, at a crew of thin, bent women picking up roadside trash under guard. Each woman wore a scarlet Iridian identifying medallion. I turned away from the window. "Well, now it has to be all of ours."

FORTY-TWO

THE HUMAN UNION CONSULATE squatted like a gray marble toad, part of the new quarter of Tressia that the Republican Socialists had built. Like most everything else about the multinational Human Union, the consulate was principally paid for and staffed by Americans.

To demonstrate the Human Union's outrage at Republican Socialist internal policy, the building had been downgraded to consulate from embassy. The Tressens cared less. The ambassador got downgraded to consul, too. Again, the Tressens cared less. But I cared because the ambassador's paycheck shrank, and he was my friend.

Human Union Consul Eric Muscovy greeted us at the consulate's double doors, waddling. More charitably, he was walking slightly splay-footed, and his lips protruded.

He hugged me, then frowned. "I hear you smarted off to Zeit today, Jason."

"Next time I'll punch his lights out, Duck." I *told* them not to send me. Time for a subject change. "Got your message. Thanks."

"I was sorry to hear. Ord was a good man." So was the

Duck. He and Ord together had sprung me from China, once upon a time. The Duck wasn't a Spook under diplomatic cover, though. He was an Asian-studies major who accepted backwater and offworld assignments that his peers rejected as disamenable, because distance from the home office conferred a measure of diplomatic autonomy. But the Duck was no privateer. "Rogue diplomat" is an oxymoron.

After greetings among Howard, Jude, and the Duck, Consul Muscovy peered across the wide boulevard. On the opposite sidewalk a brown-trench-coated Tressen in a slouch hat leaned against a lamppost reading a newspaper. The Duck smiled and waved. The man ignored him.

When the doors closed behind us, Jude jerked his head behind us toward the doors as he asked the Duck, "Ferrent?"

Ferrents were anvil-headed, beady-eyed brown amphibians the size of Gila monsters. Their most notable contribution to Tressen's pseudo-Paleozoic ecology was one singularly off-putting habit. They nosed around in other animals' dung. The Republican Socialists' Interior Police, with their sore-thumb-brown "civilian" trench coats and slouch hats, came by their nickname honestly.

The Duck smiled and nodded. "Mister Air Vice Marshall, take a glimpse of life on Tressel for citizens who aren't highly placed Republican Socialists. Jude, there's a Ferrent slouching against that lamppost twenty-six hours every day. There's another in the alley behind us, across from our back door. A Ferrent team tails everyone who goes in or out."

Jude shook his head. "Duck, the consular staff are aliens. Outer space, hostile aliens. Foreign Service personnel get surveilled in every capital—Washington, Paris, Marinus. That doesn't make the Ferrents the Gestapo."

"Oh? Last week our regular shellfish monger got replaced. The new guy couldn't catch fish with dynamite. A plant. We checked. The old monger's house was vacant. Neighbor said the family went north."

Jude furrowed his brow. "Pioneer camp?"

The Duck nodded. "And his wife and kids."

Jude shifted his weight, then shrugged. "Anecdotal evidence." I shrugged, too. Tressen's wealth, compared to its conquered rival, Iridia, came from mineral deposits in Tressen's north. It was marginally credible that a family might seek a new life on the frontier.

I eyed the walls. "Can we talk in here, Duck?"

He smiled. "The Tressens have rudimentary crank-to-ring telephones. They invented the telegraph only a couple years ago. No bug problems. On the other hand, their human intelligence collection's aggressive. Like Stalin-era KGB. So we don't let locals penetrate farther than the kitchen door out back. Like the phony fishmonger. 'Bots handle everything an embassy or consulate would normally hire out locally. We do our own dishes and change our own lightbulbs."

I nodded. "How many Spooks you got in the house?"

"None, of course." The Duck stared at me. Then he shrugged. "The cultural attaché's staff are Spooks. Don't change the subject. You've been here an hour and you've set relations back a year."

"Duck, even if we hold our noses, Zeit will never cooperate. Besides, he's dirt in a uniform."

The Duck cocked his head and pursed his protruding lips. "Economically put."

"Is Aud Planck a viable alternative?"

"Let's ask." The Duck led us down the consulate's center hallway to a door marked "Cultural Affairs" and buzzed us through a locked door.

The office was normal, but to a Tressen, or to any other non-Earthling citizen of the Human Union, the place would look like black magic, with translucent holographic images animating the space above desks. Two desks were occupied. Nearest to us a middle-aged, chipmunk-cheeked guy in a business suit glanced up from his keyboard as we entered. He looked like a hotel clerk.

When he saw Jude in neo-Gestapo black, he came up out of his chair with an aimed pistol, quicker than Wyatt Earp.

The Duck pumped his palm toward the floor. "Relax, Bill."

Bill's pistol remained sighted at Jude's forehead.

The Duck said, "The air vice marshall here's been seconded to the Human Union Space Force. His clearance at the moment is as high as yours."

Jude, stock-still, said, "I'm getting an education since I've gotten back on Tressel."

Bill dropped the pistol to his side but kept staring at Jude. "Pretty hard not to have gotten one while you were here before, Vice Marshall."

The Duck rolled his eyes. "Billy, honest people believe the lies other people tell them. If they didn't, you'd be a hotel clerk."

Which was exactly what "Bill" looked to be. Before I started adviser assignments, I thought Human Intelligence Spooks, the ones who recruited and ran local agents undercover abroad, would be ruggedly handsome blokes in tuxedos. In fact, diplomatic-covered Spooks tended to look and act just a little too slow, a little too out of it, to be suspected as spies.

The Duck asked Bill, "How's Planck today?"

I raised my eyebrows. Not, "Do you know whether Planck's still alive?"

Bill sighed, then waved up a map of Tressen that showed the country from the capital, where we stood, to the coast. The southern part of the coast was the Tressel Barrens, a vast swamp that would someday become more coal than the English dug out of Wales. The northern coast, which for the six centuries preceding the Late Unpleasantness had been the Unified Duchies of Iridia, was a smooth rock plain dotted with fishing villages.

Bill the Spook pointed at a flashing red dot that was actually slightly seaward of the formerly Iridian coastline. "Planck's hiding out in an isolated lober fisherman's blind, here. The fisherman living in it's an Iridian veteran. Planck saved his life years ago, when the guy was a POW and Planck was a Tressen platoon leader. The old guy's been nursing Planck, but the chancellor's got a fractured lower left leg and a serious head wound. One or both are infected, because he's running a couple degrees of fever."

I narrowed my eyes. "How'd you get a bug on a chancellor?"

"Sources and methods, General." Translation: no comment.

The Duck rolled his eyes. "He's Triple-A cleared. You might as well tell him."

Bill frowned. "I didn't, General. You did. You and Vice Marshall Metzger."

"What?"

"You remember after the Armistice, and before the embargo, you picked out a 'Puter at a jeweler's in Georgetown? Antique Rolex mechanical watch case, with modern guts?"

I frowned. "As a gift for Aud. The Tressens can't get used to telling time digitally. I sent it to Jude so he could hand deliver it. What does that matter?"

Bill shrugged. "Counterespionage monitors the spending patterns of everybody with Triple-A clearance or higher. When a guy who's worn a plastic Timex all his life suddenly blows four months' pay on an antique watch, they're curious."

The heat of adrenaline spiked through me. "They thought I was on the take?"

"They think everybody's on the take. It's their job. When they found out who you were having it engraved to, they passed the word to the Tressen desk."

"When I picked up the watch, the clerk said there had been a break-in. But my order was okay."

"Perfectly okay. Just midnight modified with a homer/monitor."

"You bastards." I rolled my eyes. "Did they repeal the Constitution while I was gone?"

Bill shook his head. "The Constitution's fine. The Bill of Rights applies to American citizens, not aliens. Chancellor Planck's as alien as they come."

I thumbed my chest. "I'm an American citizen."

Howard raised his palm. "Who was entrusted with information that could badly damage the national interest if sold."

I pointed at Howard. "You keep out of this! R and

D Spooks aren't real Spooks. So stop defending them."
Then I paused and sighed. I said to Bill, "You could have
asked me."

Bill shook his head. "You would have told us to go to
hell."

Jude smiled. "He's right. You would have. And we'd
have no idea where Aud was right now."

I took a deep breath. "Okay. You know where Planck
is. Do the Ferrents know?"

Bill shook his head again. "Must not. Or he'd be
dead."

I said, "I've got days to kill while the Duck presents
my credentials. Aud Planck's my friend. I want to see
him."

Bill shook his head. "You'd just lead the Ferrents to
him. And they're just old-school enough to shoot a roving
diplomat first and ask questions later."

I held out one hand, palm up. "Oh, come on! You said
it yourself. Ferrent trade craft is straight out of the Cold
War. You can't shake a Ferrent tail?"

Bill the Spook shook his head at me. "I never said
we couldn't shake a Ferrent tail. But you can't, General.
Without help."

FORTY-THREE

———

I SPENT THE EVENING IN A STUDIO in the consulate's subbasement, along with Jude. The Spooks holo'd us reading, walking around, climbing stairs. Then we did it all again wearing different clothes. The next morning the Spooks snuck us out of the consulate using a Cold War shell game with hats, dark glasses, and similarly clothed doubles. The surveillance Ferrents, who, like other Tressens, were barely accustomed to tintype photographs, would see our holos through windows or in the courtyard and be fooled into thinking we were still in the consulate.

Disguised as a fishmonger, authentic down to the smell, I arrived at a tenement apartment in the old town before Jude. The apartment was furnished with one bentwood chair and an equally talkative, stubbled Iridian resistance bodyguard armed with a kitchen knife.

Ten minutes later, Jude, in coveralls over his civvies, carrying a merchant's basket of bread, stepped through the apartment door. As the silent Iridian stepped around him to leave, Jude held out the basket. "For your family."

The man stared at the basket, then at Jude. "If my family was alive, I wouldn't risk this. You two stay put and shut up."

Jude frowned as he watched the man go.

"Still think the RS is just restoring order?"

Jude double-locked the door, then stepped alongside me. After a minute, he wrinkled his nose. "You stink."

After sunset, another resistance fighter, this one, young and holo-star handsome, gave us coats to wear, then drove us toward the coast in the backseat of a custom-bodied phaeton, top up against the cool night. Sometime in the next couple hours we would cross what had until the Armistice been the Tressen–Iridian border, and would thereafter roll through what had until recently been the Unified Duchies of Iridia. I nodded off, leaning against the phaeton's padded-leather door frame.

Two hours later, brake squeal snapped me awake.

FORTY-FOUR

"YOU TWO SHUT UP!" Our driver slowed as his head-lights lit a trench-coated Ferrent, who stood in the middle of the road ahead of us waving his arms. The flank of a sedan angled across the pavement behind him, and two helmeted infantry regulars, rifles unslung, leaned on the roadblock's fender.

The Ferrent stepped alongside our car's open driver's-side window, propped one foot on the running board, and gazed up and down our phaeton's flanks. Segmented chrome exhaust headers as thick as a woman's thigh snaked out from beneath a hood as long as a wet-navy cruiser's. "I know this car. From party rallies. It's Commissioner Kost's."

"He's my uncle."

The Ferrent raised his eyebrows beneath his slouch hat's brim. "Oh, really? Papers." He extended a leather-gloved hand, palm up.

Our driver pulled three folded documents from inside his jacket, then handed them to the Ferrent.

The Ferrent jerked his thumb at the two infantry grunts

behind him. "We're after the bastards that ambushed the chancellors."

In fact, the bastard they should have been after was Zeit, the remaining healthy chancellor. The saving grace of this mess was that my godson was seeing the reality of the Republican Socialist utopia that he and Planck thought they served. It was actually hell with better cars.

Our driver nodded. "Bastards. They should be shot."

"Oh, they will be."

Behind the Ferrent, one GI worked his rifle's bolt. I swallowed.

The Ferrent didn't unfold the papers, just poked his head through the window at us. "Who are you two?"

I fingered the white silk scarf drawn up around my throat, beneath a fur-collared coat that made me look like an organ grinder's monkey. Bad enough to speak with an offworld accent. Worse, a translator disk's rasp might not pass for natural speech.

Our driver tossed his head toward us. "Wounded veterans. Mute due to their wounds. We're bound to my uncle's place on the coast, for a holiday with him."

The Ferrent raised his eyebrows. "So late?"

"The night air helps their throats."

I bit my lip and waited for a bullet. It was the stupidest lie I'd ever heard.

The Ferrent handed back the papers as he stepped off the running board. Then he turned and waved the two soldiers to roll the blocking car back.

Five minutes later, as we drove on toward the coast, I leaned forward and said to our driver, "I can't believe that Ferrent bought that story!"

Our driver said, "He didn't."

"But you stole this car from a party wheel?"

The young man shook his head. "I drive this car all the time. Everybody in Tressen knows Waldener Kost is a blatant homosexual. He isn't my uncle, he's my boyfriend."

I cocked my head. "But we—"

"Waldener's taste runs to ménage. That Ferrent knew when to look the other way."

I squirmed in my seat. Ménage? Espionage may make strange bedfellows, but not this one.

Jude leaned forward, too. "If a party ranker is your boyfriend, why are you helping us do this?"

"I don't know what 'this' is, and don't tell me. It's enough that I know that you two are doing something to bring down the RS. The RS has sent hundreds of thousands of homosexuals north to the death camps. Including the man I loved. Kost signed his papers himself. I will bide my time with that despicable man until the day that the RS falls. On that day I will slit Waldener Kost's throat with a razor. Then I will watch the hypocrite bleed to death."

I leaned toward Jude. "The anecdotal evidence is mounting."

Jude sat back, silent, and stared out the phaeton's window until sunrise.

For the trip up the coast, another partisan took us off the driver's hands at the dock behind Waldener Kost's weekend cottage. It was a spired granite seventy-nine-room chateau "purchased" by the RS from an Iridian duke whose family had built it six hundred years before but who recently felt the need to make a new life on the northern frontier. Nobody was actually at Kost's place, least of all Kost. That suited me, because my taste doesn't run to ménage, even het.

Our new guide could have made me reconsider.

FORTY-FIVE

THE WOMAN AT THE STERN of the boxy pole boat leaned on her pole to steady the boat as it bobbed four feet below us alongside Kost's dock. She looked to be Jude's age, and she stared up at us from a dirty face beneath a broad-brimmed hat, with the deep green eyes common to full-blooded Iridians. A lober fisherman's scuffed leather armor shielded her slender frame.

I pointed at the skiff's pitching bow. "Just jump down?"

She swiveled her head, peering across the waves, one hand on a holstered pistol. "Shut up!"

I get that a lot from partisans.

She hissed, "You think rhiz hunt only at night?"

Jude had already hopped into the skiff, as lightly as a landing gull. I followed, and would have stumbled into the slop that sloshed the boat's bottom boards if he hadn't caught me.

The woman motioned us to sit, facing her, on a plank shelf while bilge that stank of shellfish lapped around our ankles.

She poled us out into the current, which ran toward

the sea, then shipped her pole and whispered, "You two watch behind us. You spot a wake, speak up." She pointed. "There's a big, bad-tempered one that's lived under a ledge over there for thirty years."

Jude leaned toward me and whispered, "A rhiz won't attack a boat almost as big as it is. But the water's so shallow here that if one swam beneath us he'd capsize us. Once we went in the water . . ."

The warmer brackish swamps of this continent's south coasts were still ruled by aquatic scorpions big enough to crush a man in one claw. Here in the continent's north, a sea colder and clearer than the scorpions liked lapped raw, bald granite. The near-shore shell fishing in tidal pools was spectacular. Trilobite done right makes lobster taste like Meals, Utility, Dessicated. The lobe-finned fishes that flopped across the tidal flats to feast on the trills were, in turn, feasted on by lifeboat-sized lobe fins that mimicked the rhizodonts of Earth's Upper Paleozoic.

We drifted with the current for an hour, past a landscape as gaunt as skulls, greened only by algae and lichen that invaded cracks in the continent's ancestral granite. The greenery was the same stuff that the Tressens cultivated, then refined, to run their cars.

I shook my head and sighed as we drifted. Most places where the Slugs had abandoned humans across the Milky Way, we hairless apes had proved ourselves a wonder of resilience and ingenuity. After thirty thousand years on the naked Paleozoic pebble that was Tressel, mankind had sprawled across this world to build a mining-based early industrial civilization, evolved without beasts of burden, without conventional agriculture, and without fossil fuels. We were, however, also beating the crap out of one another and out of the planet, which killed the wonder for me.

We passed one pole boat like ours, drawn up alongside a tide pool. The skiff's fisherman waded knee deep, staring down into the pool, his trident at port arms. A net bag at his waist, already half full, pendulumed as he waded.

Jude didn't notice. He had spent the last hour watching the woman as she mended net bags and sharpened her tridents with hands that looked more like a harpist's than a fisherman's. He pointed at her hands and smiled, the way his father used to smile at cheerleaders. "You've had practice."

She kept her eyes on her sharpening stone and shrugged. "My family's lived here a long time."

I said, "You don't like us."

She shrugged again. "You, you're all right. You smell like fish." She jerked her head at Jude. "This one stinks of the RS."

Jude stiffened.

She snorted at him. "Your pictures don't do you justice, Vice Marshall. Don't worry. I've learned to stand the smell of Planck. I can stand the smell of you."

"You know why we're here, then?"

"I will after I get to know you better. Planck thinks we're hiding him. But maybe we're holding him for ransom. I haven't decided yet."

I raised my eyebrows. "We" were hiding Planck. But "I" would decide. The pretty girl with the dirty face was calling the shots.

Another hour's drifting brought us to the sea, where Green Eyes raised a square sail, then let the wind bear us north. I scanned the waves. Bigger water, bigger predators.

The woman sat down behind us, at the skiff's tiller, and smiled for the first time. "The rhiz hunt where the small fish go to feed, in the shallows. Relax now. Enjoy the ride."

I glanced over at Jude, who hadn't taken his eyes off the woman. He was already enjoying it.

I saw no evidence of human habitation on the slick rock coast as we sailed north. The woman was as serious about hideouts as she seemed to be about everything else.

The three of us finally tugged the skiff onto a rocky beach pocked with tide pools as the sun was setting. Fifty yards away, silhouetted against the sun's orange disk, on fifteen-foot-high stone stilts, stood a peak-roofed fishing shanty bigger than a bus garage.

I visored my hand above my eyes to look at it closer. A chimney extended above the roof, but despite the early-evening chill, no smoke curled from the chimney. From a dark window slit on the shanty's wall nearest us, something poked out.

Jude reacted before me, knocking the woman and me to the rocks. "Gun!"

FORTY-SIX

THE WOMAN SHOVED JUDE AWAY. "Get off me, you idiot!" Then she rolled back on her stomach and cupped a hand around her mouth. "Pytr, it's Celline!"

The gun barrel didn't waver.

She waved at the window slit.

"Ah. It's you, Miss."

She got to her knees, brushing sand off her armor. "Pytr, we're coming up."

Judging by the algae that painted the shanty stilts two-thirds of the way up their length, we had arrived at low tide. The woman scrambled up the slippery ladder to the broad deck that fringed the shanty, its rails hung with fishing gear, and we followed.

The room inside the shanty door was large enough to park a couple of medium-sized trucks and was furnished with old and simple wood pieces. A stone fireplace at the room's opposite end ran the wall's length. Above the fire-place mantel hung a twenty-foot-long fish that looked like a fat moray eel with a head as large as a kitchen dish-washer. The rhizodont's low-hinged mouth gaped like the dishwasher door was open and had been mounted to display a forest of needle teeth.

Beneath the fish a man with shoulder-length gray hair, wearing a lober fisherman's coarse cloth tunic, knelt with his back to us. An Iridian military rifle as old as he was leaned against the fireplace. He poked a peat fire, tiny upon the immense hearth, to life and shouted louder than necessary into the peat as it blossomed into flame, "Tea in a moment."

I crossed the room to the rhizodont and ran my fingers over the cracked lacquer on its scales. "Your fish makes quite a centerpiece for your place, Pytr."

The old man stood and turned toward me. Beneath the gray hair, his right ear was missing and a scar slashed his right cheek from eye socket to chin. He cocked his head as he tried to read my lips. I repeated myself, louder.

Finally, he nodded. "Not my fish. Not my place." He pointed at the green-eyed woman who had called herself Celline. "Her grandfather built this place and caught the big fish."

My wrist 'Puter had been vibrating, at closer and closer intervals, for the last five miles as we had approached the shanty. Two closed doors led off the main room. I stepped toward the left door, and the vibration became constant.

As I stepped, Pytr snatched up his rifle.

Celline sat on a stool near the shanty's front door, stripping off her armor.

I pointed to the closed door. "The chancellor's in here." I hefted my pack. "I've brought medicine."

Celline cocked her head, made a small nod. "They *said* you motherworlders are fey. I never believed it." Then, louder. "It's all right, Pytr."

Pytr lowered his rifle, waved me to the door with its barrel.

The place was more lodge than shanty, and I found Aud asleep in a bedroom at the end of a hallway. One of Aud's legs had been splinted and elevated, a decent job. A bloodstained field dressing swelled from the side of his head.

I sat on the bed edge and whispered, "Aud?"

He stirred and muttered, eyes closed.

I felt his forehead. Hot.

I grasped his wrist, not to take his pulse but to admire his bugged watch. Without it, bless the Spooks after all, we wouldn't have found Aud, and my friend would have died.

I fished in my pack for tools, then removed the head wound's dressing.

The woman entered the room, stood behind me with arms folded while I worked. With a magnifying explorer, I located and then plucked out a metal splinter that had either been part of Aud's car or of the bomb that blew it up.

She said, "I thought you were a soldier, not a surgeon."

I lifted the magnifying explorer in my right hand. "Mag-ee makes every soldier a surgeon. Or at least a medic. As long as this little light shines green, I can poke around and pull out anything I find without hurting my patient. If things get hairy, the light turns amber and I back off. Motherworlders aren't fey. We just have good tools."

Mag-ee also prescribed antibiotics. After I inserted the cartridge that it told me to, it administered them. Recent bitter experience with Ord on Bren notwithstanding,

Tressel's bugs croaked nicely after a shot of the right Earthmade stuff.

"You have the tools to get rid of the RS. But you don't." She tossed her head in the direction of the fireplace room where Jude and Pytr waited. "The motherworld handed Tressel to the RS. You even let your young friend in there serve them."

I winced as I rummaged through the med kit Bill the Spook had provided. "The tilt? Tressen would have won the war eventually, regardless. And there would have been fewer of you left on both sides. Besides, my 'young friend' isn't even sure all the stories about the RS are true."

"Then he's naive."

"He is that. What does that make you?" I read Aud's pulse off the Mag-ee. "You had a chance to kill off this big RS fish right here. Why didn't you?"

"It's complicated."

"Try me."

"I told you. I may decide to use him as a hostage."

"Zeit doesn't want him back. Zeit wants him dead. How'd you get hold of him, anyway?"

"After the assassination attempt, the chancellor made his way here, to find Pytr. Planck was even more dead than you see him now. Planck saved Pytr's life once. Pytr insists that Planck can't possibly know what the RS has been doing. I find that hard to believe. But I'm taking a chance because Pytr's been my brains and my conscience since I was a teenager. Do you know what it's like to trust someone like that?"

I nodded as I applied a fresh dressing. "I lost someone like that, not so long ago. I know how I got to be a general. How did a fisherman's daughter come to be running the Iridian resistance?"

She scuffed the floor cobbles with her toe, shrugged. "Nobody runs the resistance. It's just pockets of survivors here and there. We keep our heads down and hope something will change for the better before the RS exterminates us all."

After I finished playing doctor, Jude and I got assigned a bedroom to share. If Pytr and Celline trusted us, they didn't trust us to split watch with them. Celline took the first watch. Jude complained, out of chivalry. I didn't, out of old age.

Jude and I lay on rock-hard cots in the dark. He said, "What do you think of Celline?"

"I think she's smarter and tougher than most fishermen's daughters."

"She's beautiful, too."

I rolled over and faced the wall. "So's the sunrise. Go to sleep and maybe you'll see it."

Outside on the decking I heard footsteps as my godson's beautiful crush padded around in the dark, armed to the teeth. Overnight, the tide had come in, so the sound of waves against the shanty's pilings metronomed me to sleep.

I woke before the others, at first light, because after a lifetime with Ord I had forgotten how to sleep late. I dressed, checked on Aud, whose fever had come down nicely, then tiptoed out onto the deck, where deaf Pytr snored with his rifle across his knees.

I stretched out kinks that I didn't have when the likes of Ord taught me to wake up too early, as I barefooted around the shanty's deck. The tide had gone out again and was now running in, the sea lapping a foot up the shanty's pilings. Ocean whisper coupled with the drone of rainbow-winged dragonflies skimming the swells like the birds that lay millennia in Tressel's future. The serenity contrasted to Manhattan, or Mousetrap, or Marinus, or the Republican Socialist sterility of Tressia.

My stomach reminded me that the dragonflies, like the pterosaurs and gulls that would usurp their ecological niche, were hunting breakfast among the waves.

Our host and hostess had each been up half the night. The nearest chicken nested light-years away, so there would be no eggs to scramble on this crisp seaside morning. Like the thoughtful guest I was, I rolled my pantlegs above my knees, slipped a trident and a shellfish creel off a rail, and tiptoed down the shanty ladder to spear fresh trilobites for breakfast.

FORTY-SEVEN

COLD PRICKLED MY NAKED ANKLES as I waded against the incoming tide. Twenty yards seaward from the shanty, I reached the nearest tide pool, where the water deepened until it chilled my knees. Trident at port arms, like the fisherman we had passed in the estuary the previous afternoon, I peered down into water as clear as aquamarine gin. Multicolored invertebrates, some spiked, some tentacled, clung to the rock bottom like an animate English garden. Among them crabbed trilobites the size of flat shrimp. All crust and no filling, the little ones were also too quick to spear, and I bypassed them.

It took me ten minutes to spot a six-pounder, fat and spiny. I slid to one side, so my long shadow thrown by the rising sun wouldn't cross him, then drew back the trident.

I held my breath, then lunged at breakfast. As the trident's tines splashed into the water, the trilobite shot away. Into its place, where my trident's tines struck, flashed a dull red streak.

"Damn!" I lifted my trident two-handed, like a full pitchfork. Impaled on the three tines squirmed a three-

foot-long replica of the lobe-finned giant that hung above
Celline's mantel. Fins as sturdy as stumpy legs, which
enabled the lober to wriggle across rock from pool to pool
and meal to meal at low tide, thrashed, and a mouth filled
with needle teeth snapped. No wonder lober fishermen
wore leather armor.

My accidental catch weighed ten pounds if it weighed
one, and lobers were better eating even than trills. The
fish's struggles subsided, and I cocked my head and said,
loud as if the fish could hear me over the tidal rush, "See?
If you hadn't gone after the little fish, you wouldn't be in
this mess."

The tidal rush had not only grown louder, it had grown
irregular, a rhythmic splashing behind me.

I turned with the trident in my hands.

Twenty feet away, a rhizodont as big as the twenty-
footer that hung above Celline's mantel eyed me head-on.
With two-thirds of its body above the waterline, its mouth
gulped like, well, a fish out of water, and its pincushion of
teeth dripped seawater like it was salivating over a snack.

Which it was.

"Crap." Slowly I turned toward the shanty. What had
I just told my victim about the perils of pursuing little
fish?

The great fish lunged toward me, lurching on thick,
lobed fins, flopping side to side like a GI low-crawling
under barbed wire on his elbows. Semi-submerged bulk
buoyed by knee-deep salt water, the fish closed the gap
between us faster than a man can jog.

I sprinted away like my hair was on fire, screaming.
But high-kneed in the tide pool, I was moving slower than
a man can jog.

When the gap had narrowed to fifteen feet, I chucked the fish and trident back at the monster as a peace offering.

The trident wedged between teeth in the beast's lower jaw like a canapé on a toothpick but didn't slow the rhiz.

The shanty ladder was ten yards away, but the rhiz was now ten feet back.

My bare foot came down through the water onto something that exploded pain into my arch like a land mine. I stumbled and fell face-first into the shallows.

FORTY-EIGHT

I THRASHED TO REGAIN MY FOOTING, gasping as I held my head above water. Salt water stung my nose and eyes, my foot burned, and I waited to hear the crunch as rhiz jaws closed around my torso.

Bang. A pause. *Bang.* Another pause, long enough for a trained soldier to work a rifle bolt. *Bang.*

No crunch.

I got to my hands and knees in the pool and looked back.

The rhiz lay still as the tide surged around it. Blood coursed from a neat line of three bullet holes above its right eye and spread in crimson tendrils through the gin-clear sea.

I staggered to my feet, balancing on one leg, and squinted up at the shanty deck. Another figure, balanced on one leg, stared down at me, old Pytr's smoking rifle in his hands.

"I thought that was you I heard! Do you visit this planet only to serve as bait?"

I shaded my eyes with my hand. The face that peered down at me was sharp, silver-haired, and familiar. "Aud?"

"Can you climb the ladder yourself, Jason? I'm afraid

I can't come down to help you up." Audace Planck, soldier's soldier turned co-chancellor, whose marksmanship had already saved me from one Tressen monster years before this, sagged against the deck rail, then collapsed.

I knelt in the water to take weight off my foot as Celline, Jude, and old Pytr's heads poked over the rail. Jude called down, "Stay there! I'll give you a hand!"

I looked back at the twenty-foot fish. "Good. I'm not cleaning this thing alone."

In fact, rhiz were sinewy and bony and tasted like muck, according to Pytr. The monster was left to the trilobites, who swarmed it like sailors chasing lap dancers. Pytr did, however, clean and sauté the lobe fin that I had landed fair and square, albeit accidentally. Pytr also removed three sea urchin spines the size of popsicle sticks from the arch of my foot, then packed the wounds with moss to draw out the poison. Meantime, my foot swelled to the size and color of an eggplant.

Pytr's treatment didn't injure my appetite.

After breakfast, Pytr put Aud back to bed while Celline, Jude, and I lingered over tea in front of the fireplace.

Celline set down her mug and stared at me with her green eyes. "We brought you to the chancellor with few questions, because your people—the quiet ones in the consulate—have earned a small measure of trust by helping us in small ways. Now I must ask you what you want with Planck."

Pieces of another universe that eat gravity. A moon stolen by an evil empire of giant snails. Black ops line items in budgets on a world so far away that its sun was invisible in her sky. Explain that to a fisherman's daughter. I sighed. "It's complicated."

She smiled. "As you say, General, try me."

"Our government doesn't like dealing with the RS butchers any better than you do."

She raised her hand. "Please. Your embargo has been hypocritical and meaningless. The truth is that a nation, a world, acts in its self-interest. As I see it, suddenly Tressel again has something that the motherworld wants. Your government sent you to get it from Planck, even though you're as bad a diplomat as you are a fisherman. Your government expected you to trade on the sentimental bond between old soldiers. But now your friend is powerless. You're farther out of water than that rhiz was."

Jude and I stared at her.

I said. "Uh. That's about it."

Pytr stepped back into the room and stood watching us, a hand cupped around one ear.

Celline nodded, then said, "But I don't understand everything. You risked your life to come here and to help Planck, because he's your friend, even though a shrewd man would know your mission is futile. You seem an unlikely general."

My current boss, Pinchon, agreed. My previous boss, Nat Cobb, agreed. Hell, I agreed. I wasn't a general, I was a historical accident.

She said, "You're not like Planck. Not like my father."

I narrowed my eyes. "Your father was a fisherman."

Pytr snorted. "Fisherman? His Grace hated this lodge."

Jude's jaw dropped as he stared at Celline. "Who are you?"

Pytr made a little bow to Celline. "If I may, Miss?" Then he turned to Jude. "You have the honor of addressing Her Grace the Duchess Celline, daughter of the late

Edmund, fifty-sixth Duke of Northern Iridia and Marshall of the Grand Army of the Realm."

I said, "Oh."

Jude frowned at Celline. "You lied to us."

She lifted her chin. "I did not! Arrogance assumes."

"Arrogant? Me?"

She waved her hand like she was swatting flies. "The title doesn't matter. It is manure now, anyway."

Pytr sucked in a breath. "Miss! Your father would be—"

She pointed at the old man, and her finger quivered. "My father would be alive but for the RS. The only thing that matters now is to gut them all."

Jude said, "The house where we met you. You knew where the fish hid—"

"That was our family's home for six hundred years."

"Your father—"

"Your RS shipped him north as an enemy of the state when they stole our house."

Pytr made another of those little six-inch bows to Celline. "Shall I see to the chancellor, Miss?"

Celline nodded, like she had been giving servants their leave all her life, which apparently she had.

I nodded after Pytr. "How long has he taken care of you?"

Celline smiled. "All my life. But you say it wrong. Pytr is like my family. Now he's old. I take care of him, and I will until one of us dies."

"The rest of your family—"

"There is no rest. Since the war, my old soldier is the nearest to family I have left."

I stared at Jude, and he at me. Wherever or whenever, war is an orphanage, and now there were three of us.

We three talked for another hour. She told us about the hierarchy of Iridia, and about the pitiful Iridian resistance, which she nominally led. I told her about Jude, about his family, which were as close to royalty as America's peculiar meritocracy came. Jude told her stories about me that made me sound better than I was.

At noon, Jude accompanied me on a rehabilitative limp, with a cane Pytr provided, inshore from the ducal fishing lodge. Pytr assured us the route was rhiz-free. Jude carried a pistol anyway.

"Jason, all these people can't be lying. What I've seen since I've been back on Tressel is no illusion. I've been criminally stupid."

I shook my head as we picked along the rocks. "You're not the first soldier who was too busy to look over his shoulder. Honest men believe other men are honest."

"I think Aud made the same mistake."

"I'll give him the benefit of the doubt."

"Do you think Celline would give me the benefit of the doubt?"

"You could ask her."

"No. After what she's seen of the RS, I need to show her who I am."

"You like her a lot."

"No."

I swiveled my head toward my godson and raised my eyebrows.

"Jason, I love her."

"Don't you think that's a big word? You've barely met her."

"How long after Dad met Mom, did he know?"

My eyes moistened, and I swallowed, then smiled. "About the time he barely met her."

That night, we three sat together again, staring into Pytr's tiny fire. Celline asked me, "What is it that the motherworld needs from Tressel?"

I told her the whole thing. She knew about the Slugs and the Slug War in an abstract way, like any Tressen or Iridian who knew her world's legends and kept up with current affairs. When I finished, she looked at us. "Will the motherworld give Zeit a free hand if necessary, in order to get at this Cavorite?"

I sighed. "That's not our opening position."

"Even provide him more weapons? To use on anyone the RS chooses?"

"Again, that's not—"

"But you have to if he insists. You know Zeit will insist."

Jude said, "Celline, you don't understand. It's not just our world at stake. It's Tressel, too."

"I do understand." She cocked her head and cast her green eyes toward the ceiling beams. "But what if Chancellor Zeit were not the only game in town? It's an Iridian expression."

I smiled at the duchess. "It's an American expression, too."

FORTY-NINE

FOUR WEEKS LATER, Aud Planck was sufficiently recovered to travel. During those weeks, I honed my trident skills without further incident and swapped war stories with Pytr. Meanwhile, the duchess of Northern Iridia and my godson talked late into every night, walked the pools together every day. Eventually and inevitably the two orphans of very different wars became an item.

Our return trip was less eventful than our trip out.

I parted with the others at an Iridian safe house, then reentered the consulate the old-fashioned way, in an upturned-collar coat and turned-down-brim hat, walking like a garden-variety passerby, then abruptly ducked up the steps and buzzed myself in the door before the Ferrents could cross the street and snatch me.

That earned me a lecture from Bill the Spook, which was cut short when the Ferrents showed up demanding that the consulate disgorge the defector and Bill had to go lie to them.

With Bill busy, I slipped up to the Duck's corner office on the top floor.

I buzzed myself in the Duck's side door, bypassing

his outer office. His inner sanctum was small for his GS grade, plain-furnished with a set of leather desk accessories he had toted over half of Earth and a smaller fraction of the Milky Way. He looked up from his screens and smiled. "Jason!" As he waddled around his desk and shook my hand, he frowned. "What happened? Where's Jude? What about Planck?"

"They're both fine. The rest is complicated. Diplomatic progress with Zeit?"

The Duck motioned me to a chair as he dropped back into his, crossed his ankles on his desk, laced his fingers behind his head, and sighed. "They're slow-playing. They don't know what we want, but they know we aren't going to offer anything for it that would strengthen them relative to us. They don't need much from us."

"While we wait for Zeit's permission to mine Cavorite, the Slugs could fry ten planets, including this one. But we have a cruiser in orbit that could fry Zeit first."

The Duck swung his feet to the floor and leaned across his desk toward me. As he spoke, he poked his finger into his desk blotter. "We've been through this together before, Jason, on Bren. We've both been ordered to make a deal, not a war. If a public servant can't carry out an order, his option is to resign, not to whine. You'll never quit. So quit whining!"

"That's what I thought you'd say."

I reached inside my jacket, removed a paper sheaf and pen, signed the top sheet, then slid the sheaf across the desk.

The Duck poked it like it was a dead rat. "What's this?"

I pointed at page one. "Acceptance of Relief and Retire-

ment. Pre-signed by my boss. If retiree is posted outside
the continental United States, Copy A of this document
may be delivered to any United States Embassy or similar
facility for transmittal to the Army Officer Personnel Directorate without charge for postage. Retiree's separation
will be backdated to the date of delivery to said facility."

The Duck snorted. "Jason, that just fixes your pension
pay start date. You can't quit."

"You just dared me to."

"We're at war. You could be shot for desertion."

I reached beneath my jacket again, unholstered Ord's
.45, laid it on the Duck's desk blotter, then stood back,
hands on hips. "All you have to do is cock it. Then shoot
me."

The Duck's eyes bugged.

I unbuttoned my jacket and stuck out my chest. "Go
ahead!"

"They were right to retire you. You're nuts." The Duck
stared at the pistol in front of him with his palms on his
desktop for thirty seconds. Then he sighed and closed his
eyes. "Okay. What do you want?"

"Recognize me as spokesperson for the legitimate
government of Iridia."

"Jason, there is no Iridia. Zeit's made it part of Tressen."

"Read the Armistice. Zeit's police powers over Iridia
are temporary until the indigenous government of Iridia
chooses to restore itself."

"Jason, the indigenous government of Iridia can't
choose jack. The Armistice became a dead letter when
Zeit's goons killed the last Iridian duke a year ago."

I walked to Duck's coatrack, tugged his coat off it, and
chucked it at him. "Let's take a walk."

The Duck covered his face with his palms and muttered through them. "France. For this, I turned down France." Then he stood and walked toward the door, slipping an arm into a coat sleeve.

"Almost forgot!" I raised my index finger, then leaned across the Duck's desk and scooped Ord's pistol off the blotter.

As we got to the office door, I fished an object out of my trouser pocket.

I tapped the pistol's clip back into its butt while the Duck stared at it, jaw dropped.

I shrugged. "I'm not nuts. But you might have been."

Once the Duck gave the orders, it took only an hour for Bill the Spook to shuffle us out of the consulate and set us loose in the old town, free of Ferrent escort.

FIFTY

SUBVERSIVES IN DOWNTOWN TRESSIA were as likely to seek out the tenements on the north side as antelope were likely to seek out lion dens. The Ferrents knew it and ignored the neighborhood. That was why the gray three-story apartment building to which I led the Duck overlooked the departure point for "pioneers" bound north.

We paused on the building's grimy stoop and looked back at barbed-wire enclosures filled with gray Tressen motor coaches waiting to be filled with lines of grayer people.

"Just one smart suborbital down the Interior Ministry chimney, Duck? One?"

He gritted his teeth as he stared at the coaches. "Don't push the cuteness, Jason. Just show me whatever magic beans you're peddling."

In the tenement's stairwell, we passed an old man, head down, mopping the stone first-floor landing. As we passed, he moved his bucket and its rattle echoed upward.

The second sentry's hand was inside his jacket when we stepped to the door of the first apartment on the second floor.

Pytr opened the apartment door while he held a pistol in one hand, an antique weapon even by Tressel standards.

Aud and Jude stood in front of us, both in threadbare civvies, like defendants in the dock. Aud leaned on a cane.

The Duck nodded to Jude. "Good to see you safe." He made a little bow to Aud Planck. "Chancellor."

Aud made a smile. "Your courtesy is overstated, Consul. We both know there's only one chancellor now. And I hope you believe that I am as appalled at what you can see from the stoop of this building as you are."

Jude said, "And so am I."

The Duck looked from Jude to Aud, and back to me. Then he shook his head. "Gentlemen, it doesn't matter whether I believe you or whether I think you're both gallows-converted hypocrites."

Both Jude and Aud drew back like they had been slapped. I stepped across and stood with my godson and my friend. Aud Planck had risen from his sickbed to save my life—yet again. He might have been too trusting, but he was no Nazi.

The Duck pointed toward the barbed-wire pens beyond the building. "The reason it doesn't matter is because that abomination out there is the internal affair of a duly constituted government recognized by the Human Union." The Duck turned to me. "Jason, I've bent plenty of rules for you over the years. I've bent plenty more before you ever got here, for the sake of my own conscience. But I can't pretend that Chancellor Planck here is the successor to the legitimate government of Iridia. The union won't play king maker between squabbling generals. Which is what this looks like, no matter what my conscience tells me."

I crossed my arms. "Are you done?"

The Duck crossed *his* arms. "Are you?"

"Perhaps he is, Consul. But I am only beginning." Celline stood in the doorway that led to the apartment's second room.

Clothes may not make the woman, but they make a duchess if she looks the part to start with. Celline was so pure-blood royal on both sides of her family tree that her rank survived her father's death. Chin high, Celline, fifty-seventh Inheritrix of the Duchy of Northern Iridia, and last surviving successor to the common throne of the Unified Duchies of Iridia, lit the gritty tenement. Her business suit was the color of a fawn in autumn, and her blond hair was drawn back so that her eyes looked bigger and greener. Her jewels of rank, as if she needed any, were what the netbloids would call understated, a tiara set with grape-sized emeralds that matched her eyes.

I held my breath, partly because, well, Celline merited it. Partly because we couldn't produce jack squat in the way of credentials if the Duck didn't believe Celline was the duchess.

The Duck stared at her.

My heart pounded.

"Your Grace favors her mother." The Duck bowed.

I exhaled.

Celline cocked her head and smiled. "You are too kind. Have we had the pleasure?"

The Duck didn't have to work at smiling. "I would surely remember, Your Grace."

I leaned toward Jude and whispered, "She's really good at this."

He whispered back, "I liked her better barefoot."

After ten minutes of diplomatic slap and tickle, Celline turned and motioned to two vacant chairs in the room's corner. "Sit with us, Mr. Muscovy." After they sat, she crossed her legs, then knit her fingers over her knee. "Consul, we must inquire as to the union's intentions as a cosigning guarantor of the Armistice."

The Duck cocked his head. "Your Grace?"

"We are not rabble. We are the duly constituted government of Iridia. We no longer require Tressen assistance to maintain order. We intend to expel Tressen by such force as required, as is our right."

The Duck nodded. "That is your right. That is what the union agreed to." He glanced across the room, where deaf old Pytr stood guard at the window with a single-shot pistol. "But I'm not authorized to alter the current—ah—imbalance of force."

Celline shook her head. "We're not asking for starships, Mr. Muscovy. Or for unrewarded charity." Celline leaned toward the Duck and gave him a look that, I suspected, had been the last thing many a sea monster had seen. "Give us the tools to defeat these butchers and we'll give the union Cavorite to choke on."

A smile and a tiara will get a girl only so far, even with a man of conscience. In the subsequent negotiation, the Duck insisted on Cavorite first, within a month, tools of revolution after. The Spooks would prime the pump with a sprinkling of weapons, communications gear, and intelligence dope. America had handed out under-the-table party favors like that since the Cold War. But there would under no circumstances be any military or Spook hands-on participation, not even real-time intelligence if things heated up, except to haul away Cavorite when and if my new boss and her "reformed government" delivered.

Considering that my new boss's negotiating muscle consisted of maybe a double handful of resistance fighters as fierce as old Pytr, we shouldn't have expected any more generous terms. The Duck had no choice but to hedge his long-shot bet, which he was placing with his employer's chips. If we failed, the Human Union needed to be able to plausibly deny connection with these misguided rebels when it knuckled under to the RS, and to knuckle under fast.

So job one was to deliver Tressel's weapons-grade Cavorite to the Human Union within a month. But a planet's a big place, and I didn't even know where to start. However, I knew who did.

FIFTY-ONE

WITH THE SPOOKS' HELP, I met Howard Hibble the next day, at the Tressen National Museum of Natural History, a logical place for a person of Howard's peculiar predilections to visit. I found him in a basement storage room that reeked of formaldehyde.

Howard was standing on tiptoe, reading labels of shelved specimens, when I closed the door behind us and locked it.

Howard said, "What a great place! Couldn't you just spend the day?"

"Howard, we have twenty minutes before your Ferrent tail figures out that isn't you upstairs in the library."

Howard reshelved a jar packed with trilobites the size of kosher dills, then sighed. "That's not the only clock that's running."

"What have you heard?"

"Nothing. That's the problem. We have no idea how the Pseudocephalopod will use its new Cavorite. Our best alternative is to do unto It before It does unto us."

"Which we want to help you with."

"We?"

"I'm retired now."

"I heard that. They say the dental plan's awful."

"I take it that the Tressel Cavorite fall didn't land in the middle of nowhere. If it had, you would have just snuck down here, mined what you needed, and snuck away. Without telling the Tressens a thing."

Howard's eyes widened. "You think I'd do that?"

"Not think. Know."

He sighed. "The Joint Intelligence Directorate wouldn't let me."

"Assuming we can deal with the fall's location, wherever it is, what will it take to get the meteorites out?"

"Weapons-grade Cavorite behaves like it's less dense even than the Stone Hills Cavorite we mine on Bren. Each meteorite's as light as a tennis ball, so they don't burrow or burst on impact, like nickel-iron meteorites would. The fall took place forty thousand years ago, give or take. But the environment around it is static. We estimate that forty-two percent of the bolides remain at or near their individual points of impact, exposed on the surface. We designed these terrific 'bots that would scuttle around the surface and harvest them like tomatoes."

"Where are your 'bots now?"

"Pasadena."

"California?"

"Actually, there's just the prototype. It cost as much as a main battle tank."

I sighed. "Could people just go around and pick the rocks up off the ground?"

"That would be simpler, wouldn't it?"

"How long would that take?"

He shrugged. "Depends on how many pickers you

have. If you had a thousand pickers, a week or so. Once the bolides were gathered to a central point, one Scorpion could fly in, pick up the whole kaboodle, and be gone inside an hour."

I narrowed my eyes. "That's too easy."

Howard sighed. "I haven't told you where the Cavorite fell."

FIFTY-TWO

TWO WEEKS LATER, pounded by a two a.m. downpour, Aud Planck and I carried cheap civilian suitcases down an alley in Tressia's old town. Despite healing accelerants, Aud gritted his teeth as he disguised his limp, more so because he, like me, had to pretend his suitcase was no heavier than a normal traveler's valise.

From other compass points, Jude and Celline, and six other groups of two, converged on our destination, with the modest objective of saving the human race and the more local benefit of beginning the end of Republican Socialism on Tressel.

We rounded a street corner and bent forward into the wind that drove the cold rain. Down the cobbled pavement of the dark street we entered snaked a double line of people bent like us, bundled like us, and carrying luggage like us.

We slipped into the line, and a shivering woman, clutching a scarf around her head, leaned out to peer toward the line's head. "How much farther?"

A chubby soldier alongside the line motioned her back into her place. "Not far. Not far now. These coaches will be crowded, but when you get off, there will be stoves where you can dry your wet clothes."

I leaned toward Aud. "What a crock!"

Aud shook his head and whispered, "Jason, the coaches just run a few hours north, to the Ice Line. That's where it begins to dawn on these people. It's brilliant. Not even these soldiers know what's really going on."

Neither that guard nor any of the other guards spaced every ten yards along the dutifully shuffling lines glanced at Aud or at me. We shuffled past them with all the others, and on toward the coaches. Breaking out of a death camp might be hard, but breaking in was a can of corn.

The coaches had their seats removed, to hold more of us, and we shivered, standing packed together while they rolled north. At three a.m. the coaches halted and we spilled out onto a glassy, moonlit plain. Fifty yards from us, a blocky black wall ran until it disappeared into the night in both directions.

I blinked back tears pricked by the icy wind. It wasn't a wall, it was a coupled train of iron-sided ore sledges. Each sledge stood fifteen feet high from runners to wood-plank roof, and a greatcoated soldier with a rifle paced atop each sledge.

Paleozoic Tressel was too young for coal, and its human colonizers had bypassed the age of steam and rail-roads, on the way to the industrial revolution. North of the Ice Line, the latitude above which rivers stayed frozen nine months of each year and nonnavigable the rest of the time, the Tressen mines were linked to the populous South by trains of sledges towed up and down the frozen rivers by spike-wheeled engines that ran on fuel oil re-fined from algae.

A man at my elbow, who carried a cello case swaddled in oilcloth, said, "Those have to be the luggage vans. They must be bringing up the passenger coaches after."

A sign between us and the ice train read "Resettlement buildings are well heated, but outside temperatures can be uncomfortable in winter. Don't be concerned if you have underpacked. Suitable outerwear is available for loan at the Northern Terminus." The beauty of this operation was that people believed the soothing whoppers because to believe otherwise was simply too horrible. The guards didn't search bags. That would have been inconsistent with the lie. There would be ample opportunity to recover the dead's valuables at "the Northern Terminus."

I set my suitcase down on the frozen river, and its contents clanked. Nobody noticed. Then I flexed my fingers as I whispered to Aud, "You see the others?"

He nodded. "Jude and Celline just boarded the sledge forward of us. Freder and Maur are two coaches back."

The inside of the sledge stank already, and the fresh dry moss on its floor, dim in the narrow moonlight bars that penetrated the car's ceiling slats, only looked inviting. A guardhouse like an ice-fishing shed sprouted from the roof of each sledge, with a helmeted guard seated in each, rifle between his knees, already shivering.

When the crowd in our iron box had packed in shoulder to shoulder, a small man in a red moustache, who had told someone else that he was a shopkeeper, called, "Please! I'm claustrophobic!"

A guard shouted in, "It's just to keep you out of the wind while we couple to the main train. Move closer! Others are chilled out here."

How thoughtful. People, even the claustrophobic shop-keeper, shuffled closer together.

Rumble.

Our sledge's door slid shut, then iron clanged on iron as it was latched. I swallowed. This was beginning to seem like a terrible plan.

Two hours later, my legs ached, people were swearing, and the smell of wet clothing mixed with sweat generated by shoulder-to-shoulder overcoated bodies had overpowered the ore box's stink.

Thump.

The sledge rolled the first six inches north, and a man in a long black coat and a matching hat, which on Earth would be called a homburg, lurched against me. "Sorry."

"No problem."

"You don't sound Iridian."

I said, "I'm not."

"I'm not, either. This is a mistake, you see. I'm a physician."

He didn't know the half of it. Over the next six days, which was the one-way-trip time that Spook intel had predicted, we and the other pairs in other sledges would try to recruit and educate a little army in each of our moving prisons about what was really going on and what they could do to save their own lives.

The ice train hissed into darkness.

I dozed standing up.

When I woke, thin gray daylight trickled between the ill-riveted wall plates, and the thump-thumps as the sledge runners crossed pressure ridges in the river ice had become a steady growl. The physician faced me, close enough that I smelled something like onion when he breathed out beneath a pencil-line black moustache. He stared at Aud, false-moustached in the daylight. The physician frowned, then his eyes brightened. "Chancellor?"

Aud's head swiveled toward the question, only a half inch, but it was enough.

The physician's face lit. "Yes! It is you! Thank God, it's you!" The physician turned to a woman beside him. "You see? It is a mistake! If Chancellor Planck himself is in this box, it's all a mistake!" He threw back his head and screamed at the ceiling, "Stop the train! Stop the train! It's all a mistake! The chancellor is in here! Chancellor Planck is in here!"

I hissed, "Shut up!"

"Why? Don't you see? They'll let us go!" He threw his head back again and screamed so loud that his hat popped off his bald head, rolled off an adjacent shoulder, and disappeared onto the iron floor.

I wrestled enough space to draw back my fist and coldcock him.

"No!" Aud caught my forearm.

"Shut up down there!" The guard's boot stomped the ceiling.

"I tell you I know him! He's right down here beside me!"

"And Puck the Fairy is up here beside me! Shut the fuck up!"

Two minutes later, the physician screamed out again. "Just look! That's all I ask! Just look down here and see for yourself."

Boots thumped the car's roof as every face in the car turned up toward its ceiling.

I swallowed, but my mouth was dry. If the guards

found Aud in here, our plan was done. Ord's pistol nestled in my shoulder holster, but a shot now would solve nothing.

The roof trapdoor creaked open, and daylight flooded in and blinded us.

The physician pogoed up and down, staring up and pointing at Aud. "Here! He's right here!"

With my fingers splayed in front of my eyes to block the light I said to Aud, "Fuck! You should have let me slug him!"

The guard's helmeted head and greatcoated shoulders darkened the square of daylight above us as he peered down, broad nosed and scowling. His shoulder seemed to move.

A breath tweaked my ear as something flew past it.

Thump.

The physician screamed. The brick struck him full on the forehead, and crushed brain and blood and bone sprayed the shoulders and faces that stared at the physician.

The guard shouted, "I told you people to shut the fuck up! If I run out of bricks, I got a rifle!" He slammed the hatch and left us in the dark.

People shrank away from the physician's body until it slumped to the floor.

In a distant corner, someone prayed. A woman sobbed.

Beside me, Aud whispered, "What have I done? What have I done?"

The physician's bowels evacuated when he died, the harbinger of a problem that would not improve over the next six days.

The next day, Aud and I began whispered recruiting.

A woman beside me covered her ears and began reciting nursery rhymes to herself. Few of our car mates would even meet the eyes of either of us, or of anyone else.

Before the sun set for the second time, someone found the physician's hat, and people began using it to pass human feces from one person to another until they could be dumped, more or less successfully, outside the car through the openings between the wall slabs.

The matter of the dead man's hat, and the communication and cooperation that began with it, opened the doors between us and our fellow death-row inmates. And as we plotted, we didn't have to worry about anyone ratting us out to the guard.

As the hours inched by, the mass of people in the sledge orbited, so each would take a turn at the wall opening, to enjoy light and the fresh air sucked through the open sliver. As the ice train rumbled farther north, driven snow on the wall joint could be licked off, to supplement the buckets of snow that the guard periodically lowered through the hatch.

When the rivers ended, the ice track continued, hewn from the frozen ground. The farther north we traveled, the less prized became the time a person spent exposed to the frigid wind that knifed between the wall slabs.

The physician, and a frail woman in a cloth coat who didn't wake up on the third day, were slid to the windward side of the sledge, where their bodies froze and also provided useful windbreaks.

After a lifetime, five days, twenty-two hours, and six minutes according to the wrist 'Puter hidden beneath my coat, Aud and I snapped out of sleep as the ice train slowed down.

FIFTY-THREE

I TUGGED UP THE MASK that shielded my face and pointed a mittened hand. "There!"

The moments between thumps lengthened as Aud and I stood together squinting out through the side slits at endless white beneath a hard blue sky. Aud and I took longer turns standing at the frigid, windward wall of our sledge because, forewarned, we had come equipped with more effective cold-weather clothing than most of the others.

In fact, the Spooks had forewarned us about much that we would see. Tressel's North Polar region actually more closely resembled Earth's South Pole, a wind-scoured continental plain bisected by razor-peaked mountains, its moisture so frozen in its ice and snow that its air was as dry as a desert.

Bits of black appeared in the distance, peeking from snowy ridges.

I said, "That must be the wire. Makes a lousy snow fence."

Parallel to and a mile from the trackway that knifed toward Tressel's pole ran the barbed-wire boundaries of the first "resettlement camps." Hidden beneath the wind-blown snows between us and the wire slept Iridian children, Tressen professors, homosexuals of all nationalities, and anyone else unfortunate enough to differ from or with Republican Socialism. The simple brutality of the scheme was more breathtakingly bleak than the Tressen Arctic.

Aud spoke through his scarf as he shook his head. "I should have seen this. I should have seen this."

"Aud, Zeit wasn't exactly advertising the truth. Good soldiers doing their duty have been fooled before. I sent you that biography, about the field marshall whom the Nazis poisoned for plotting against them."

Aud shook his head. "A soldier can hide behind his duty. I abandoned that excuse when I swore on the chancellor's book. And at the last, your Rommel tried to do the right thing."

"Which is what you're doing now."

The ice train wasn't slowing because we were almost there, it was slowing because it was going uphill. According to the Spooks' mapping, the early mass graves continued for ten miles, then the single track climbed through a mountain pass and descended to another plain. On that next plain the newer barbed-wire enclosures resumed, the drifted snow low against them, and at that spot were garrisoned the troops who kept the survivors penned until exposure and starvation finished them.

The presence of that military garrison had been the problem that had scuttled Howard Hibble's plan to burgle Tressel's Cavorite. Because beneath the snows of that new plain, amid the corpses, lay the fallen stars of Cavorite that controlled the fate of mankind. Spooks and the politicians they serve love covert ops. But politicians fall out of love quickly when covert ops go wrong.

Within twenty minutes, the ice train crept slower than a walking man. It rolled through a dynamite-widened pass that was still so narrow that from the sledge I could have reached out and touched the vertical granite walls, and so deep that its shadows darkened the box like sundown.

My 'Puter's altimeter pegged the pass crest elevation at nine thousand feet, and the Spooks' mapping said the canyon rim topped out fully one thousand feet higher. Growing up in Colorado, the rule of thumb had been climb a thousand feet and lose three degrees Fahrenheit. But it felt like we couldn't get colder.

Forty minutes later, the thumps of the runners over the ice road had increased in frequency again, as gravity accelerated the ice train down the pass backside, toward our destination.

I turned to the man next to me, dozing standing up with his arms crossed, and nudged him until he opened eyes that the last five days had sunken in their sockets.

I said, "Showtime!"

FIFTY-FOUR

As SOON AS OUR SLEDGE ROLLED through the gate into the wire rectangle within which our train would unload, Aud and I began loading, then redistributing, the weapons our recruits had been dry-firing during the trip north. The pistols in our suitcases were obsolete Iridian single-action service revolvers. They were the only small, simple, plausibly deniable weapons that Bill the Spook could score in the Tressen black market on a few days' notice.

My unmittened fingers were so numb that I dropped one round for every six I loaded. Then I passed each pistol to Aud, who in turn handed it off, so it could be passed to one of the prisoners whom we had trained to shoot.

"Trained" overstated things. It typically had taken Ord and me months as advisers to train partisans. Here and now we lacked that gift of time. Nonetheless, if things were running according to plan, the scene was being repeated in six other sledge cars. But there were risks in this that planning simply couldn't help.

Few of the prisoners in this caravan had ever fired a weapon. The RS had long since exterminated most veter-

ans who had served on the wrong side in the war. Most of
the unfortunates who were rounded up and shipped from
Tressia were city dwellers who had never plinked a tin
can on the East Forty.

We hadn't risked handing out loaded weapons earlier,
so there would be shooters scared to death the first time
their pistols roared and kicked in their hands. There would
be shooters who didn't cock hammers, shooters who lost
their pistols in snowdrifts, shooters who couldn't hit a
cow's rump with a bat, and shooters who simply were too
petrified to shoot.

On the positive side, the waiting camp guards were
going to be less prepared than Bo Peep would have been
if her sheep had gone postal.

With a thunk, then a hiss, the ice train stopped. After
six days, the silence of the empty wilderness rang like an
alarm between my ears.

I peered out between the iron wall slabs. Two hundred
greatcoated, helmeted guards awaited us, drawn back a
hundred feet on the featureless snow, rifles slung. They
stamped feet, smoked, and batted their arms against their
chests.

A thin cry echoed from one of the other sledges. "Dear
God! Please! Let us out!"

A dozen guards, scarves to noses, rifles still slung,
trudged to the cars, then unlatched and slid back each
sledge's door. They retreated to the line of their buddies,
to escape not the prisoners' wrath but their stench.

There was no need to order prisoners out of the iron
boxes. After six subhuman days, those who remained am-
bulatory leapt, stumbled, crawled, and tumbled into the
snow alongside the icy track. Many wept. A few crammed

handfuls of snow between parched lips. Most were too weak even for that.

After five minutes, a different dozen guards walked the train, peering into each box. If they found halt, lame, or dead inside, they wrenched prisoners from the snow and forced them to unload those unable to unload themselves.

As each sledge was cleared, the guards padlocked its door shut. No shelter for the new arrivals. Then each sledge's guard climbed stiffly down from his guardhouse and joined his colleagues.

The emaciated prisoners, if any noticed, offered no more protest than so many pieces of frozen meat, which they would be soon enough.

I scanned the milling, kneeling heaps of prisoners, until my heart thumped. Jude, and then Celline alongside him, saw me, too, and Jude nodded to me. I had never been so glad to see two people who looked like hell. I nodded back.

The Spooks had flown a Mechanical up here to monitor ice train arrival procedure for us, so we knew what came next. By the time the engine crew, the guards, and the others had reassembled, the Arctic sun slid low along the horizon, at our backs, as a noncomm called roll of our jailers.

Years of experience had taught these troops that there was nothing to fear from the hopeless, decimated "enemies of the state" who tumbled from each ice train into the snow. The only way a guard up here could get himself hurt was to wander off, then be left behind on the plain to freeze, like the prisoners he was guarding.

When all the guards were accounted for, all of them,

some with rifles slung, others with them over their shoulders, stocks backward like pickaxes, turned their backs on the people in the snow.

The guards trudged, heads down against the wind, toward the distant barracks and machine-shop complex that lay outside the wire, toward warmth and beds and hot food. The more energetic among them opened wooden crates, plucked out dynamite sticks, then lit and flung them to explode snow fountains. Others tossed empty cartridge boxes up into the wind, ahead of them, while their buddies whooped and shot at the boxes like skeet clays. Disposal of deteriorated stores, perhaps.

Tressel's civilization poised on that historic cusp where Earth's had teetered almost two centuries before, proud to have invented dynamite, but not yet guilty enough to fund a peace prize with the profits of sale.

Bored, stupid, lazy commanders begat bored, stupid, lazy troops. Bored, stupid, lazy troops became dead troops. What we were about to attempt wouldn't give these troops the benefit of a fair fight. But the last thing a good commander wants to give the enemy is a fair fight.

As the Spooks' Mechanical had forecast, the prevailing wind howled toward the casual mob of guards, into their faces and ours.

Therefore, the guards didn't hear us as we rose, in groups of twos and threes, and began walking mute toward the unsuspecting guards' backs. Surprised shouts of other prisoners vanished in the wind and among the moans and delirium of others. We had formed a ragged skirmish line, ninety in all, forty-five on each side of Aud and me, and had come within twenty yards of the guards when I saw the first prisoner, stumbling forward, ten yards to my right, raise his pistol.

For these novices, the range remained too great. I had drawn Ord's pistol and carried it muzzle-down at my side in my unmittened hand. I waved it at the guy as I stage whispered, "Not yet! Crap! No, no, no!"

Bang.

Even a blind pig finds an occasional acorn. The first shot of the prisoner's life, and the first shot of the Battle of the Northern Terminus, struck the last guard in line in the nape of his neck, between the skirt of his helmet and his jacket collar. He went down noiselessly, like a flour sack, so that his buddies noticed neither his loss nor the pistol shot amid the skeet shoot ahead of them.

Within two heartbeats, nervous pistols crackled like popping corn, as the prisoners fired at will into a massed target too big for even novices to miss.

By the time the guards realized what was happening and stopped, the gap between prisoners and guards had closed to ten yards. Forty guards lay in the snow.

By the time the guards unslung rifles, the gap was five yards, and just a hundred of them remained standing. I, Jude, and Aud spent our effort running back and forth behind our skirmish line, screaming and tugging our shooters, trying to keep any from getting out ahead or from falling behind, so that no one would be shot by a buddy. I lunged for one man too late, and he took a round in the back of his thigh from another prisoner.

More guards fell, shot point-blank.

The remaining guards, blinded by the sun at our backs, reflexively standing and fighting when they should have run, were overrun before they could get off more than wild shots.

Prisoners fell on their tormentors three or four against one, firing pistols into screaming mouths, beating and kicking, pummeling guards with their own rifle butts, until guards' heads cracked like dropped melons.

Then there was no sound but wind howl and the crying of wounded.

Two minutes had passed since the first shot.

I stood panting, hands on hips, facing back at the litter of bodies in the reddening snow.

Aud limped up alongside me. "I think we lost four."

A prisoner beside me aimed his pistol ahead of us, cocked the hammer, and pulled the trigger. The hammer clacked on a spent cartridge. "Dammit!"

I turned and looked where the pistol's muzzle pointed. A lone guard ran, bareheaded, coat flapping, toward the distant fence and the barracks beyond.

It was barely possible that with the wind, the oncoming darkness, the cover provided by the guards' rowdy firing, and the sloppy state of this garrison that the troops remaining in the barracks complex could be surprised. In fact, we had half planned on it.

But not if the runner got to the garrison before we did.

I knelt in the snow, swung Ord's pistol up, and sighted on the runner. In the fading light, he looked back over his shoulder as he ran. It was the broad-nosed boxcar guard who had killed the physician.

A decent shot with a service .45 can bring down a man at forty yards. An expert might stretch that to seventy-five yards. Liars claim one hundred.

Ord always claimed that, if I practiced more, I could

be the best shot he had ever trained. He also claimed that his personally gunsmithed pistol was the most accurate .45 ever built.

I made the range ninety yards and growing.

More Slug Warriors had died beneath my hand than I could count, but they were, according to the Spooks, mere organic automatons. Human beings had died beneath my hand, too, when, as a soldier, lawful orders had required it.

But this was my decision. Like Ord had said, I was on my own.

The range opened to one hundred yards. I breathed, exhaled, paused, and fired.

The broad-nosed guard ran for his life. Toward, perhaps, a wife, children, a place in the church choir.

His arms spread wide, as if he was trying to fly like Puck the Fairy. His head snapped back so that his face turned toward the darkening sky. Then his body arced forward, fell in an explosion of snow, skidded, and stopped.

The wind in my face pricked gun smoke into my eyes, and I holstered the .45, then wiped them.

The prisoner with the dead pistol clapped my shoulder. "That was good!"

Aud limped past me. "We must press our attack! But so far, so good."

The two of them left me standing alone, staring at the distant, dead soldier, facedown in the snow, then staring at the bodies all around me. So no one heard me say, "Goodness has nothing to do with us."

FIFTY-FIVE

IN THE LONG DUSK OF ARCTIC AUTUMN, our accidental army redistributed ammunition, cannibalized rifles and clothing from the guards' corpses, and moved out toward the garrison's barracks with Aud Planck on the lead, as always. Or, as his troops had said of Erwin Rommel, *an der Spitze.*

The flat buildings' smoking chimneys and yellow-lit windows, promising warmth and life, drew not only our minutes-old veterans, but the rest of the prisoners who could walk or crawl. A ragged human wave rolled toward the barracks, its only sound the creak of thousands of numb hands and feet against dry snow.

Aud's point group reached the gate that led outside the twelve-foot-tall barbed-wire fence, to the barracks complex fifty yards beyond, before a clang like iron against a hung iron triangle alarmed the garrison.

The gate, untended and unlocked, was swung aside as soldiers, pulling up suspenders and fumbling with rifles, tumbled out of barracks doors. The lucky ones were cut down by bullets poorly aimed but as numerous as hornets.

The second engagement of the Battle of the Northern

Terminus was no more a fair fight and no less a massacre than the first. In all, fourteen prisoners died of wounds sustained in the fighting, but mercy was an uncommon commodity among their peers. None of the five-hundred-man Interior Guard garrison survived.

An hour later, Jude, Celline, and I walked the plain in the darkness beyond the barracks. The oil tanks that fueled the sledge trains and the barracks stoves, set alight in the fighting, painted the snow flickering orange. We plowed the drifts with shuffling feet. My foot struck an object that gave way easily, and I grunted.

Jude said, "Another ration can?"

I bent, felt for my boot toe, then grasped the object and stood. "Gotcha!"

I turned the apple-sized meteorite in my hand, lit by the oil tanks' flame. The rock felt as light as cork. "Doesn't glow like a Stone Hills nugget. But it isn't supposed to."

Celline said, "I know the next step is vital. But these people are half dead."

I said, "Some of them will bounce back by the morning. We should have plenty of hands to harvest in a couple days."

Jude said, "We're ahead of schedule."

So far, the plan, horrible and bloody as it was, had exceeded even optimistic expectations.

We had neutralized the hostile force that had sat atop Tressel's weapons-grade Cavorite. We had moved a motivated workforce of nearly a thousand people above the Arctic Circle of Tressel by the only transport that existed to move them there. We had a week left before the Duck's deadline, during which we would gather the meteorites together, then call down pickup.

The call itself would be as easy as sending out for pizza on my wrist 'Puter.

Cruisers that had visited Tressel over the years had quietly left behind geosynchronous-orbiting surveillance and communications satellites. CommSats were, as Howard put it, surprisingly affordable if you didn't have to ground-launch them or opt for encryption. Since the Tressens had barely invented the telegraph, encryption for eavesdropping protection seemed a safe option to cheap out on.

We weren't allowed to ring up the Spooks from my 'Puter until we were ready to have the Cavorite picked up. But by the week from now when the Ferrents would first notice that the return train from the Northern Terminus was overdue, the Cavorite would be long gone.

Jude and Celline continued to scuff meteorites from the snow while I stared at a group that dragged stiff bodies to the tank farm fire to be cremated.

I could tell myself that the broad-nosed guard whom I had killed had himself brutally, unnecessarily, and without remorse killed an innocent man. I could tell myself that, if the man I had killed had in fact left behind a widow and children, the greater good produced by his death would save their lives and all mankind. I could tell myself that he, as a soldier, had accepted the risk.

But, finally, I would have to tell myself that I had arrogated to myself the right to take the life of another.

"Jason!"

I ran toward the sound of Aud's shout, Jude alongside me.

FIFTY-SIX

AUD PLANCK STOOD IN THE DOORWAY of a room in the camp commandant's quarters hut as I ran up. The windowless room wasn't more than an oversized closet, and its only furnishings were a simple table, a chair, and a sputtering oil lamp suspended from a ceiling beam.

A figure in Tressen colonel's uniform slumped in the chair, head down across the table. One hand clutched a service revolver that had been inserted in his mouth, and what had been the back of his head splattered the far wall of the tiny room.

Presiding over mass murder, in a frigid, forsaken outpost, would drive a normal human being near suicide, I supposed. Facing up to the reality that your sloppy command had gotten all your troops killed could drive a soldier the rest of the way. Or maybe he had been a fanatic, more afraid of having let down his RS bosses than of burning in hell.

Aud said, "I wondered why we hadn't found the camp commandant." Aud stepped to the table, slipped his pistol's barrel beneath the empty hand of the dead man, and lifted it. Beneath the hand was a wood slab with a pivoting brass arm six inches long fixed above it.

Jude stared first at the body, then at the brass and wood device, then swore.

Jude turned to Aud. "You think he transmitted anything?"

Aud shrugged. "He could have been transmitting for the last hour."

"Or not at all."

I raised my palm. "The Tressens haven't invented radio."

Jude pointed at the wood block, and at bright copper wires that curled away from it, then disappeared over the table's real edge. "Telegraph. It's so new that it's more a parlor trick than a practical system. At least that's what I thought."

"I looked out of that sledge for six days. I never saw one pole."

Jude shook his head. "Wood's rare here. Insulated cable would be buried in the roadbed."

I shrugged at Aud. "It could be nothing." I didn't believe myself, but there was also nothing we could do now.

An hour later I sat on the edge of a barracks bunk, cleaning Ord's pistol. My wrist 'Puter vibrated. I scrolled through functions. It wasn't an alarm. It was an incoming call.

I picked up.

"General Wander?" It was Bill the Spook. Howard's bargain satellites delivered terrific sound quality.

"Bill? I thought phone calls were off limits."

"Officially, they are."

"This contact is freelance? You could lose your pension."

"The dental's awful anyway." He paused. "That was a rough trip you took."

The Spooks may have been forbidden to help us, but that didn't mean their overhead eyes weren't watching us while they tracked the 'Puters that Aud, Jude, and I wore.

I shrugged, invisible to him. "I've had better."

"But it looks like your operation's off to a good start."

"Successful's a better word." I shifted on the bunk.

"You have company coming."

Hair stood on my neck.

"Some local eyes reported that Forty-fifth Infantry started scrambling onto a sledge train pointed north thirty minutes ago."

The Forty-fifth Tressen Infantry, the Quicksilver Division, took its name from the commander that had made it into Tressen's best outfit, prematurely silver-haired Audace Planck.

I swore.

Bill said, "I dunno what tipped them."

I did. The camp commandant had tapped out a warning that had also served as his suicide note. "Bill, there was a telegraph line running south from here."

Silence. A good Spook took a failure of combat intelligence personally.

"Sorry."

"So we got, what, six days?"

"They're loading on a streamliner, not a slow freight like you came on. And the Forty-fifth is garrisoned on the northern frontier to begin with. The only good news is it's a passenger train. They're leaving their artillery at home."

Why bother? Artillery to quell a mere prison riot?

"That's a small favor. You got an ETA?"

"The best eight thousand infantry on this planet are gonna land on your doorstep in forty-eight hours, ready to rumble."

"Can you bring the rain?"

"The Duck's been ragging the *Tehran*'s skipper for an hour. But the rules are set. No fire support. No nothing. No exceptions. It stinks, but you're all hung out to dry."

I stared at my 'Puter, numb. "Thanks for the heads-up, Bill. Tell the Duck thanks for trying. And tell Admiral Duffy thanks for nothing. See you around, Bill."

Silence. Then he said, "Sure."

FIFTY-SEVEN

IN THE NEXT MORNING'S SPARSE DAWN, Aud, Jude, Celline, and I stood together in the wind shadow cast by the train that had brought us, which had been reversed on a spur overnight, so that it pointed back toward the spiked black mountain range through which we had come, ten miles to the south. Smoke from the smoldering oil fire overhung the plain like dirty gauze in the pre-sunrise calm.

Around us by twos and threes, those of our companions who had been revived by a meal and a night in barracks bunks that their captors no longer needed already scoured the snows. They bent, gathered meteorites, then stuffed them into knapsacks and into the pockets of coats for which their captors also had no further need. Periodically, someone gasped as, beneath the snow, they touched the frozen corpse of an earlier and less fortunate arrival.

In the midst of the vast and unmarked graveyard, Aud knelt in the snow and pointed at his makeshift sand table map. A line of stones bisected the flat, swept area that represented the plains south and north of the mountains. A red string, laid south to north, represented the ice road line. The string snaked across the stone "mountain range" wedged into Aud's paper-narrow "mountain pass" like dental floss.

He pointed at the north end of the red string. "We're here. Without the refueling oil we planned on, this ice train can barely reach here." His finger slid along the string, then stopped above the "pass" that ran north to south through the mountains.

He swung his arm around the plain at the stone gatherers. "We need to buy time to finish this work. The mountains are impassable. If we overturn this ice train in the pass, we'll force Forty-fifth Division to dismount their train and advance toward the pass on foot. A small force using the sledges and engine as breastworks can hold the pass even against a division."

I asked Celline and Jude, "Assuming volunteers, how many can you spare from gathering and still meet the deadline?"

They looked at each other. Jude shrugged. "We planned on a thousand pickers. Could you manage with two hundred?"

"There were three hundred Spartans at Thermopylae," I said. But there were eighty thousand Persians on the other side.

Celline frowned. She knew Thermopylae like I knew how to stir trilobite bisque. But she said, "We'll manage with a hundred less, then."

I didn't tell her that the three hundred had been the finest troops in their world, maybe in any world, not starved, frostbitten shopkeepers. I also didn't tell her that the Spartans lost. Big.

There was another similarity to Thermopylae. I shaded

my eyes with my hand as I pointed at the eastern shoulder of the distant mountain pass. "The Spooks mapped this. There's a way around the canyon. A ledge a goat could walk, eight hundred feet above the canyon floor, along the east wall. It's a long way 'round, but once the Persians outflanked the Spartans the battle was lost. If the Quick-silver Division can move a battalion over that goat track, it can swing in behind the bottleneck in a day."

Aud shook his head. "I know the Forty-fifth. But I also know the commander who succeeded me. Folz is deliber-ate. Unimaginative. He'll pound away at the pass fron-tally for days before he resorts to maneuver. But you're right. Eventually . . ."

I pointed at the "shoulder" of the pass on Aud's sand table map. "They widened the main route through the can-yon with dynamite when they built the railroad. There's still one case left in the machine shop, even after the GIs played with it. It's not enough to close the main pass, but it might be enough to drop a narrow spot on that ledge, cut that path. Your old troops are good, Aud. But they can't fly."

Aud shook his head again. "We'll just have to take our chances. I can't spare a man. And none of these people can handle dynamite."

I said, "I can."

FIFTY-EIGHT

"ON THREE!" Aud and I, in line with twenty others, strained against a cable spooled through a block and tackle stripped from the camp machine shop, tied to an eyelet on an ice sledge. The sledge's runners squealed, then groaned as the great iron box crashed onto its side like a dying mammoth. The echoes died against the canyon's stone-cold walls, even as other cars toppled by others of the three hundred volunteer shopkeepers fell into place.

We were overturning sledges so that their iron floors became parapets that blocked the canyon bottleneck from vertical stone wall to vertical stone wall. Aud set the first line of our barricade six hundred yards up the canyon, near its crest, where the thousand-foot-high walls bottlenecked down to a twenty-yard width.

That way the front line of an entire division of attacking troops, even shoulder to shoulder, could never amount to much more than sixty soldiers. And those sixty would be advancing uphill, unprotected, for six hundred yards. Meanwhile, our guys, even if they weren't marksmen, would hunker behind cover and mow their attackers down, then mow down the ranks behind them, until we ran out of ammunition or the attackers ran out of enthusiasm.

There's a schoolyard simplicity to infantry tactics once you remove air power from the equation.

Boom.

The last sledge toppled across the canyon like a beached whale as Aud stepped alongside me, batting dust off his long coat with mittened hands. He craned his neck, up along the canyon's east wall, where the narrow ledge overlooked both us and the plain to the south from which the attack would come. He sighed. "There's no point in placing marksmen above. We have no marksmen but you."

"I'm taking a rifle and a hundred rounds up on the ledge with me."

Aud shook his head. "Your most vital job is to destroy the flanking route, not to play at target practice. Just set the charges, light the fuses, and run. Live to fight another day."

I looked around. Men stacked rocks on the parapets. Others cleaned weapons or unboxed cartridges. Each shopkeeper busied himself to avoid the reality that they would die in this canyon. "Nobody else seems to have an exit strategy."

I knelt, then swung up the pack with the dynamite. Aud grasped the pack's handle, centered the load on my back. "Jason, I know you. You intend to return from the pass, then rejoin us here. You return to the camp. If the stones aren't delivered, this sacrifice will count for nothing. Honor me, and these men, by making sure we all died for something. Promise me that." He laid a hand on my shoulder.

I laid my hand over his, stared up at the late afternoon sky. "I better go. The only thing I hate worse than heights is climbing them in the dark."

It might once have taken me a few hours to make my way back north along the canyon, then east to the steep, narrow route that switched back and forth toward the ledge that overlooked the canyon, then up the trail that climbed a fifth of a mile.

By the time I not only made it to the trailhead, then climbed to the ledge, my skinned knees and elbows trembled beneath my coat's sweaty bulk, and the cotton that had once been saliva crusted my lips, and it was midnight, according to the Tressen pocket watch I carried. The only Spooknet-capable 'Puter the Spooks would allow us I had left behind with Jude, so that he could call for pickup of the Cavorite in case I didn't make it back.

I lay on the ledge in the dark, too exhausted to fear the sheer drop that began inches from the blisters inside my boots.

I had no heated armor to keep my fingers and toes from going numb, no helmet water nipple, no padding when I slipped and fell, and no optics to keep the dark from blinding me. I huddled in a crevasse, snugged my clothes up to keep as warm as I could, and dozed.

I woke at four a.m.

The moonless Tressel night was frigid, black, and still.

Except for a faint glow on the southern horizon that shifted position back and forth. Like a train winding north.

FIFTY-NINE

WITHOUT NIGHT-VISION EQUIPMENT, I had to wait for dawn to begin my work. I was in no hurry. Among the things that had terrified me since childhood were heights and explosives.

My hands shook as I stuffed black-powder-cored fuse lengths into dynamite sticks. I had to take off my long coat and mittens to scramble down the rock face below the narrow ledge, wedge the old dynamite into cracks and joints in the granite, then pay out fuse to the place from which I would light it.

If I had done it right, a fifty-foot section of the ledge should shear away, so no infantry could either slip behind or get an angle to fire down on Aud's unlikely Spartans.

By the time I finished, I couldn't feel my fingertips.

I sat rubbing back the circulation while I stared toward the horizon, where the train's glow had shone in the early-morning darkness. I focused on the quivering image of a tiny black worm against a white sea. The troop train was perhaps an hour away. I shouted a warning down to the defenders.

If it were spring, or even winter, there might be enough

snow on the rock above the canyon for my shout to trigger an avalanche. That happens in the holos, not in real life.

I inched south along the ledge, cringing from the edge, until I found a notched boulder from behind which I had a clear field of vision and of fire over the train track and adjacent avenue of approach.

I had promised Aud—technically, I had avoided promising, but that was semantic crap—that I would return to camp, not to the canyon floor. I didn't promise him when.

I loaded the rifle, a bolt-action Tressen standard, with a telescopic sight that was little more than lenses fitted in a tube bolted above the receiver that was as long and slender as a walking stick. Then I laid out ammunition on the rock ledge in front of me.

The train showed clear now. It streamed oily smoke that scudded above the flat whiteness, and it slithered closer minute by minute.

Sound echoed up crystalline from the canyon floor. Rifle bolts snicked, a dropped cartridge case jingled over rock. Voices whispered and prayed.

From my vantage, I could see the train. But an observer on the train wouldn't be high enough to peer into the canyon's shadows and see the blocked path. Minutes crawled by before the troop train visibly slowed.

When the train finally stopped, I estimated the range to the engine, an iron hedgehog with its great spiked wheels, at two thousand yards. If our attackers had bothered to bring artillery, they could have stood off and simply shelled the canyon. Our first tactical victory had been won for us by our opponent's disdain.

A single patrol emerged from the first coach behind the engine's oil tender and advanced along both sides of the ice trail.

I sighted the rifle not on the patrol, which was well out of range, but on the trench that we had dug to block the ice road to the canyon. An army could fill a trench fast, but not so fast if the trench was covered with aimed fire. Four hundred clear-shot yards away from and below me, the enemy wouldn't be able to repair the trench as long as I kept sniping his repair crews. But our main purpose was not to kill repairmen but to prevent our enemy from using the train as an armored approach vehicle, or worse, as a battering ram.

We needn't have worried. The train was Forty-fifth Division's ride home. Their commander wasn't about to put it in harm's way. I swore to myself and wished for artillery, for a smart bomb, even for enough explosives to have improvised a train mine out there on the plain.

The patrol didn't come within my rifle range before it spotted the trench ahead of it, then turned and double-timed back to report.

Deliberate the Forty-fifth's commander proved to be, as Aud predicted. I smiled. Deliberate was fine by our side. If the Forty-fifth sat back and sized up the situation for a week, until Jude, Celline, and their pickers gathered all their meteorites, great.

Twenty minutes passed. Then the engine's spiked wheels flailed, gained traction on the ice, and the ice train crept forward eight hundred yards. The commander didn't know how well equipped we might be. He was willing to gamble that we had no artillery, but he stayed beyond the range of a Tressen mortar, just in case we had one.

A half hour passed, then a battalion fell out from the train into the snow, formed a skirmish line on both sides of the ice track, and advanced on line along the track's axis.

I focused the rifle sight on individual soldiers. Lean, grim, and purposeful, they and their gear outclassed our shopkeepers and the junk we had scrounged from the prison guards.

The skirmish line drew close enough that I could have plinked a GI. But at best that would have revealed my position and highlighted the flanking route if the attackers were unaware of it. And it would only have cut the odds against us down to 7,999 against 301.

Once the skirmish line closed to where it disappeared below my line of sight, I inched back along the trail until I could see down to the canyon floor.

The Tressen troops on point zigzagged or low-crawled as they made their way up the canyon. Aud's shopkeepers had removed every rock or snowdrift that offered so much as a shred of cover. They held fire.

When the nearest attacker had low-crawled within one hundred yards of Aud's iron parapets, the shootout started.

When the infantry advanced, they were cut down. When they retreated, they were cut down. When they lay as still as turtles, shopkeepers' bullets eventually found them.

The attackers finally scrambled and stumbled back down the canyon, leaving behind fifty-four motionless bodies.

I panned the scope's tiny view field across the caps, crooked helmets, and shoulders of the defenders but saw no evidence that any of them had suffered a scratch.

Screams of relief and disbelief echoed up to me from the mouths of the shopkeepers. A quarter mile below me, the men pumped their rifles up and down and slapped one another on the back.

I inched back on the ledge, sat with my back to the rock wall, and sighed to nobody, "Seven thousand nine hundred forty-six to go, fellas."

SIXTY

AUD PLANCK KNEW HIS ENEMY. Over the next four hours, the Tressen commander squeezed two more futile frontal assaults into the canyon meat grinder.

After each withdrawl, Aud sent a half-dozen shop-keepers forward to drag left-behind bodies back behind the parapet, rather than leave them on the killing ground. Nothing sentimental. The corpses would have provided the attackers cover in subsequent assaults.

One of the recovery team, a delicate, red-moustached sort, whose wife remained back at the camp, had, along with another man, dragged a body until they were within twenty yards of the boxcar parapet when the red-moustached man spun like a dervish, then collapsed, bleeding from the throat.

The crack of the sniper's bullet snapped down the canyon in the same instant. The red-moustached man was the first casualty among the three hundred. The remaining two hundred ninety-nine kept their heads down after that.

After dark, which came early in the canyon's shadows, the attackers tried to work scouts and sappers up the canyon. One scout made it to the parapet, slit the throat of a man dozing on guard, then was shot.

Darkness blinded the Tressen snipers, too. Aud sifted men forward, dragging tins of the remaining oil from the overturned locomotive's tender. Aud's men set fires down the canyon to deprive the infiltrators of the cover of darkness. Cinders that cracked from the fires lit the dead's uniforms, and the smoke and stench of burned cloth and flesh roiled up the canyon walls like a crematory's chimney.

I haven't seen hell. Yet. But I'll bet my agnostic's pass to heaven that a battlefield at night comes close.

Dawn brought light but not heat. I had slept in the crevasse bent, and it took minutes before I could straighten my original-equipment arm. The prosthetic, which was actually younger tissue, woke sooner and more supple. I crawled back to the notched boulder overlooking the plain to the south, dragging my rifle, then peeked below. "Crap."

Eight hundred yards from me, on both sides of the track, clustered six groups of three soldiers each. A disc of snow twenty feet wide had been tramped down around each group.

I raised my rifle and squinted through the scope. Each group of three men busied itself around a black metal tripod. Each tripod's rearward leg tilted toward the canyon and was as thick as a stovepipe. The Tressens had left their artillery at home, but mortars broke down into loads a couple of crew members could backpack.

As I watched, the leftmost crew scurried around their tube, then all three ducked away as the mortar platoon lobbed its first shot toward the canyon.

If you ever want a demonstration that whatever goes up

must come down, watch a mortar. The trajectory is steeper than a roller coaster, both up and down. Smooth-bore mortar rounds travel slower than bullets, even at the moment they exit skyward from the mortar tube. If you look closely, you can follow the round as it ascends, finned like a backyard science-project rocket, and scarcely bigger.

Thok.

The round dropped toward me, and I curled into a fetal position behind the rocks. "Crap, crap, crap!"

Blam.

The round impacted fifty yards above me, on the canyon's opposite wall, and exploded shrapnel and shattered granite chips that clattered down onto the shopkeepers eight hundred feet below. I cocked my head, nodded. Not a bad-ranging round. From the gunners' standpoint.

Once all the tubes were similarly laid, the rain would become unbearable for Aud's troops.

I crawled back into the boulder's notch and peered through my rifle's scope. The mortar crew members' tight-wrapped scarves scarcely rippled. There was little wind to correct for, here or near the target. The scope on my rifle would never be mistaken for even the last-generation optics in an Eternad armor helmet, but it was good enough.

There had been no time to zero the rifle, and my first round puffed snow, unnoticed and yards wide of my target. When the sound reached the mortar crews, some flinched, but they kept beavering away, heads down, around their tubes.

Mortars have been the same for centuries and across light-years, one of those unbroke things that nobody screwed up by fixing. A Tressen mortar is little more than a steel pipe on legs, open at the top, with a sharp vertical pin at its closed bottom. A finned artillery shell, with a percussion-fired explosive cap in its tail and an explosive charge in its nose, is dropped down the mortar bore. Cap strikes pin, driven down by the shell's weight. Boom. Round out. Do it again.

My second shot struck a mortar crewman in his torso as he hung a round above the tube. The round didn't drop cleanly and hung inside the tube. A hung round puckers mortar men anywhere, and Tressen explosives were, as mentioned, unstable.

One of the unwounded crewmen knelt, laid the tube on its side, then tilted the tube mouth toward the snow, to coax the live round out. My third shot struck him between the shoulder blades, and the round detonated. Not only was the first mortar destroyed, it looked like crewmen in adjacent crews took shrapnel, also.

I kept firing, as fast as I could mark targets and work the rifle's bolt. Consternation ensued below, followed by a rapid retreat out beyond rifle range, dragging wounded and mortar tubes.

It was past noon before the mortars resumed, from out on the north forty, where I couldn't get at them. Of course, they couldn't so easily get at us, either. Trying to hit a target with a mortar is like trying to pitch a penny so it drops down a stovepipe. The farther you stand back, the flatter your trajectory, and the harder to drop the penny in without rattling it off the inside of the stovepipe.

Therefore, the Forty-fifth Division cooled its heels—above the Tressen Arctic Circle, not a figure of speech—for the rest of the available daylight while its mortar men tried to pitch pennies down a distant stovepipe. The closest round penetrated to four hundred feet above the canyon floor before it detonated against the rock wall. Shrapnel and cobbles showered harmlessly down on the shopkeepers. Otherwise, the mortar crews merely rearranged the mountain scenery with explosives and kept their off-duty comrades awake.

At dusk, I slipped back down to the ledge and glanced over the side. Far below, the shopkeepers had gone to school on the mortar attack and had improved their overhead cover, roofing over their little fortress with boulder-reinforced boxcar doors.

But eventually, pennies would drop to the bottom of the stovepipe, and the boxcar doors wouldn't be umbrella enough.

In the second half of the twenty-first century, Earthlings beat one another's brains out largely at night. But without night-vision technology, wireless communication, and remote sensors, war keeps bankers' hours.

The night raced past in silence. The most likely reason for that was that Forty-fifth Division's commander intended to rest his troops, in order to make full use of the upcoming daylight hours.

SIXTY-ONE

THOK. THOK. THOK. THOK. THOK.

I opened my eyes staring into dawn-lit frozen granite, in the crevasse that had become my home. The mortar men were up early.

Blam. Blam. Blam. Blam. Blam.

Early, but still inaccurate. Evidently, the Forty-fifth's commander had a trainload of mortar ammunition that he didn't care to haul home as "deteriorating stores." I shrugged. He wouldn't be the first commander who failed to win a battle because he stood off and shelled an enemy to avoid the unpleasantness of digging them out of their holes. Of course, the Forty-fifth's commander didn't know that in his case failing to win—and win quickly—was to lose.

I crept back to my vantage at the notched boulder and swore. The Forty-fifth's commander had awakened on a more aggressive side of his Pullman berth.

Across the twilit snow a scout company, their torsos cross-slung with ropes, jogged not toward the canyon mouth but toward, well, me.

Through my scope, their faces looked grumpy and

purposeful. In the pantheon of military nobility, snipers like I had become occupy an unfavored niche. Also, I suspected, the slaughter of the last couple days had persuaded Forty-fifth's commander to seek a way around the canyon. Which the scouts would soon locate and secure if I didn't do something about it.

I set to work with my rifle and left too many scouts facedown in the snow.

The survivors, also too many, finally disappeared beneath me, under the mountain's curve, invisible and no longer shootable by me.

I shook my head and shrugged into my pack. "Checkout time."

It was no longer a question of whether my position would become indefensible, but when. I had no way of estimating how long it would take the scouts to scale their side of the mountain, and I dared not cut my primary responsibility, to deny the enemy the flanking ledge behind me, too fine.

Meanwhile, out on the plain, troops formed up in black phalanxes against the snow. There had to be four thousand troops out there. I swallowed. The theory was that an inferior force could hold perfect terrain indefinitely. "Indefinitely" was about to become a precise term.

My panting smothered by the incessant, percussive rain of mortar rounds, I crabbed back across the narrowest fifty feet of the ledge, above the explosives-packed string of joints and crevasses that crisscrossed below the ledge.

From there, I could see down into the canyon, where lead elements of the Forty-fifth and the defenders had already engaged, rifle crackle intertwining with the constant crump of the mortars. I still had fifty rounds for the rifle, and I put forty to good use.

After an hour, a mortar round whistled clean between the canyon walls and burst in the center of the defender's position. I counted thirty motionless bodies and heard more wounded than I could count. One silent, bleeding figure who remained defiant on the parapet was Aud Planck.

The attack wave crested, then receded. But the defense was wearing ever more rapidly. If it were outflanked, or grenaded from above, the end would come too soon.

I tugged out a box of wooden kitchen matches and crept to the bunched fuses. I had test-burned some back at the camp and figured these would burn through in ninety seconds.

Two hundred yards away, down the ledge, the first scout's helmet peeked above the ledge.

I struck my match, but it broke in my numbed fingers. I grabbed for it and spilled the rest of the box, the tiny sticks floating down the eight hundred feet to the canyon floor like dandelion seed.

Spang. A scout's bullet exploded granite six feet above my head, then sang away into the distance.

I peered into the matchbox. One left.

My unpracticed fingers shook as I struck the match once, twice without result. I cursed my smoke-free lifestyle, then tried again. The match burst into yellow flame, and I cupped it with my other hand around it, then lit the fuses.

They spat and crackled as they burned toward the dynamite.

Another scout bullet struck the ledge, in front of me.

I spent a remaining round to keep the scouts' heads down while I begged the fuses to burn faster.

The count in my head reached ninety seconds.

Nothing.

I counted ten seconds more, then peeked out to see whether the fuses were burning.

Spang.

I earned a near-miss and a stone chip through my cheek for my curiosity.

Boom!

Boom! Boom! Booomm!

The explosions lifted me off the ledge, then belly-flopped me on the stone.

Granite flew.

Acrid smoke billowed.

The noise level returned to the background sizzle of small arms and the drum of mortars.

As I got to my feet, head lowered, and turned to pick my way north away from the battle, I muttered, "You cut that too close."

I glanced back.

The smoke cleared. Jagged gaps had been torn in the granite.

But the ledge was still there.

SIXTY-TWO

"CRAP! CRAP, CRAP, CRAP."

I swayed there on the ledge. I had no more dynamite, five more bullets, and no plan. The rational thing to do was escape before the scouts noticed. And leave Aud Planck's shopkeepers hung out to dry.

I ran to the narrow ledge span, smoke still curling from its crevasses, up between my boots. I jumped up and down on the ledge but it remained as immovable as, well, granite.

"Goddamit!" I reversed my rifle in my hands and jammed the stock into a smoking crevasse, as if I could pry the mountain apart.

A bullet struck between my feet, and I looked up. A scout charged toward me along the ledge, screaming and firing. The sniper's scope on my rifle probably earned me no love. Behind him four more scouts single-filed toward me.

I had wedged my rifle immovably in the crevasse, but I still had Ord's pistol, albeit bundled beneath layers of clothing. I needed to buy time.

I released the rifle and raised my hands.

The scout slowed and shuffled toward me, rifle trained
on me from the hip.

He stopped fifteen feet away, panting steam. He didn't
look like a Nazi. He looked like a thousand other soldiers
I had known, a kid who needed nothing in this world but
a shave and a three-day pass.

It would never work, and this kid didn't deserve it, but
I was out of options. I lowered one hand slowly toward
my jacket lapel, toward the pistol, while I sighed and cast
my eyes to the sky. I said, "Crap," as my plan became
irrelevant.

SIXTY-THREE

THE DESCENDING MORTAR ROUND plummeted across my vision in less than a blink, silhouetted against the cloudless blue sky, then scraped the edge of the ledge behind the kid, and alongside one of the other four scouts, so hard that its steel sparked orange against the granite. Out of sight below the ledge, the round burst.

For a moment, nothing happened. Then the kid's eyes widened as they met mine. The ledge beneath him and the other four scouts sank like an elevator's floor.

He dropped his rifle and stretched out his hand.

I reached for it, but he was gone, tumbling and flailing, staring up at the sky, along with the other four scouts and, all around them, the spinning shards and blocks of granite that had been the ledge, eight hundred feet to the canyon floor below.

The rock beneath my feet sloughed away, too, and I fell on my back, scrabbling and grasping. Finally, I lay staring up past the canyon rim, sucking air and shaking.

When my heart slowed a fraction, I rolled onto hands and knees and peered over the edge of the ledge that was now severed by the impassable gap completed by the mortar round's explosion.

Below, Aud's former soldiers and his new ones struggled hand-to-hand atop the overturned sledges. He strode, chest out, dragging one bandaged leg behind him, along the makeshift battlement while shells burst around him, until he reached an object that protruded from beneath a new-fallen boulder.

Aud Planck tugged my splintered sniper's rifle from beneath the boulder, then turned and looked up, shading his eyes with one hand. He pointed the rifle north, in the direction I was supposed to go, then saluted with his other hand.

I leaned out above the battle, returned his salute, then turned and started down the ledge.

We stared at each other through the smoke, then we both turned away from one another for what we both knew would be the last time.

I reached the junction where the down trail's northern end joined the plain at sunset. From the canyon, the rumble of battle continued, without me. Unflanked, what remained of the unlikely three hundred fought on. I couldn't save the shopkeepers who remained alive. But maybe I could help to make their sacrifice count for something.

Blood trickled from one ear, an eardrum burst by the mortar round's concussion, and from my cheek. A granite splinter had torn through my sleeve and lodged in my birth-equipment forearm. I hadn't eaten in four days, nor drunk anything but melted snow. What wasn't bruised, ached. I began walking north into the frigid darkness, on feet I could no longer feel, then shifted gears to an airborne shuffle trot that would get me back to the camp by sunup.

As I shuffled, I snorted to myself, "Some retirement."

In fact, at four a.m. I arrived at the southern wire that demarcated the camp. It had been visible for miles across the plain, as oil lanterns carried by meteorite pickers crisscrossed the snow like fireflies.

A shopkeeper sentry saved my life by firing at me high and wide while intending anything but.

It took until five a.m. before I reached Jude and Celline, who pored over a camp map penciled with a search grid.

I reported the battle results like Pheidippides returning from the plain of Marathon, then asked, "How close are you?"

Celline ran her fingers down a tally sheet as she handed me back my 'Puter. "Close enough. Call your vessel down now. We need every second."

I nodded. Before the Forty-fifth Infantry and the burned-out oil supply had entered the picture, our plan had been to deliver the Cavorite, then return the survivors on the commandeered ice train as far south as possible, then abandon it. The newly numerous Iridian resistance would melt into the population and become, like Mao's guerillas, fish in the sea.

Jude unrolled another of the camp commandant's maps. Now, with no transportation, and the pass south blocked by an advancing army, the survivors' only hope was to outrun the Forty-fifth Infantry, east across the Arctic, until they reached the eastern end of the mountains, where they could turn south and make for the more hospitable climate of the north Iridian coast.

An emaciated army of cellists and fishmongers and shopkeepers' widows would flee battle-hardened troops, across four hundred miles of frigid wilderness.

Jude shook his head. "I won't tell these people, but the journey would be barely survivable even if we didn't have an army chasing us."

Celline said, "But if we stand and fight, we die. And hope dies with us."

I pointed at my 'Puter in Jude's hand. "You do it. Call down the ship. My fingers can't work the buttons anymore."

Then I tugged off my boots and sat on the edge of a camp cot, kneading my toes with my fingers and feeling neither. "I think I'm gonna lie down here for a minute."

The next thing I knew, Jude stood shaking my shoulder. "Jason! The ship's here!"

SIXTY-FOUR

THE HUMPBACKED SCORPION drifted down toward Tressel's snow, a white ceramic teardrop against the steel-blue afternoon sky. Its pilot throttled back to subsonic to remain silent but jinked at right angles and sprinkled heat-seeker-fooling flares, though "hot" was the last adjective that described this landing zone.

The hundreds of survivors healthy enough to gather stones that were spread across the vast white graveyard plain drew toward the alien ship like iron filings to a magnet. Most had seen newspaper drawings or grainy tintype photographs of the motherworld's flying machines, but the reality must have shocked them like a flying saucer, which, essentially, the Scorpion might have been.

The Scorpion dead-stopped and hovered three feet above the snow. The Scorpion's hull, scorched by its passage through Tressel's upper atmosphere, boiled off snow in a hissing steam cloud that rose into the scalded air shimmering above the ship.

The Tressens formed a silent, spectating ring around the Scorpion as a rear ramp whined down from the modified Scorpion's bulbous tail, lifting the former fighter's weapons pod like a stinger.

The forward canopy rose as the cargo ramp dropped, and the pilot extended the ship's ladder above and across the hull, then clambered across and down. He splashed through the slush his ship had melted, straight-backed, chest out, comm and life support leads swinging in the breeze in time with the silk scarf that dangled around his neck.

Jude, Celline, and I stepped forward out of the circle, and he stopped three feet in front of us. A "Whizard" call sign stencil painted his pilot's helmet, and a multicolored, embroidered patch of a scowling pelican wearing boxing gloves crested the chest of his unzipped brown leather bomber jacket. He saluted and grinned. "Package pickup service!"

It was only as I watched the grin melt into his smooth-shaven cheeks that I realized how gaunt, filthy, and emaciated we all were. Jude's and Celline's eyes peered from pits sunken in faces grayed by oil smoke and stretched by starvation. Their faces were scarved with rags, and their swollen coats were torn everywhere they weren't soiled. We no longer noticed how we stank.

The kid's eyes flicked around the silent hundreds who stared at him, who looked worse than we did. The face of war was softer when your enemy was a dot on a screen and physical hardship was wardroom coffee gone cold.

I returned the young pilot's salute by careerlong reflex. "Glad to see you. Jason Wander."

His jaw dropped. "General?"

"Retired."

His eyes widened as he looked around again at the silent Tressens. "Sir—Mr. Wander—I just got the one ship. My orders are to pick up cargo. Quick and quiet. I can't—"

"I know. They know. We're walking out."

He turned his ear toward me as though he hadn't heard. "Sir?"

I pointed at the ramp of his ship, where Tressens were already lining up, holding bulging sacks and bins piled high with stones. "Could you make sure they load your bay the way you want? We need to be out of here quick and quiet, too."

He trotted to the ramp.

I turned to Jude and jerked a thumb at the Scorpion. "The second seat on that ship's empty. You're the best pilot we've got. Your place is in a cockpit. Finish this thing. For your family."

Jude put one arm around Celline and swept the other around at the queued and gritty little army. "This is my family." He nodded toward the leather-jacketed pilot. "Jason, I could never be that guy again. There are plenty like him who can deliver Silver Bullet. The Slug War is your generation's—it's your war to finish. My war starts here. Now."

Ord's last words echoed in my head. I was on my own now.

I jerked my head south, toward the canyon where Aud Planck and three hundred shopkeepers had held back an infantry division. "The lookouts say the Forty-fifth is through the pass, route marching north, already. No head start will be enough."

The Scorpion's cargo ramp whined as it clamshelled

shut. The pilot walked to the three of us, peeling off his flight jacket. Beneath it he wore a Zoomie sidearm in a shoulder holster. "We're loaded. General—Mr. Wander— Admiral Duffy said I'm to bring you back with me."

I said, "Why?"

He shrugged. "Just in case, he said."

"In case of what?"

"Can't say, just now."

I shook my head. "Then fuck off."

"The admiral said you'd say that. Sir, the skipper gave me a direct order to get you into that cockpit. At gunpoint if necessary." The kid didn't smile.

Jude said, "Go, Jason. You know this war can still be screwed up. You might not be able to prevent that up there. But you sure can't prevent that from down here."

Celline touched my sleeve. "Iridians say that a thousand miles' journey begins with one step. But if we falter, we need to know that we took that step for a purpose. You go, and be sure that these stones win your war. And tell the story of how we tried to win this one."

The pilot held out his jacket to Celline. "I got another one just like it upstairs, ma'am. Looks like somebody down here can use this."

The duchess took the jacket in a mittened hand and smiled. "A loan. Return for it in a few years, when we've won."

I hugged Jude, then Celline, then I stood still and looked at them.

The pilot shivered in his coverall, then turned to me. "General Wander, my ship's a sitting duck on the ground like this. And we've still got work to do."

SIXTY-FIVE

THE SCORPION'S CANOPY whined down and sealed me in alongside the pilot. The cockpit looked familiar, exactly like the modified ship in which Jude had given me my flying lesson back on Bren, before so much had changed.

The pilot scanned instruments, adjusted controls, and punched touch panels rowed across the canopy top like a concert pianist playing upside down.

The screens lit, the canopy seemed to disappear, and we drifted into the sky.

As we rose, the pilot pivoted the Scorpion, so we gazed out across the Arctic wilderness, toward the black mountain wall that stretched for three hundred miles to the east, around which Celline and Jude would have to lead the malnourished army huddled below us. He whistled. "Quite a walk. But I wouldn't bet against that lady."

"The walk's not the problem. The company is. There's a Tressen infantry division ten miles behind them and gaining."

When the altimeter read fifteen thousand feet, the pilot flipped back the hinged, red-striped shroud that covered the weapons console as he drifted the Scorpion south along the railroad.

I pointed at the console. "You can't fight this ship."

He nodded. "Correct, sir. Engagement within the airspace of Tressel's strictly forbidden. We weren't even permitted to load defensive armament for this pickup."

"Then what . . . ?"

"Admiral Duffy determined that the *Tehran* was carrying deteriorating stores."

"Huh?"

"We can always jettison deteriorating stores that endanger the ship into nonorbital space or into deserted country." He pointed below us. "Sir, could you have a look to assure that area below us is just deserted country?"

Below, a column of black specks stretched a hundred yards wide for a mile on either side of the railroad, as Forty-fifth Division gave chase to my godson, Celline, and their tiny band of innocents.

My jaw hung slack. "Eddie'll get relieved without pension for this."

"The admiral said that, too, sir, to me and the four red jackets that volunteered to load the pod. He said to tell you the dental plan's lousy, anyway."

"Son, this is no joke." However, as I said it I mentally retracted every curse I had placed on the head of Eddie Duffy.

"The admiral's log will say deteriorating stores were jettisoned above the Arctic Circle of Tressel. Only me, the admiral, and the four red jackets can say different."

"And me. Why am I here?"

"The admiral wanted somebody spotting who knows

where the friendlies are, where the bad guys are, and the target characteristics."

I jerked my thumb over my shoulder, toward the stinger pod. "What are you packing?"

"Radar-guided Area Denial Explosive. Basically bundled cluster bombs that arrange themselves as they fall. The radar identifies moving targets and shifts the cluster units for maximum efficiency."

I pointed below as we hovered unheard and unseen high above Forty-fifth Division's quick-marching GIs. "There are no friendlies down there."

He nodded as he laid his hand on a selector dial. "They got any hard-shell vehicles or body armor? RADE burst fragments behave like razor blades."

I shook my head. "Dismounted light infantry. Cloth coats, steel helmets."

"Then they're toast."

They weren't toast. They were human beings, as cocky, imperfect, and mortal as he was.

The targeting screen winked on, the pilot tipped the Scorpion up, and the fuselage shuddered as the cluster bombs released and began their tumble, three miles above the unsuspecting marchers.

Onscreen, a wavering green rectangle materialized as the munition sized up its target. Then dozens of red lights swarmed like gnats within the rectangle as cluster-bomb units rearranged themselves in free fall, so their bursting bomblets would perforate every square foot of the target.

I peered down at the undulating smudge on the snow that was thousands of infantrymen shuffling north while cursing their blisters.

Ting.

The only sound we heard, as the munition detonated three miles under us, was a chime from the Scorpion's targeting 'Puter.

A silent, rectangular snow cloud snapped into sight below. Prevailing wind at the point of impact, which the targeting 'Puter read at sixteen miles per hour, blew away the snow. The smudge that remained on both sides of the railroad track didn't undulate anymore. Among the bodies, at most a few dozen moved. They would freeze solid by the next morning.

On a perpetually snow-covered graveyard isolated at the top of this world, the bodies would soon be snow-covered thousands among already-dead thousands. The magnitude of the carnage, perhaps even the fact of it, much less its cause, wouldn't be apparent for years.

I turned my eyes north and let them rest on the tiny line of rebels that snaked its way east.

The pilot pointed below, as the targeting 'Puter retracted. "Stick a fork in 'em. They're done."

I suppose I should have congratulated him.

Then the Scorpion shot upward toward the *Tehran*.

SIXTY-SIX

———

By the time the *Tehran* came in sight of Mouse-trap, so many cruisers, Scorpions, transports, and tenders drifted dispersed in space around the moonlet that Mouse-trap seemed enveloped in light fog, the way Bren's Red Moon had looked when the Slugs cordoned it off.

Howard had returned with me on the *Tehran,* to shep-herd the stones, and we split up when we off-shipped. The first thing I did when I off-shipped was check the port registry. The *Emerald River* was here, but her skipper was listed as a name I didn't know. Mimi's name appeared nowhere among the personnel of the vast fleet. Whatever had become of Mimi's request for transfer back to a ves-sel command, it hadn't landed her at Mousetrap. My next stop was Off-Station Communications, otherwise known as the post office. I had checked Jeeb's doghouse there and reclaimed it.

The clerk scrolled his screens. "Nothing, sir. Not under 'General' or 'Mr.' If you've got outgoing, I can take it in, but Mousetrap's been on lockdown since the push started last month. Nothing in or out."

I toted Jeeb's container with me to the Spook Pent-

house on level forty-eight, to see Howard Hibble. The MP
at the tube was the same one who had been on duty my
last visit. He blocked my path.

"What's up, Corporal?"

"Restricted area, sir."

"I'm cleared."

He shrugged, hand on his holstered sidearm. "Not in
my 'Puter. Sir."

Howard eventually came out and vouched for me,
which shouldn't have worked, but did. Even a retired general has a certain avoirdupois.

We sat in Howard's office.

I scowled at him. "From the armada around this place,
I gather the final push is cranking up. You could have
told me."

"You don't have a clearance since this retirement
business."

I rolled my eyes. "That was just a paper game to shock
the Duck. I'm going up to AOPD and unretire as soon as
we're done here. When do we jump off?"

Howard crossed his arms.

"Howard. This is me."

He sighed. "Weaponization of the stones we brought
back should take a month. The *Tehran* will refit in the
meantime. The rest of the fleet's been on alert for two
months."

I nodded. "Good. I can use the rest."

Howard shrugged.

I pointed at the deck beneath us, beyond which, out in
the space of the Mousetrap, the great human fleet drifted.
"Howard, when that fleet leaves, I leave with it. I *will* see
the end of this war."

My next stop was on level twenty-nine, where the adjutant general's office operated a branch of the Army Officer Personnel Directorate. The branch consisted of a compartment the size of a gang shower, occupied by one overweight, overworked, pug-nosed second lieutenant who was sufficiently junior that she was saddled with all administrative matters for the post.

I sat in front of her desk, leaning forward in my chair.

She ran her finger across a line on a flatscreen, then nodded. "Yes, Mr. Wander. Your paperwork came through from the Human Union Consulate on Tressel and was processed. Your initial pension check was direct deposited on the first, just before we locked down."

"It's *General* Wander. I want to unretire. It was a mistake."

"It's not that easy."

"What I mean is I just needed some time off to attend to something I couldn't accomplish as an army officer."

She shook her head. "That's not what your file says."

I squirmed. "I know what I intended."

"If you intended to abandon your post in the field during wartime, you intended to desert. Says here the judge advocate general's office declined to prosecute only because Consul Muscovy included his sworn affidavit with your papers. The consul swore that he forced you to retire to avoid an interplanetary incident detrimental to diplomatic relations with the government of Tressen. You're lucky you kept your pension."

"What do I have to do to unretire?"

She cocked her head. "You're too old to enlist again." Then she brightened. "File a two-oh-two stroke seven. You might be reinstated at a reduced rank."

I exhaled and closed my eyes. "Yes! Print me one."

She shrugged again. "Sure. But it's gotta be approved in Washington. And we're on indefinite lockdown, so it can't be transmitted off Mousetrap."

I leaned forward with my elbows on the desk. "What am I in the meantime?"

She sighed, and swiveled her chair to face a different screen. "A ward of the Veterans Administration, Mr. Wander."

I stood, planted my fists on her desk, and leaned forward. "I've been in this war from the beginning. I'm going to be in it at the end. Even as a spectator. Can you get me on a ship? Any ship. As a dishwasher or something?"

"Ships are classified areas. You aren't cleared to enter a classified area. You can't get cleared because—"

I exhaled so my lips flapped and made a motorboat noise. "Clearances have to be approved through Washington, but we're on indefinite lockdown."

She smiled. "I knew you'd understand. But as a retiree lawfully on a military post, you can access all unclassified areas."

"Being?"

She rolled her eyes to the compartment ceiling and ticked off on her fingers. "This office. The post office. Bachelor Officers' Quarters—you're entitled to lodging there on a space-available basis. You have Officers' Mess privileges. You can make purchases at the post exchange, including the package store if you're of age."

"What can I do besides sleep, eat, shop, and buy booze?"

"There's the Mousetrap Library."

"Is it any good?"

"It will be when I get time to start it." She shrugged for the last time as she snatched a paper file off a stack. "Oh. And you can use the Officers' Club."

I smiled. "Perfect!"

SIXTY-SEVEN

———

TWO HOURS AFTER I LEFT AOPD, I stepped through the hatch into Mousetrap's consolidated Officers' Club, with a brown paper bag under one arm. Mousetrap's O Club served all branches of the Human Union Forces, which looked suspiciously like the U.S. Army and the U.S. Space Force, with a sprinkling of Brits of all stripes, Euros, Asians, Afros, and Outworlders.

The O Club's decor was early Neon Beer Sign, with a pool table and bowls of plausibly nonhydroponic cocktail peanuts on the tables, and the place was half-full of the swabbies who had flooded Mousetrap like a tsunami.

My quarry, alone at a table with a neat whiskey and a paperbook history of the Boston Red Sox, looked up and smiled. "Jason!"

He waved me over, and I sat.

He pointed at the bag I held. "Whazzat?"

"A congratulations present on the occasion of your new command, Eddie. And I owe you for Tressel."

"Nothing happened on Tressel."

"Of course not." If there was a rule bender to be found on Mousetrap, it was Eddie Duffy.

Eddie's cheeks glowed redder than usual. "The *Abraham Lincoln*'s a great ship. But I'll miss the *Tehran*." Then he frowned. "Not as much as I suppose you miss things. I heard about the retirement."

I shrugged. "I miss not getting a ticket to the finale. I've earned my seat. I don't miss the responsibility. I just want to see it, not be it."

"After what you've been through, I don't blame you. If there was anything I could do . . ." He reached across the table, tugged at my brown paper bag, then raised his eyebrows and smiled. "Hewitt's! How did you know?"

"We killed the last bottle I bought you six years ago."

He narrowed his eyes. "You needed a favor then."

I stiffened and widened my eyes. "Surely you don't think I—"

"As long as it's a small one."

I held my hand up between us, with the thumb and forefinger so close together that a cocktail peanut wouldn't fit between them. "Tiny."

SIXTY-EIGHT

___

SIX WEEKS LATER, Eddie and I were still together, chasing a six-legged mechanical cockroach through intragalactic space, or at least through that part of space that hurtled along just forward of the *Abraham Lincoln*'s Bulkhead One Twenty.

Whenever we had shipped together in the past, as admiral and embarked-division commander, Eddie Duffy and I jogged together every day. On this voyage, as admiral and his stowaway, we continued the routine because Eddie was my shipboard protector, because we were friends, and because we were the only people on this ship who either of us could keep up with.

"Gimmee a minute." Eddie raised his palm, panting in silence broken only by the metallic skitter of Jeeb's six legs against the deck plates.

The *Abraham Lincoln* was deserted from forward of Bulkhead One Twenty on forward to Bulkhead Ninety. Normally, Bulkhead Ninety back to Bulkhead One Twenty was overcrowded with the infantry division that a cruiser packed, in addition to the cruiser's Space Force crew of twenty-two hundred.

But the people back on Earth like my former boss General Pinchon had invited no infantry to the party that would, they were sure, win the Pseudocephalopod War.

Just aft of Bulkhead One Twenty the launch bays made a belt around the ship.

As a stowaway, albeit one vouched for by the skipper if anyone asked, I stayed between Bulkhead Ninety and Bulkhead One Twenty, except for meals. I puttered with equipment leftovers in the infantry armory, wrote letters to Mimi and to Jude, which weren't going to be delivered for a long while, and played with Jeeb by the hour.

Unlike Mousetrap, the *Abraham Lincoln* had an excellent library. Eddie had routed me through his own 'Puter via the ship's net, so I could read from my stateroom and, for that matter, see what he and the ship were up to, without showing myself forward of Ninety.

Each launch bay had a drinking fountain, and we stepped through the hatch into Bay One. So early in this mission, most of the flight deck's thirty-six bays were as deserted as the infantry billets. Months from now, as we neared the Pseudocephalopod homeworld jump, the flight deck would bustle. But today, flight deck personnel tended the three Early Bird Scorpion interceptors, which every cruiser kept on alert 24-7, on the other side of the ship, and the very special Scorpion in Bay One.

While Eddie rehydrated like a beached hippo, I stared at the Scorpion locked on to Bay One's launch rails. Its canopy was raised, and a bay crew member helped one alert pilot out after his watch so another could strap in.

I stood, puffing, hands on hips. "On that oversized watermelon seed ride the hopes of mankind, Eddie."

Dripping sweat and bent forward hands on knees, he shook his head. "Not all of them."

The Silver Bullet munition that Howard's Spooks had fabricated essentially worked like a bundle of last-century MIRV warheads, the biggest cluster bomb in history. Bigger bombs split into smaller bombs and so on down to spherules smaller than sand grains. The grains would rain down evenly spaced Cavorite over an entire planet, in a pattern so uniform that it would kill a maggot that had the mass of the Eurasian Crustal Plate. That's how big Howard's Spooks had calculated that the Pseudocephalopod was, give or take Scandinavia.

The Scorpion was kept on alert even now, months away from the fleet's objective, not so that it could attack or defend anything. The cruisers and clouds of Scorpions screening us took care of that. The Scorpion was on alert in case mechanical failure, mutiny, appearance of marauding gypsies, or anything else threatened the Scorpion's mothership. If anything like that happened, the Scorpion could move to another cruiser. The Space Force and the Spooks had thought of everything.

The Spooks had even made two Silver Bullets, just in case. Half of the Tressel Cavorite we had worked so hard to get made this bomb. The other half was in a bomb in a Scorpion aboard the *George Washington*, with Howard babysitting.

I had picked up lots by eavesdropping on Eddie's 'Puter. Still, I scratched my head. Stowaways don't get briefed. "Eddie, the *Abraham Lincoln* and the *George Washington* are old designs. Why are the old warhorses carrying the heavy freight?"

He stood, rapped against a hull girder, and the sound

of his knuckles echoed in the vast bay. "The newer cruisers can't take a punch like these old girls. The rest of the fleet's here strictly to keep the maggots off us, so we can deliver the two Scorpions to the last jump."

The human race had put all its eggs into two sturdy baskets, then told the mightiest fleet in human history to watch those baskets. I didn't have a better idea, and if I did, nobody cared what a retired general thought. "Eddie, you really think we're gonna have to fight our way in to the last jump?"

He shrugged. "We planned for a fight. But we hope to be pleasantly surprised."

We stepped back through the hatch and resumed our daily torture. I grimaced not so much from the exercise as from my concern that the maggots' surprises were seldom pleasant.

SIXTY-NINE

TWENTY-FIVE JUMPS, and more daily jogs than I cared to remember, later, I floated weightless in the deserted observation blister on *Abraham Lincoln*'s prow. Spangled blackness glided around me as the ship rotated. Dead ahead beckoned the lightless disk of the next, and presumed last, insertion point, its gravity already accelerating us forward. Invisible over my shoulder, and all around us, the fleet surrounded this ship, dispersed over spans longer than the distance between Earth and the moon.

Jeeb perched on the blister's handrail alongside me, and one of his legs squeaked loud enough in the stillness that I winced. He stared up at me with polished optics, and I tasked him. "Accelerate left third locomotor replacement."

In response, his internals clicked, so faintly that only I would notice, as he reprogrammed.

I rested one hand on the rail beside Jeeb, and my replaced arm throbbed. By now, Jeeb and I each resembled George Washington's hatchet. One hundred percent original equipment, except for six new handles and four new heads.

But Jeeb, for all the humanity I saw in him, was so immortal that he could survive a near-miss nuke, and he was selfless in the way that only machinery can be. We humans were all too mortal and all too selfish. And that, my life had taught me, was the essence of being us. We understood our mortality, yet we sacrificed everything for others, the way Jude's father and then his mother had, the way Audace Planck had, the way Bassin was prepared to, and the way countless others had over the course of this war.

Sometimes the calculus of sacrifice was simple, one life for six thousand, or for all mankind. Sometimes the calculus was one arm for nothing explicable. I feared that only more sacrifice would win this longest and broadest of wars for us. I believed that we would overcome the Pseudocephalopod because, in our best moments, we overcome our selfishness.

From the speaker in the handrail, the bosun's whistle lilted. I grumbled because it never stopped calling me. I sighed, then somersaulted, and floated aft, in the direction from which I came. "Let's go, Jeeb. We're not done yet."

Jeeb and I drifted, then walked, back to infantry territory. As I stepped through the Bulkhead Ninety hatch, it slammed me in the back like a bulldozer.

SEVENTY

———

DEPRESSURIZATION KLAXONS HOOTED. I shook my
head to clear it. Behind my back, the hatch locked down,
separating Bulkhead Ninety and aft from areas forward.
Had I been in the hatch, instead of through it, it would
have snipped me in two like a salami.

I was still breathing, so the problem had to be with the
deck forward, not with where I was. I swiveled around,
then laid my cheek against the hatch. That way, I could
peer through the eye-level quartzite peephole in the hatch
to see what was wrong on the other side, between Bulkhead Ninety and Bulkhead Eighty-nine.

I swore and wiped the peephole, but it was black.
Something on the other side had smeared the peephole so
I couldn't see through it.

I blinked, then squinted through again. Little points of
light swam in the blackness, and something the size and
shape of an old beer can with its top peeled back tumbled,
weightless.

I blinked, then squinted again. "Crap."

The *Abraham Lincoln* forward of Bulkhead Ninety

rolled slowly in space, a mile away and drifting farther from me by the second.

"Crap, crap, crap." I ran to my cabin and punched up my wireless library patch to Eddie Duffy's computer. "Eddie?"

Silence.

"Goddamit, is anybody left up front?"

"Jason? Where are you?" Eddie!

"In my cabin. What the hell happened?"

"Dunno. Viper, maybe."

I swore. As little as we understood about Slug tools and motives, we understood the Viper least of all. The Spooks figured that Vipers were dense lumps of Cavorite-powered matter, maybe no bigger than refrigerators, that the Slugs left loitering in space near things they thought were important, like mines afloat in vacuum. Vipers were triggered by sensors that looked like Slug-metal footballs that also were sprinkled around strategic points, like electronic trip wires. When a football sensed something it was programmed to dislike, the Viper accelerated to a speed in excess of .66 C, being two-thirds the speed of light, homed on the little football sensor, then smashed the living crap out of whatever the football had detected.

Kinetic energy is a product of velocity and mass, so a single refrigerator-sized Viper can put a hole in central Florida bigger than Cape Canaveral. In fact, one had, and I still bore the physical and mental scars.

"Then why are we still here, Eddie?"

During the First Battle of Mousetrap's opening moments, a Viper had smashed headlong into the *Nimitz* and vaporized it.

"The Viper took us abeam, not head-on. Sliced us clean. I dunno how many we lost. Gotta go."

The Slugs hadn't figured out what cheap human gangsters had figured out centuries ago. A high-velocity bullet may pass through a body wreaking less havoc than a fat bullet, or than a bullet that fragments. So, I was alive, albeit a castaway, because the Slugs weren't diabolical enough to invent the dum-dum bullet.

An hour later, while Eddie Duffy tended to the catastrophe that afflicted his crew of over two thousand, most of whom had been forward of Ninety when the Viper split the *Abraham Lincoln,* I inspected the life raft upon which I had been cast adrift in space.

My first discovery was the worst. I ran, Jeeb clattering across the deckplates in my wake, until I reached the flight deck. The starboard launch bays, where all the Early Birds and their crews had been, had been crushed. The port side was little better. The red lockdown light flashed above Bay One's hatch.

I peered through the hatch peephole. The *Abraham Lincoln*'s hull, and the bay bulkheads, had peeled away, so the bay deck and the Silver Bullet Scorpion on its launch rails stood naked against space's blackness, like a house chimney left standing after a Kansas tornado. There was no sign of the bay crew, the Scorpion's canopy was up, and the harness straps of the empty pilot's couch dangled up in a windless vacuum.

I pounded my fist on the sealed hatch. The Viper had struck during watch change, when the bay crew were milling around, and both incoming and outgoing pilots were exposed.

Whether it was Rommel on D-day eve, traveling home

for his wife's birthday, or Nagumo's aircraft caught on deck rearming and refueling at Midway, or a Hessian picket who might have been satisfying a natural need when he should have been looking for Washington crossing the Delaware, military history often turned because somebody took an ill-timed break.

Mankind's saving grace in this catastrophe had been Howard Hibble's preparation of two Silver Bullets, not just one.

I returned to my cabin and punched up Eddie on my flatscreen. He didn't answer. I tapped into the video feed that, as captain, Eddie could access to view his bridge displays from his cabin.

Damage Control reported two hundred dead or missing, among them the Air Wing pilots who were meeting in their wardroom, starboard. But the ship's forward section was airtight and fire-free, although drifting as dead as a log.

Evidence of the status of my end of the ship was circumstantial, mostly what had been observed from the forward section and was now reported on the main 'Puters. The impeller rooms, far aft of me, appeared to be split open like pea pods. The ship had shut down the drive faster than a human could think, so inertia kept the two pieces in motion at a similar speed and trajectory, which was why the *Abe*'s dismembered parts remained within sight of each other.

Seated in front of the screen, I paused and breathed. In the billions of cubic miles of interstellar space that the fleet occupied, the *Abe*'s passage close to some unseen, drifting Slug football, and the Viper attack that passage had triggered, must have been pure rotten luck. Clearly,

the Slugs had laid a Viper minefield in front of the final
Temporal Fabric Insertion Point that separated us from
the Pseudocephalopod homeworld, which in retrospect
seemed only logical. But the chance of a football drifting
into a cruiser in the three-dimensional vastness of space
had to be as remote as a collision between two dinghies
drifting from opposite sides of the Pacific.

I toggled over to Eddie's externals to see what progress
the rest of the fleet was making in coming to our aid.

There was static, so I had to squirm in my chair, lighter
than I had been as the ship's aft section slowed its rotation, while I waited for the link.

SEVENTY-ONE

THE AUDIO LINK CAME UP an instant before the flatscreen's visual.

"Break right! Break—"

Then I was watching the same display that the captain
had selected, during that moment, to show on the forward
screen of the *Abraham Lincoln*'s bridge. The onscreen
showed a heads-up visual through the front of a Scorpion's canopy. When a cruiser's 'Puter displays for mere
human eyes, it adjusts to human sensory frailties. The
audio lags a beat, and a display like a Scorpion-canopy
image is slowed to the speed of a World War I dogfight.
Otherwise, all a watching human would perceive would
be flashes and blurs.

Ahead of his wingman, from whose viewpoint the display appeared, a Scorpion leader broke at a right angle
to their path. That probably meant something was on the
two ships' tail.

As the lead Scorpion broke, it exploded in a red flash.

A beat later, a voice crackled out of my flatscreen,
"Slug heavy!"

The wingman, the sound of his breathing pumping

through the audio, stopped his Scorpion dead. Then a red light on the heads-up display floating translucent on his canopy winked green as he deployed a missile.

A Firewitch shot by the wingman, high right, cork-screwing through space, as the purple traces of fired heavy mag-rail rounds lasered from the tips of the eight spread arms that made an open basket at the Firewitch's prow.

Beat. "Fox one." The wingman's voice.

Slow motion or not, the missile's exhaust flashed like a red laser toward the Firewitch and exploded the mammoth Slug fighter in a vast purple cloud. The wingman pivoted his Scorpion back over front, searching for threats and targets.

Eddie Duffy's voice overrode the audio. "Enhance the furball, please, Mr. Dowd."

I swallowed. So much for my theory about a random collision of dinghies in the Pacific. The Slugs had jumped the fleet as it prepared to launch the two stealthy modified Scorpions that would win the war.

The Bridge's enhanced display substituted enlarged images of distant ships for the pinpricks that maneuvering ships would show as when dispersed across hundreds of thousands of cubic miles. The display wasn't pretty. The *Abe,* faithfully rendered in two pieces, drifted in the center of a massive dogfight, aka "the furball." Around us were arrayed a half-dozen cruisers, where there should have been twelve. Whether the others had fallen to Vipers or in ship-to-ship combat I couldn't tell and didn't care. The fact was that the fleet had already taken a beating.

One of the six remaining cruisers drifted, like the *Abe.*

Against the backdrop of starlit space, Scorpions and Firewitches by the hundreds darted and spun in a silent cloud around the great pearlescent cruisers, the fighters' marker traces boiling like red, green, and purple thread.

Audio crackled with chatter, from controllers and among Scorpion pilots.

So many fighters burst, then winked out, that the furball was like watching fireworks on holo with the audio off.

"Jason?" Eddie spoke to me over his audio while the battle raged.

"I'm fine. Keep doing what you're doing."

"Is the Silver Bullet Scorpion flyable?"

"Huh?"

"We can see the modified Scorpion, Jason. It's standing on the launch rail, in what's left of Bay One."

"I saw it myself, from in here. I couldn't see any damage. But I don't know what to look for." My heart thumped. "Eddie, is there a live pilot back here?"

Eddie said, "The *George Washington*'s sustained damage, like we have. She's unmaneuverable but alive. But Silver Bullet II's destroyed. We need to get Silver Bullet I off the *Abe* and onto another cruiser."

"Once you stabilize the battle."

"Now. Both halves of the *Abe* are getting sucked into the jump."

I swallowed again. A cruiser, or, theoretically, a modified Scorpion, dove into a jump, dodged other debris, slingshot past the ultradwarf star mass core, then powered safely out the other side in new, folded space, light-years away.

An unpowered cruiser, or a piece of a cruiser, that got sucked in didn't power out. It would simply crush in upon itself, until it became part of an ultradwarf star mass smaller than a golf ball.

"Can't somebody come take us all off?"

"They're busy. Whether we all get off the *Abe*'s unimportant. But that Scorpion back there with you's got to find a home on another cruiser. So a pilot can fly it through the jump and deliver the bomb."

"You said there was a pilot alive back here, somewhere."

"I said—never mind. Who've you seen alive back there?"

I shrugged, to no apparent purpose. "Me. Jeeb. I can't get to the impeller rooms."

Eddie paused, and I heard his breath through the speaker. "You ever fly a Scorpion, Jason?"

"Hell, no!" I paused. "Actually, kind of."

"It's a very forgiving ship. All you gotta do is ease it off the rail and slide it over to a cruiser. Then somebody can talk you through maneuver and docking."

"Can't they talk me through it first?"

"Jason, we have four cruisers left healthy enough to receive that Scorpion. Pretty soon, we may have none."

Boom.

The back half of the Abe shuddered so hard that Jeeb wobbled, perched above the flatscreen.

Waiting here for the fleet to ride to the rescue was no option.

"Crap!"

"Now what?"

"Eddie, I have to cross a hundred feet of vacuum to get from the bay hatch into the Scorpion."

Eddie's breath hissed out again.

Thumps and shudders shook the deck every few seconds now. The Slugs could be potshotting the *Abe*'s carcass, or the hull could just be breaking up.

Above the flatscreen, Jeeb swiveled his head at every thump and whined, like he wished he could hide himself in a suit of armor.

I leaned my head on my palm, with my elbow on the shelf in front of the screen. "Okay. I have an idea."

SEVENTY-TWO

THE INFANTRY ARMORY aboard the *Abe* hadn't been stripped just because she was carrying no infantry this trip. A half-dozen Eternad infantry armor suits hung from racks behind a repair and refit bench. With the ship's rotation now virtually stopped, the weightless suits' legs bounced every time a new impact shuddered the ship's dying carcass, like a robot chorus line. Eternads are made airtight and oxygen-generating principally to protect a GI from chemical and biological agents, but as a field-expedient space suit, they had worked for me in the past.

The second suit I tried on fit well enough that it should have been able to hold pressure once buttoned up. In Eternads, I could cross the open-to-space bay deck, clamber into the Scorpion's cockpit, close it, and pressure the ship up.

The trouble was that the hatch that separated the destroyed bay's vacuum from the shirtsleeve comfort in which I then resided wasn't an airlock. Once I depressurized the flight deck, so I could open the hatch that led into Bay One, I would have no refuge to return to. If the Scorpion had been damaged, it would become nothing more than the most streamlined retired veteran's coffin in history.

Ten minutes later, I stood at the Bay One hatch, listening as all of the flight deck's air hissed through a bleed valve into vacuum while my heart pounded so hard that I heard it above the hiss. So far, I had ascertained that the suit had been down checked because its radios didn't work. That did not, of course, mean that it hadn't also been down checked for lack of pressure integrity, in which case I would blessedly pass into unconsciousness before I decompressed to death.

An hour ago, the human fleet had stood poised to launch the two Scorpions through the jump into which this derelict was now falling. The scorpions would drop a couple of bombs, and mankind would declare victory, without a single additional human casualty. We might still salvage victory, if I could limp this Scorpion to a pilot aboard another ship. But at best victory would come at a previously unimagined price.

The Slugs approached war with the blunt simplicity of a caveman with a club. Somehow all of our collective cleverness was never enough to anticipate what the Slugs, in their alienness, would do. I suppose we shocked the hell out of the Slugs just as often. But mankind had, until now, muddled through by the skin of its teeth and the individual initiative and sacrifice of our disparate, imperfect parts.

The pressure around me equalized with the pressure of the rest of this universe, which was none. The hatch status light flashed amber, its chime soundless in the vacuum I had created.

I undogged the hatch, and Jeeb stepped through with me.

If the *Abe* had been rotating, Jeeb and I would have been spun off into space, where gravity would still, eventually, tumble us to be compressed into the insertion point's core. Instead, I was able to creep across the deck, grasping the tie-down loops spaced across the plating, while Jeeb clung to my back with all six locomotors, like a treed cat. If there is a benefit to weightlessness, it is that even though it's the ultimate form of falling, you don't feel like you're falling, but rather like you're floating in a pool.

I hand-over-handed up the launch-rail ladder, stopping and manually releasing the clamps that locked the Scorpion to the rail. I wedged myself into the pilot's couch, which was designed to fit a slim kid in a G-suit, not a gorilla-sized armored infantryman, and wriggled into the shoulder harness. Then I found the canopy closure lever, held my breath, and slid it forward.

Nothing moved.

My heart, which was already rattling at the red line, skipped.

Eternads could generate oxygen for a long time and would keep their wearer warm as long as his movements recharged their batteries, but this was not good. Finally, I looked at the instrument panel. Red flashing letters read "Check Harness," just like the seat-belt light on a family Electro.

Ord's pistol in its shoulder holster, which I had reflexively strapped onto the Eternads somewhere along the way, bulged, so the harness clasp hadn't latched.

With gloved, shaking fingers I forced the clasp shut. The red light winked off.

The canopy sighed closed, and the cockpit pressured

up and warmed within sixty seconds. I replaced the armor helmet with the pilot's helmet clipped alongside the headrest and dialed in the tactical net. "This is Scorpion . . ." I read the nose number. "Sierra Bravo One."

After two heartbeats, a Zoomie's voice crackled back. "Roger, Silver Bullet One. Are you good to launch?"

"I've never done that part. Which ship am I bound for?"

Silence.

"Okay. Big John's still got one bay operable."

A chill settled in my stomach. "That's it? We're down to one cruiser?"

"We're stalemated with the Slug fleet, but we've taken some damage, fleetwide."

My correspondent displayed a knack for understatement.

"What do I do, then?"

"Wait one, Silver Bullet."

Jeeb perched on the seat alongside me, his optics dilated wide. My optics were probably as wide as saucers, too.

A different voice said, "Okay, Silver Bullet, look to your upper right."

"There's a box." My heart skipped yet again. "There was no box last time!"

"That's the 'Puter that guides the ship through the jump. Don't touch it!"

I dropped both hands in my lap. "Okay. Not touching."

"Drop your right hand alongside the pilot's couch. You should find a lever about the size and shape of a banana."

"Got it."

"Don't move it!"

I jerked my hand away like I had been scalded.

"That's the throttle. Look forward, out the canopy windscreen."

Ahead of me I saw nothing. The insertion point was so close now that light couldn't escape it.

But beyond the ruined tin of the launch-bay bulkheads, a white teardrop hung motionless in space. The other Scorpion's stinger rear doors were clamshelled open.

I said, "Is that my guide?"

"We're making this up as we go, Silver Bullet. We need you to ease the ship up the rail, then just drift. The ship ahead of you will back up to you, then pinch your stinger pod with its clamshells. That ship will drag you into the bay on the *John Paul Jones*."

"What do I do?"

"Go along for the ride. Just don't mishandle the throttle. You'll take off like a goosed cheetah."

I licked sweat off my upper lip. "Do I need to do anything with my stinger pod first?"

"No! The pod controls are inside the weapons console. So's the principal munition deployment control. Put the weapons console on your list of things not to touch."

I drew a breath. "Okay. Do I pull the banana lever now?"

"Like you were petting a cobra. You can't be *too* gentle."

I wrapped my fingers around the throttle and grasped it tight.

The Scorpion lurched and leapt off the rails.

"Lay off!"

Around me, ships darted, spun, and exploded in silence. My mere touch on the throttle had shot me into the furball.

One ship slid close to me, its stinger clamshell doors open.

In my ear a feminine voice cooed, "Come to momma . . ."

The pilot slid her Scorpion closer, oblivious to the battle around us.

Screee.

Metal scraped ceramic as the inside of my tow truck's clamshell doors clamped my Scorpion's stinger skin.

"Fuck!" Not so feminine.

I gulped. "What fuck?"

"Relax. I dinged your impeller lift slats. Doesn't affect you."

For the next ten minutes, my tow truck's pilot tiptoed us, ignored and as tiny as watermelon seeds clamped back-to-back, through the vast dogfight.

Ahead, Big John grew as we approached. As huge and white as an iceberg, she maneuvered amid the twine ball of purple tracer hosing from her own surface turrets, as well as from the swarm of her defending Scorpions.

Firewitches dove on her, singly and in pairs, head-on, at her flanks, and from aft.

We closed in on the black rectangle that marked the open bay in Big John's slowly rotating hull, and her turrets spat a protective steel tunnel around us.

Clang.

The attending Scorpion detached as Silver Bullet and I floated into the open bay as slowly as a man walks. In the transparent bubble on the bay wall, the bay boss bent over his control panel. Alongside him a pilot in coveralls, helmet in the crook of his arm, waited to take Silver Bullet back out and through the jump.

I sat back and sighed to Jeeb, "Whew!"

I punched up the aft screen to glimpse my tow truck's departure.

The feminine voice purred in my ear as the Scorpion rotated back toward the fight. "Curbside delivery, Silver Bullet. You can leave the rest of the driving to a profess—"

The Scorpion exploded in the instant that the purple flash of a Slug round flickered.

Boom.

I pitched forward against my shoulder straps as my Scorpion struck the bay's back wall and tumbled.

A male voice. "Silver Bullet! Get the hell out of there!"

"How do I—"

"Now!"

Ahead, the wall disappeared as the tumbling Scorpion pointed out toward the black rectangle of space.

I yanked the banana throttle. I blinked, saw blackness ahead, and slammed the throttle closed. The little nudge I had given the Scorpion felt like no motion whatever inside the ship's gravity cocoon. I looked around to see what happened.

There was nothing there.

The male voice said, "Silver Bullet!"

"Yeah. What happened?"

"You did well to get the ship out of the bay." The voice turned flat. "You may as well switch on the jump-guidance box."

"Huh?" I couldn't see a thing. It finally dawned on me that this was because I was hurtling into a black hole.

"You've traveled fifty thousand miles and counting. A

Scorpion's impeller's not strong enough to back you out now."

"I'm gonna die?"

Pause.

"Switch on the box. Let it try to guide you through the jump and out the other side."

"Then what?"

"Then you're on your own. In a few seconds radio waves won't be able to reach—"

SEVENTY-THREE

I'VE JUMPED WITHIN THE GRAVITY COCOON of a captured Slug Firewitch, which hurt. I've jumped within the cocoons of a half-dozen different cruisers, which was always a nonevent. I don't recommend jumping inside the cocoon of one of the only two Scorpions modified to jump a Temporal Fabric Insertion Point, unless you enjoy nosebleeds, blood in your urine, a head that feels like it's been in a punch press, and nausea.

On the other hand, the jump itself is over before you can blink.

If the Pseudocephalopod had mined the backside of Its front door like it had the front, I should have been dead, or at least attracting attention the way the fleet had.

But the way things were supposed to work, the Silver Bullet Scorpion was supposed to be too unexpected and too undetectably small to attract attention.

I had the throttle wide open—why not? Never slow down, something might be gaining on you. The Scorpion flashed through the emptiness of new space at thousands of miles per second. Flying a Scorpion in atmosphere, as I had with Jude, was not only slower, and therefore easier, it provided a frame of reference. I didn't know where I had been, or where I was going. However, I was making great time.

Theoretically, I could turn this crate around, jump back through the T-FIP, and let the fleet figure out how to deliver the bomb that filled the bay behind me. But there was no way of knowing whether the jump-guidance box worked for a return trip, or how to work it, with no one to talk me through things. I didn't know how many, if any, back-to-back jumps this Scorpion could withstand. I didn't know whether the fleet, if there was anything left of it, could make use of this ship if I returned it.

I clipped out of my harness, stripped out of the Eternads to make elbow room, then bent over the controls, searching for whatever a Scorpion carried that corresponded to the Navex in a rental car. I rooted around behind the pilot's couch, under the second couch where Jeeb perched, and in the stores locker, for water and survival ration packs.

A day later, I woke to Jeeb's whistle. He stood tiptoed on all six locomotors while his optics bulged forward, toward the windscreen.

I looked up and saw a pale yellow star, growing visibly brighter as we plunged toward it.

Twenty-three hours later, the star looked as bright as Sol did from Mars, and a dark shape the size of two poppy seeds, one large and one small, became visible with the Scorpion's forward optics, silhouetted as it inched across the star's disk.

Hair rose on my neck.

It could be nothing. Or it could be the end of a journey that had begun for me as a civilian when the first Slug

Projectile struck Earth in 2037 and that was now ending for me as a civilian four decades later.

After another twenty hours, the Scorpion's ranging optics measured the planet as ninety-six percent the size of Earth. Its equatorial mean temperature was fifty-eight degrees Fahrenheit, but the planet was cold enough at its poles to sport white polar ice caps. Its rotational period was twenty-four point four hours. North and south of the poles, blue ocean glistened beneath white cloud swirls. The continent that girdled the planet at the equator showed from space grass-green.

It could be just another Earthlike planet. They were rare enough, but not every one was a guaranteed Slug nest.

Except that the satellite that orbited the planet, in an orbit barely higher than the planet's exospheric atmospheric shreds, was red, smooth, and familiar.

I stared for thirty minutes as the Scorpion shortened the distance between me, the planet, and the transplanted Red Moon.

The planet's continent, eight thousand miles long, stretched four thousand miles from the planet's arctic to antarctic circles. The Scorpion's spectrometer said the whole thing, eight thousand miles long, four thousand miles wide, and at least a half mile deep, was all organic compounds.

I shuddered. It was no continent. It was a living thing. It was the unseen enemy I had fought against all of my adult life.

But more than frightened, I felt cheated. Howard's Spooks had predicted that the organism at its center would look like this. But somehow I expected some Moby Dick–

sized Slug in a cape, slouched on a throne. Something that I could stab through its black heart with a fixed bayonet. Or at least something that I could finally ask, "Why?"

I didn't know what plans lay within the Pseudocephalopod's vast mind, now that It possessed the Red Moon. But I knew what mankind had in mind for the Pseudocephalopod. I whispered, as though It could hear me, "Hello after all these years, you bastard."

I raised the red-striped, hinged lid on the Scorpion's weapons console.

SEVENTY-FOUR

I HAD STUDIED THE SCORPION'S modified weapons console for hours on the flight in. The normal controls to deploy weapons rearward, from the stinger pod, remained unchanged but were useless with no weapons in the pod.

Three simple switches had been added to deploy the Silver Bullet munition. The first was a red one-finger toggle that armed the munition and opened the rear hatch. The second toggle, labeled "Deploy," ejected the weapon. The third was a removable wedge, shaped like a grip exerciser or an oversized spring clothespin, labeled "Abort."

I flicked the first switch and armed the munition. Behind me, hydraulics whined as the bay opened and exposed the bomb cluster.

Jeeb whistled, and in the same moment the "threat" buzzer sounded. Up from the planet's surface, a half-dozen Firewitches hurtled toward me, growing from gnat-size to bird-size in a breath. The threat 'Puter crackled. "Defensive armament unavailable." The Scorpion's weapons pod was filled with Silver Bullet, instead of something that could shoot down an onrushing Firewitch.

The 'Puter asked, "Commence auto evasive maneuvers?" Better than me trying to fly the ship.

The first Firewitch rounds flickered up toward me.

I thumbed the "Deploy" toggle before I auto-evaded.

The Scorpion shuddered.

The Silver Bullet munition burst into a swarm of subdividing cluster bombs too small for Slug technology to shoot or chase. Some would drop directly below the deployment point. Others would arc in decaying orbits toward the planet's surface. In the planet's stratosphere, each bomb would burst again, into smart bomblets that would rain evenly down on the surface, then count down before they burst, poisoning the only other intelligent species in the known universe.

When the cluster bomb ejected, a bundle of satellites, really just little radio signal relays the size of tennis balls, ejected, too. Up until the bomblets detonated, the abort remote could transmit a signal through them and shut down the whole show. I snatched the abort remote from the console and tucked it in my coverall pocket. "Fat chance!"

Whump.

The first Slug round grazed the Scorpion. On the console, a button the size of a biscuit flashed "Commence auto evasion."

I pounded the button with my fist, and the Scorpion spiraled down toward the planet, with a half-dozen Firewitches on its tail. In atmosphere, a Scorpion could outmaneuver portly Firewitches indefinitely.

I said to Jeeb, "We can dodge around the sky until the bomb goes off—"

A purple streak flashed beneath us as a Slug round barely—too barely—missed.

On the overhead display, a new light flashed red. Its label read "Lift impeller slats."

Great. My tow pilot hadn't been concerned about dinging this ship's lift impeller slats, given the needs of the moment. But now, in atmosphere, we could dodge down, but we couldn't dodge up. We were going to run out of sky.

Six minutes later the Scorpion dodged five hundred feet above a landscape that looked like a neverending green sore, unreeling below us in a blur. Firewitches potshotted us from behind.

The Scorpion juked left, clipped the surface below us, and cartwheeled.

SEVENTY-FIVE

THREE MINUTES LATER, the Scorpion came to rest, listing to the right, its hot skin crackling. Crashing a gravity-shielded ship isn't physically traumatic; it's like watching a crash holo from an armchair. But this crash killed the auxiliary systems. The Scorpion's canopy was as opaque to our surroundings as a coffin lid.

I sighed to Jeeb, "The eagle has landed." I shrugged back into my armor, drew Ord's pistol, then triggered the manual canopy release.

Outside, the sky was blue. According to my helmet displays the air was chilly Earth-normal, but too oxygen-poor to breathe for more than two minutes. The Scorpion rested on endless tissue that looked just like the Ganglion blob Howard Hibble and I had captured on Weichsel, about a million years ago. Surrounding us a thousand yards away stood a solid wall of Slugs, without Warrior armor. But some carried mag rifles.

Of course. The Scorpion's Cavorite impeller kept the Slug Warriors back the way a campfire discouraged wolves. But we sat on the One Big Slug like an unimaginably small flea biting an unimaginably big dog.

I glanced at my helmet display. Distributing a cluster bomb across an entire planet took time. Detonation of the bomblets was hours away.

To my front, a dozen Slugs inched forward. If they came too close, the Cavorite in the impeller would kill them, but Slug Warriors didn't care. I raised Ord's pistol, fired, and dropped the lead Slug like a punctured water balloon.

I fingered the two clips in the ammunition pouch on Ord's holster as the Slugs drew closer. Give or take, at one round per Slug, I was short a minimum of fifty thousand rounds.

Twenty minutes later, kamikaze maggots swarmed the Scorpion, Jeeb, and me three deep while I pounded on them with Ord's empty pistol.

Nobody really knew what happened to GIs who had been overrun by Slugs over the course of the war. But these didn't shoot me with their mag rifles, nor stab me with the blades on their rifles' edges, though they could have.

When poisoned Warriors fell away, others replaced them, until they had dragged me, with Jeeb on my shoulder, squealing and flailing his locomotors at them, out onto their big daddy's skin. When they were far enough away from the Scorpion that the new Warrior crop could surround me without poisoning themselves, they drew back fifty yards, then just sat there.

Jeeb sat alongside me. My helmet timer ticked down, too slowly. Eleven hours before the bomblets went off. I smiled a little. The bomblets strewn across this planet would kill the Pseudocephalopod. The Slugs couldn't stop that onrushing train, even if they knew they were stuck on the tracks.

My smile faded. With my ship wrecked, and on the wrong side of a black hole anyway, I would be marooned here on my enemy's corpse, with Jeeb, my 'Bot Friday, until I starved. But I still wanted to be the last species standing.

"*Brrrruuummm!*" The rumble knocked me over, and I bounced on the Pseudocephalopod like a kid on a mattress.

"*Brrruuu. Mmmm. Uuuummm.*"

I stared down alongside me. The vibration was real enough. But the noise was coming from Jeeb's audio output. A TOT, a Tactical Observation Transport, was designed as a battlefield snoop. In one turkey-sized package, it incorporated sensors not just to see the enemy from above or from ground level, but to hear the enemy. It eavesdropped on communications, decrypted ciphers, translated foreign languages, even ones it didn't know, then spat out what it processed, like a spaniel retrieving an old print newspaper for its master.

In forty years, no TOT had ever intercepted Slug-to-Slug communication, though Howard's Spooks had tried.

So the Pseudocephalopod wasn't talking to its minions that held us at mag-rifle point. It wasn't talking to itself.

It was talking to me.

SEVENTY-SIX

As HISTORIC STANDOFFS GO, this didn't look like much. For the next ten hours I sat, pistol holstered, arms clasped around my armored knees, in the center of a mass of motionless Slug Warriors, which were no more separate from the organism I sat on than white corpuscles.

Meantime, as the timer counted down toward Slug Armageddon, Jeeb's circuits chittered back and forth with the Pseudocephalopod as Jeeb deciphered the communication he monitored.

Above, the captive Red Moon orbited around the planet's equator, south of us. The Red Moon had set when syllables began to trickle from Jeeb's audio, then words. Finally, I heard the Pseudocephalopod, its voice a flat, mechanical simulation.

"Man. You have come to harm me."

A Slug of few words. After another few hundred thousand exchanges, the translation would be smooth and idiomatic. For the moment, the meaning was plain enough. The Big Slug was on to us, more or less.

"You already harmed us. Many of us."

"I have not harmed man."

"There is more than one man. You have not harmed all of man. But you have harmed man." By the millions. Without remorse.

"I have learned this. Man has many . . ." Jeeb's translator stumbled. "Identities."

The Spooks had always thought that this unitary intelligence couldn't understand the concept of mankind, or any other kind, as multiple individuals.

The adrenaline of rage surged through me. "My mother. My lover. My friends. Infants. Old people. You harmed them all." I kicked the vast skin beneath my feet as though the thing could feel it. "Have you learned that I—this identity of man—can kill you now? I'm bringing the rain on you." The green numbers of my helmet display timer winked down to nine minutes. "And you can't stop me. Then I'll beat feet out of here." The last was bravado. This was a one-way journey for me. But at least it was ending at a worthwhile destination.

"I have learned this. But I have the . . ." Jeeb's translator stumbled. "Cavorite."

I frowned and glanced again at the timer as it spun down. "You've had Cavorite for a long time before this. What's changed?"

"As I am immersed deeper in this universe I suddenly understand more."

I snorted. "You and Archimedes."

"What is Archimedes, man?"

"Not what, who. Archimedes was the name of a separate identity of man. He immersed himself in a water tub and then suddenly understood a great truth about the universe. Each separate identity of man has a name, so we can communicate."

Pause.

"I wish to communicate, man. Say your name."

"Lieutenant General Jason Wander, retired" would require explanation of socioeconomic designators, surnames, and given names, which was pushing the envelope with a hermit. "Jason."

"Jason, you will call me Archimedes."

"I'll call you whatever I want to. Murderer. Dead Slug walking. Archimedes already took that name."

"Then bring Archimedes."

"I can't. He's dead."

"What is dead?"

I snorted again. "Harmed. No longer able to immerse. Returned to dust. Like what you did to sixty million of man's identities. And now like you, Archie."

"Man can still immerse. Therefore Man is not dead. Archie can still immerse. Therefore Archie is not dead."

My jaw dropped so far that I blipped my helmet's chin control. This thing really didn't get it. One day a half-million years ago, Archie had realized that he existed. Over the half-million years since that day, he had never seen any other of his kind die, because there were no others of his kind. So he couldn't understand the difference between dead and alive. As far as he was concerned, he had done no more than trim mankind's fingernails.

What if he wasn't going to use the Red Moon to exterminate mankind?

"Archie, why did you take the Red Moon?"

"Archie is fully immersed in this universe. Archie wishes to immerse in another universe. Only the Red Moon will allow Archie to beat feet."

I nodded to myself. After a half-million years alone, in

one place, even a big, interesting place, I might yearn for new challenges. In fact, I did, in a lot shorter time.

Archie wanted a change of scene. But Archie had no feet, no wheels, no cruise liner. He was like a curious infant who had grown up on a desert island. The only life raft he possessed was what he had stumbled onto in his youth, Cavorite. And because Archie had developed a serious weight problem in middle age, he needed lots of it in order to travel.

I said, "You've rebuilt the Red Moon to transport you to the edge of this universe."

"No. To transport Archie to the adjacent universe."

I rocked back on Archie's skin, surrounded by his white corpuscles. The scourge of mankind was telling me that he wanted to cede the field of battle to us after thirty thousand years. Blow town? Catch the 3:10 to Yuma? I shifted my weight and felt the abort remote in the cover-all pocket beneath my armor. Then, inside my helmet, I shook my head. "How dumb do you think I am?"

"Archie does not understand."

"You're lying."

"What is lying, Jason?"

I smirked at the speaker on Jeeb's carapace. "Okay. I'll play. Not telling the truth."

"What is truth?"

"Come off it. You've enslaved a galaxy. But you don't understand truth?"

Archie didn't answer.

Inside my helmet, I cocked my head. What would Howard Hibble say about this?

Logically, it takes a minimum of two separate identities to lie, the liar and the lie-ee. So Archie didn't know truth, at least as opposite to untruth. He shouldn't have developed the capacity to lie. Howard had always said, and it was true, that the Slugs, that this simple-talking monster, didn't deceive us. The Slugs approached us head-on. Push, they pushed back, harder. Deceive, they bought our deceptions. A liar would have learned.

I said, "Archie, truth is saying what is, instead of what isn't."

"There is only what is, Jason."

Archie had seven minutes to live. I had seven minutes to decide whether to kill the sworn enemy that had consumed my life, or to risk the future of mankind on a conversation so bizarre that it could be a figment of my imagination.

"Come with Archie, Jason."

"What?"

"Beat feet also. Archie and Jason will immerse together."

It doesn't take an orphan long to learn that he wants to be part of a family.

"You don't understand, Archie. How long is the journey?"

"If Archie knew all of the journey, Archie would not wish to go."

Ha-ha. I think.

Archie said, "Approximately two hundred thousand jumps."

"No, Archie."

"No?" Jeeb's translator lacked ability to impart inflection, beyond a question, but I heard a sob in the word.

"Archie, I can't. I'm too fragile. My identity will die long before two hundred thousand jumps." Then more words tumbled from my lips. "But it sounds great. Really." If Archie couldn't tell a lie, he certainly couldn't recognize a white one when he heard it.

"Jason would die?"

I nodded as if Archie could see me. "Jason would die. Jason does not want to die."

The timer winked down to three minutes.

"Then Archie must go alone. Jason, Archie also does not want to die."

SEVENTY-SEVEN

I SAT HERE, tiny, somewhere in some galaxy. I was on my own, obliged to decide the fate of two races, with nothing but the lessons of an accidental soldier's life to guide me.

I hadn't realized it until this moment, but suddenly, lonely Archie and I were both, in our own way, orphans. Decades before, I had been the first modern human to encounter this being. Today, one way or the other, I would be the last.

A soldier in a life visits both poles of mankind's nature. I had seen men enslave other men on Bren and make war incessantly to no purpose. But I had also seen men like Bassin sacrifice to change that for the better. On Tressel, I had seen men commit unspeakable atrocities. But I had seen men like Audace Planck sacrifice everything to change that for the better.

Did all our arrogant cruelty, not just to ourselves but to the world around us, disqualify us from the survival sweepstakes? If Archie were lying, would he be doing this universe a favor by wiping us out?

But what about Archie? The simplicity of voice and

outlook that rendered him as charming as a transgalactic sock puppet was just a product of an obsolete translation algorithm. Did it change the reality of what he had done? Without remorse, he had slaughtered and enslaved the only other intelligent race in his universe.

The choice became simple. End the imperfect life of one race to preserve the imperfect life of another? Or risk that both could survive, and become better?

I took a deep breath, popped the seal on my helmet, and stripped off my armor until I could get at the abort remote in my pocket. By the time my fingers closed around the remote, blackness clouded the edges of my vision. I reached for my helmet to try to draw a breath. The timer display numbers read fifteen seconds.

Fourteen.

I fumbled with the remote, then fell forward onto the only other intelligent species in the universe as consciousness vanished.

I closed my eyes.

SEVENTY-EIGHT

I SAID, "I don't want you to die, Archie. I'm tired of making things die. I'm tired of man making things die."

"Wander? You're awake?"

I stared at the ceiling, then at the Space Force lieutenant commander who stood alongside the bed in which I lay. I rasped, "Where the hell am I?"

"In the commander's cabin aboard the *JFK*."

I rubbed my hand beneath me and felt cool synlon. "What happened?"

"We were hoping you would tell us. We recovered you from a derelict Firewitch, seventy-two hours ago. You disappeared through a jump eight days before that in a Scorpion."

I rubbed my eyes and sipped water from a plasti he handed me. "Thanks. God, I get tired of waking up in strange beds. Who're you?"

"Lieutenant Commander Maxim Shaloub."

He ran his hand through black hair, what military barbering left of it, that curled like steel wool. I eyed his collar brass. "Judge Advocate General's Corps?"

"I feel morally obliged, though I'm not legally so obliged, to tell you that this interview is being holo'ed."

"Why?"

"That depends."

"On what?"

"On whether you were serving as an officer who disobeyed standing orders or you were a civilian stowaway who misappropriated government property. Your status remains unresolved."

I rolled my eyes and sighed. "Whatever. If you think I'm gonna tell you what happened, the problem is I don't know half of it."

He pointed behind me, to the top of my bedframe. Jeeb perched there, diagnostics purring. "Wouldn't your mechanical have recorded something?"

"You tell me. Your techs have had seventy-two hours to download it."

He smiled. "Don't think they haven't tried. You've evidently programmed it with a secure download algorithm. Which of itself raises questions about what you have to hide."

I sighed and closed my eyes. "Jeeb. Rewind. Spill the beans."

Jeeb didn't move. I added, "Please."

Jeeb whirred, then the flap in his carapace that covered his download port opened.

Shaloub frowned. "Oh."

Jeeb spilled the beans, as requested.

According to his records, as I collapsed, I aborted Silver Bullet's detonation, with all of four seconds to spare.

The attending Slugs loaded me and Jeeb into a Fire-

witch, which stood off from Planet Archie, while he lit
off his Cavorite express. Jeeb's holo couldn't do justice
to the spectacle of an entire planet accelerated from its
orbit by the most powerful engine ever conceived, at least
in this universe.

When Archie left on his orphan's journey, his Firewitch shot back through the jump with Jeeb and me. Then
it did what Archie's detached instrumentalities had always done when cut off from his direction. It just drifted.
The last thing on the recording was Archie's mechanical
voice. "Archie does not want Jason to die, either."

The JAG prosecutor stepped back and leaned against
the cabin's desk. "We won the war. You won it."

"No. Both sides won. We're alive. The Pseudocephalopod is alive. Still want to court-martial me for desertion? Or try me for treason?"

He blinked. "It's not up to me."

"No, it isn't. I've been through this kind of thing before. By the time we get home, the politicians will pin
medals on you and me and everybody involved and claim
credit for the result."

He crossed his arms and shrugged. "Probably. But
it's not up to them, either. We're fourteen months from
Mousetrap. The vessel captain is the law out here. As a
matter of law, you're more likely to get summarily ex-
ecuted than get a medal."

Medals. I stared at the ceiling's blank whiteness trying
to remember all the heroes of this war that had consumed
my life, trying to remember all their sacrifices. A lump
swelled in my throat. There were too many, and the re-
membrance too painful. There would be time.

Finally, I sighed. I cocked my head at the JAG officer.

"You said this is the *JFK*. The *JFK* isn't scheduled to enter service for two years, even from now."

He rubbed new paint that covered old on the bulkhead. "This isn't the new *JFK*. This is the *original John Fitzgerald Kennedy*. They demothballed her two years ago. Maximum effort and all. She's so old that we move between jumps on antimatter bottles. We fell so far behind the fleet that we were authorized to turn back, but the skipper wouldn't. Still, we got here too late."

I smiled at him. "Not from where I'm lying."

He managed a thin smile. "There are a lot of people aboard who would say that. Because the skipper didn't turn back, we were able to pick up survivors from a half-dozen ships. We have people hot-bunking in the companionways. A Colonel Hibble sends his regards, by the way. He's splitting bunk time with Admiral Duffy. The brig's already converted to a dormitory, so the skipper opted to confine you here, surprisingly."

"Why surprisingly?"

The prosecutor shook his head. "Because there's no pricklier commander in the fleet. They say the skipper actually had to *beg* for this rust bucket and runs it tight so nobody can take it away." He rolled his eyes. "Don't expect leniency from Admiral Ozawa."

Capitol City Statesman
The Clear Voice of Roth's World

Harvest 16th, 2116 Standard

Herd on the Street

Today the Rancher's Club of Roth's teams with the Historical Society to welcome guest speakers from the Inworlds. At the speakers' request, the club has been opened to the public, and the buffet will be provided with the speakers' compliments. There are 'goon ribs and there are the Rancher's 'goon ribs, so arrive early!

Mr. Jason Wander is a true-born Earthling, and one of the last surviving veterans of the Slug War. So is his lovely wife, the former Mimi Ozawa, also true-born, who will speak, too.

Your Social Editor caught up with the Wanders yesterday, while they rode the Stepper out to see Ruby Falls. That view never gets old!

The Wanders are, Mrs. Wander says, "About sixty years old, subjective." But, because of near-light travel dilation, they are "a bit older, standard." On the Wanders' wedding day, the entire Human Union was just fourteen worlds, Mrs. Wander says!!

Perhaps, but your Editor should look so good! Mrs. Wander says they have visited one hundred forty-four worlds, counting Roth's. They have no plans to stop traveling.

The couple married late, so they never had The

Blessing. But, Mrs. Wander points out, on some worlds the problem is too *many* children. The War orphaned Mr. Wander, but he says that his life has taught him that all the people of the Human Union are his family. And the Wanders travel with Jeeb, a lap-sized Mechanical as old as they are, which "we spoil like our own child."

Both Wanders will tell about their experiences in the Slug War, which Mr. Wander says were "average."

But he says the true reason they speak on the outworlds is so no one ever forgets the sacrifices, made by so many soldiers, that saved two races and brought peace to the galaxy.

It sounds like a good story.

Acknowledgments

Books, they say, are marriages. Of ink to paper, of author to material, and of reader to story. *Orphan's Triumph* is for some of us an anniversary and for others a spring wedding.

So, my thanks. To something old (child-bride appearances notwithstanding), senior editor Devi Pillai and agent Winifred Golden, both present at the creation, and Alex Lencicki and Jennifer Flax, veterans of the reissued series. To something new, my U.K. editor Bella Pagan and marketing executive Darren Turpin. To something borrowed, the U.K.'s gift to Orbit U.S., publishing director Tim Holman. And something blue, Calvin Chu, who outdid himself with *Triumph*'s icy, cerulean cover. And to everyone else at Orbit for their great work.

And, as always, to Mary Beth for anniversaries past and better ones to come.

extras

orbit

meet the author

ROBERT BUETTNER is a former Military Intelligence Officer and a National Science Foundation Fellow in Paleontology, and he has published in the field of natural resources law. He lives in Georgia. His Web site is www.RobertBuettner.com.

introducing

If you enjoyed ORPHAN'S TRIUMPH,
look out for

THE COMPANY

by K. J. Parker

Hoping for a better life, five war veterans colonize an abandoned island. They take with them everything they could possibly need—food, clothes, tools, weapons, even wives.

But an unanticipated discovery shatters their dream and replaces it with a very different one. The colonists feel sure that their friendship will keep them together. Only then do they begin to realize that they've brought with them rather more than they bargained for.

For one of them, it seems, has been hiding a terrible secret from the rest of the company. And when the truth begins to emerge, it soon becomes clear that the war is far from over.

Teuche's father knew the soldiers were somewhere in the parish. He'd met Tolly Epersen as he was driving the herd back to the sheds for evening milking, and Tolly reckoned he'd seen them, a dark gray blur on the slopes of Farmoor. Teuche's father was worried, naturally enough. His sheep were on Big Moor, a hopelessly tempting prize for a large body of hungry men. He considered the risks and options: if Tolly had seen them on Farmoor an hour ago, even if they were coming straight down the combe, it'd still take them four hours to reach the pasture where the sheep were. There should be plenty of time, therefore, to get up to Big Moor and drive the flock into Redwater combe, where with any luck they wouldn't be noticed. Normally he'd have gone himself and left the milking to Teuche, but as luck would have it, he'd put his foot in a rabbit hole and turned over his ankle two days earlier and was still limping badly. He didn't like the thought of sending the boy out where there might be stray soldiers, but he couldn't risk anything happening to the sheep. He called Teuche out of the barn, where he'd been mending hurdles, and told him what to do.

Teuche clearly wasn't wild about the idea, but he could see that it had to be done and that his father was in no fit state to do it. He whistled up the dogs, put some rope in his pocket just in case he did meet any soldiers (if the dogs ran ahead, they'd give him away; once he got up on the top he'd put them on the lead, just in case), and set off up the course of the dried-up stream. It wasn't the shortest way, but he figured he could keep out of sight behind the high banks on that side if there turned out to be soldiers on the moor.

The streamed ran down the steepest side of the hill,

but Teuche was young, fit, and in a hurry. Because he was keeping well over to the lower side, in the shade of the ninety-year-old copper beeches his great-grandfather had planted along the top of the bank to act as a windbreak, he could neither see nor be seen, and the wind in the branches made enough noise to mask any sound he made, though of course going quietly had long since been second nature to him. It took him no more than an hour to reach the gate in the bank that led from Pit Mead into Big Moor. There he paused, pulled himself together, and peered over the gate to see what he could see.

To begin with, he had no idea what they could be. They were far too dark to be sheep, too big to be rooks or crows. If he'd been a stranger to the neighborhood he might well have taken them for rocks and large stones, not an unusual sight on the top of the moor, where the soil was so thin and the wind scoured more of it away every year. But, thanks to his great-grandfather's windbreak, Big Moor was good pasture with relatively deep, firm soil; there were one or two outcrops down on the southern side, but none at all in the middle, and these things, whatever they were, were everywhere. His best guess was that they were some kind of very large birds—geese, perhaps.

At first, they only puzzled him; he was too preoccupied by what wasn't there, namely the sheep. He curbed the impulse to run out into the field and look for them. If they weren't there, it might well mean that the soldiers had got there first and were down out of sight in the dip on the eastern side. By the same token, the sheep might be down there, too, though they tended to crowd in down there only when they needed to shelter from the rain. He couldn't decide what to do for the best, and as he tried to make up his mind, he considered the unidentified things scattered all over the field, not sheep or rooks, not stones, and there had to be hundreds of them. Thousands.

He stayed in the gateway for a long while, until he realized that time was getting on and he still didn't know where the sheep were. Very cautiously, he climbed the gate and dropped down as close as he could to the bank, where he'd be harder to see. His idea was to work his way along the bank as far as the boggy patch, where he could use the cover of the reeds to get far enough out into the field to spy down into the hidden dip. It was a good plan of action. In spite of his anxiety, he felt moderately proud of himself for keeping his head in a difficult situation.

The first one he found was lying in the bottom of the narrow drainage rhine that went under the bank about a hundred yards down from the gate. Because of the clumps of couch grass that edged the rhine, he didn't see him until he was no more than five feet away. He stopped dead, as though he'd walked into a wall in the dark.

The man was lying on his face, his arms by his sides, and Teuche's first thought was that he was drunk, passed out and sleeping it off in a ditch, like old Hetori Laon from Blueside. He noticed that the man had what looked like a steel shell that covered his top half, from his neck down to his waist, and under that a shirt apparently made out of thousands of small, linked steel rings. Then he realized that the man's face was submerged in the black, filthy water that ran in the rhine. He ran forward to see if he could help but stopped before he got much closer.

He'd never seen a dead man before. When Grandfather died, his mother had made him stay out in the barn; when he was allowed back inside there was no body to be seen, just a long plank box with the lid already nailed down. Maybe as a result of that, he'd always imagined that a dead body would be a horrifying, scary sight; in the event, it was no such thing. It looked just like a man lying down—a man lying down drunk, even, which was comedy, not tragedy—but he could tell just by looking at it that it wasn't human anymore; it wasn't a person, just a thing. Teuche wasn't afraid of things. He went closer.

He knew the man must be a soldier because of the steel shell and the ring shirt. From the available facts, he worked out a theory. The soldier had been drinking; he'd wandered away from the rest of the army, fallen asleep sitting against the bank, somehow slid over and ended up facedown in the rhine, where he'd drowned without ever waking up. It struck him as a sad thing to have happened, sad and stupid but understandable. Something of the sort had happened to a tinker last year out over in Spessi, and the general opinion had been that it had served him right.

But he didn't have time for any of that now, he reminded himself; he had to find the sheep and get them down into the combe. It occurred to him that the soldier's friends might be out looking for him, so he carried on down the bank toward the reeds, keeping his head below the skyline. He'd nearly reached the outskirts of the wet patch when he made the connection in his mind between the dead man and the things he'd seen lying in the field.

Once the idea had occurred to him, he felt stunned, as though he'd just stood up under a low branch and cracked his head. If the gray things lying in the field were all dead men . . . but that couldn't be possible, because several thousand human beings don't just suddenly die like that, all together at the same time, out in the open fields.

But, he thought, they do, if they're soldiers, in a war. That's precisely what happens. He knew all about the war, and wars in general. He'd always liked hearing stories, both the old ones about the heroes of long ago and the more up-to-date ones about how our lads were slaughtering thousands of the enemy every day, in victory after victory. It was almost impossible to believe, but maybe that was what had happened right here, on Big Moor; General Oionoisin had managed to catch up with the enemy and cut them to pieces, right here, on our top pasture . . .

He tried to think about the sheep, but he couldn't. He wanted to go farther out into the field, to look at the bodies, but he couldn't bring himself to do it, in case some of them were still alive, wounded, dying. Shouldn't he try to do something for them, in that case? But the thought made him feel sick and terrified; the last thing he wanted to do was actually go near them, dying, as if fatal injury was something contagious you could pick up by touch. Nevertheless, he crept out from the fringe of the reed bed and walked quickly and nervously, as though he was trespassing, up the slope toward a clump of the things clustered 'round a gorse bush.

There were five of them. They all had the same steel shells and shirts; one of them had a steel hat with ear flaps. It hadn't done him much good: there was a wide red gash in his neck, through the windpipe. The blood was beginning to cake and blacken, and the last of the summer's flies were crawling in it, weaving patterns with their bodies. The man's eyes were wide open— he had a rather gormless expression, as if someone had asked him a perfectly simple question and he didn't know the answer. There was another gash on his knee. His right hand was still clutching a long wooden pole, splintered in the middle. The other four men were face-down, lying in patches of brown, sticky blood. Teuche noticed that the soles of their boots were worn almost through. A little farther on, he saw a dead horse, with a man's body trapped under it. There was something very wrong about it, but it took him quite some time to realize that the body had no head. He looked 'round for it but he couldn't see it anywhere.

He tried to think what he should do. His first duty was to see if there was anybody he could help; but there were so many of them, and besides, what could he do? Suppose there were two or three, or five or six or ten or twenty or a hundred men lying here still alive, capable of being saved, if only someone came to help them. That made it too difficult. One man, one stranger, and he'd feel obliged to get him down the hill, somehow or other, back to the house, where Mother and the other women would know what to do. Just possibly he could manage one, but not two; and if there were two, or more than two, how the hell was he supposed to know how to choose between them? Besides, he told himself, these people are the enemy. They came here to kill and rob us and take our land. They deserved it. More to the point, he had to find the sheep.

He reverted to his original plan of action, though he knew it had been largely overtaken by events: down to the dip, where he found no live enemy soldiers and no sheep. That more or less exhausted his reserve of ideas, and he felt too dazed and stupid to think what to do next. After a minute or so wasted in dithering, he climbed up on the bank beside the southern gateway, where he knew he could get a good view of the whole of the river valley, from Stoneyard down to Quarry Pit. Of course, that wasn't Kunessin land; it belonged to the Gaeons, Kudei's family, but he knew they wouldn't mind if he went onto it to get his sheep back.

But there were no sheep, no white dots, only a scattering of the gray ones, stretching down the valley until they were too small to make out. That's it, then, he thought: the sheep have gone, the soldiers must've taken them, after all. He knew without having to think about it that that was really bad, about as bad as it could possibly get. He tried to feel angry—bastard enemy coming here, stealing our sheep—but he couldn't. After all, the enemy had been punished enough, General Oionoisin had seen to that, and what good had it done? Thirty-five acres of dead meat wouldn't make up for losing the sheep. Then he told himself that the government would probably pay compensation, sooner or later; it stood to reason that they must, because otherwise it wouldn't be fair. You can't have armies come onto your land and kill thousands of people and steal a valuable flock of sheep and not expect to pay for it. The world wouldn't work if people could behave like that.